"You've remembered something?"

Whatever it was, Michael knew it had obviously shaken her.

Briana took a steadying breath. "I can't locate my partner, my firm doesn't exist...and no one seems to be able to find my grandmother...."

The sudden, devastatingly lost look in her eyes made his heart lurch. "It's all right. You're just confused—"

"That's not all, Michael. I—" She stopped, as if unable to go on. "I'm afraid to tell you. It's so absurd."

"Briana, you never have to be afraid to tell me anything. I'm here for you. Besides, believe me, we psychiatrists live on the very edge of absurdity."

Her eyes met his and steadied. "This isn't my face." She swallowed. "The first time I saw this face was when I woke up this morning and looked into the mirror. Michael, I'm not just missing three weeks. I'm missing my face."

She paused to laugh with no mirth at all.

"You said you lived on the edge of absurdity?" she asked. "Well, it looks like I've just dropped off it."

Don't miss out on any of our special offers. Write to us at
Harlequin Reader Service, or see our website for more
information. Customer Service:

U.S.: 3010 Walden Ave., P.O. Box 1325, Buffalo, NY 14269
Canadian: P.O. Box 609, Fort Erie, Ont. L2A 5X3

ABOUT THE AUTHOR

The Dream Wedding is the sequel to *The Dream Doc*, a short story featured in Harlequin's September anthology, *Fortune Cookie.*

M.J. Rodgers is the winner of *Romantic Times* Career Achievement Award for Romantic Mysteries, two-time winner of their Best Intrigue Award and is also winner of B. Dalton Bookseller's top-selling Intrigue Award. She loves to hear from readers and will autograph a sticker for placement inside your copy of *The Dream Wedding* if you send an SASE to her at P.O. Box 284, Seabeck, WA 98380-0284.

Books by M.J. Rodgers

HARLEQUIN INTRIGUE
102—FOR LOVE OR MONEY
128—A TASTE OF DEATH
140—BLOODSTONE
157—DEAD RINGER
176—BONES OF CONTENTION
185—RISKY BUSINESS
202—ALL THE EVIDENCE
214—TO DIE FOR
254—SANTA CLAUS IS COMING
271—ON THE SCENT
290—WHO IS JANE WILLIAMS?
335—BEAUTY VS. THE BEAST*
342—BABY VS. THE BAR*
350—HEART VS. HUMBUG*
375—LOVE VS. ILLUSION*
392—TO HAVE VS. TO HOLD*
423—ONE TOUGH TEXAN
*Justice Inc. miniseries

HARLEQUIN AMERICAN ROMANCE
492—FIRE MAGIC
520—THE ADVENTURESS
563—THE GIFT-WRAPPED GROOM

M.J. Rodgers
THE DREAM WEDDING

Harlequin Books

TORONTO • NEW YORK • LONDON
AMSTERDAM • PARIS • SYDNEY • HAMBURG
STOCKHOLM • ATHENS • TOKYO • MILAN
MADRID • WARSAW • BUDAPEST • AUCKLAND

"The future belongs to those
who believe in the beauty of
their dreams."
—Eleanor Roosevelt

ACKNOWLEDGMENT
With special thanks to
"NetSleuths, An Information Brokerage"
{email:patrickm@sprintmail.com}
for finding what everyone else said
wasn't there.

ISBN 0-373-22445-1

THE DREAM WEDDING

Copyright © 1997 by Mary Johnson

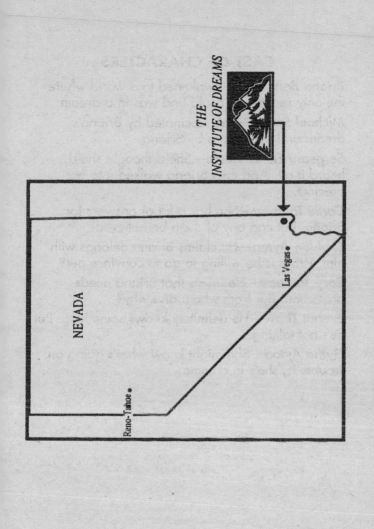

THE
INSTITUTE OF DREAMS

NEVADA

Reno-Tahoe •

Las Vegas •

CAST OF CHARACTERS

Briana Berry—She awakened to a world where the only reality she could find was in a dream.

Michael Sands—He's fascinated by Briana's dream and even more by Briana.

Sergeant Elena Vierra—She'd thought she'd heard it all. And then Briana walked into her precinct.

Carlie Taureau—She has a lot of answers for Briana. But can any of them be believed?

Sheldon Ayton—He claims Briana belongs with him. What is he willing to do to convince her?

Rory Taureau—He insists that Briana needs protection. But from whom and why?

Everett Thaw—He definitely knows something. But he's not talking.

Gytha Ayton—She might know what's going on. Trouble is, she's in a coma.

Chapter One

Michael Sands knew something was amiss the instant he walked into the spacious rotunda of the Institute of Dreams.

He halted immediately, listening carefully, his muscles tensing in readiness for whatever he would face. Only a deep, empty quiet beat against his ears.

Michael's eyes quickly swept over the gleaming white marble floors and walls to the unmanned guard desk in the middle. Nothing stirred, save the twinkling Christmas lights on the twenty-foot Scotch pine standing in the corner.

His gaze rose to the glass-domed ceiling bulging high into the heavens. The night's black velvet drape was a jeweler's case, the stars within it a thousand sparkling diamonds.

All was serene at the Institute of Dreams.

And yet that odd sense of disquiet remained with Michael, as though a sense apart from his normal five had been breached.

Michael enjoyed pursuing these rare nudges originating from beyond his normal awareness. Following them had often led to the unusual and unexpected.

Unfortunately, this nudge had not appeared at an opportune time. He had three parties he had promised to swing by tonight, two sponsored by prominent patrons of the institute. He was already late to them all.

Michael took one last quick look around before continuing toward the front doors and the parking lot.

The second he rounded the guard's desk, he saw her. And she stopped him dead in his tracks.

Michael's whole life revolved around dreams—those wonderful wisps of other worlds that the unconscious cavorted in at night, when the conscious was fast asleep. He knew that dreams could be absurd, astonishing, outlandish, outstanding.

He also knew they could contain important questions, and provide even more important answers to the concerns of waking life. For years he had probed their meanings, their power, their magic.

But he had never met one in the waking world before.

She was lying beneath the institute's giant Christmas tree. And she was definitely too lovely to be anything but a dream.

He stood absolutely still and stared.

She was long of limb and slim, the gentle swells of her breasts and hips beneath the white satin of her gown taking his active male imagination on a quick, exciting trip. The thick waves of her hair were pure flame and flowed past her shoulders, fanning the white marble floor.

He couldn't see her face. It was hidden behind the diaphanous white lace veil of her spectacular wedding outfit.

Michael approached in a disbelieving daze. He went down on one knee beside her. Only when he took her hand in his and felt its warm smoothness did he begin to trust what his senses were telling him.

She was real.

He felt for her pulse. It throbbed beneath his finger in a relaxed but steady pace.

Slowly, he drew back her veil.

Her face glowed beneath the twinkling Christmas-tree lights, a perfect oval sculptured by full cheekbones and chin. Her skin had the translucent shine of fine white linen. Her eyebrows rose into gentle auburn arches above the lush sweep of her long eyelashes. At the end of her small, straight nose were lips as full and delicately stained as a coral sunset. He couldn't tell what color her eyes were, for they were closed. Her chest rose with a gentle, rhythmic swell.

It seemed it was she who was fast asleep, not he.

Michael leaned back on his heels, his forehead furrowing into a frown. Dream or no, she was still too ravishing to be real. What was this beautiful bride doing asleep beneath his tree?

And then it hit him.

Of course! This dream bride had to be one of his friends' not-so-subtle fix-ups. A "gift" to him on this Christmas Eve.

Michael chuckled. It was an incredible prank, but then, his friends would know it would have to be something incredible to capture his attention.

Which one of them had this much imagination and flair for the dramatic? And who was this perfectly lovely lady they had recruited to play pretend bride?

Michael couldn't wait to find out.

He was about to shake her shoulder to do just that when the cell phone in his tuxedo pocket pealed away. He answered it.

"Michael, it's past ten, and the party is way into its swing," Dr. Nathaniel Quinn's irritated voice said in his ear. "Where in the hell are you?"

"I had some last-minute things to finish up at the institute, Nate. Are you the one who left the unusual Christmas present for me here under the tree?"

"What unusual Christmas present?"

Michael smiled down at the sleeping bride. "The one wrapped all in white."

"Our 'present' is wearing black, in both her dress and her expression. You were supposed to have been here an hour ago."

"Don't tell me she's another one of Laura's friends," Michael said, shaking his head.

Nate's exhale sounded slightly exasperated. "It's one of those women things. Laura likes you. She hates to see you alone during the holidays."

"Nate, I am *never* alone during the holidays unless I choose to be, as you very well know."

"Yeah, I know. But you said yourself you hadn't met anyone interesting this year. And besides, the ladies you generally choose to spend holidays with aren't exactly the lasting type. Why not spend some time with one of Laura's friends for a change?"

"Because they are the lasting type."

"Come again?"

"Nate, they're perfectly nice women. Attractive, even bright. But they're either single and looking for a husband and father, or divorced with a couple of kids and looking for a husband and father."

"Marriage isn't that bad, Michael. After two months, I highly recommend it. You'd be surprised how great it is to have someone to come home to and share dreams with."

"For ten years women have been sharing their dreams with me," Michael said. "Believe me, no woman could surprise me."

As Michael said those words, he looked again at the beautiful sleeping bride and saw her eyes moving beneath her closed lids. She was dreaming?

"Look, Nate, I have to hang up now. There's something urgent I have to attend to here."

"But you're going to make it to the party?"

"Sorry. Looks like I'll be too busy with the present that was left for me here."

Nate exhaled in exasperation. "What do I tell Laura's friend?"

"The truth. I'm not into the family thing. I would have just disappointed her."

Michael flipped his cell phone closed.

"So you're not a gift from Nate," he said to the sleeping bride. "Not Fay, surely? No, our Fay's far too subtle for such a splashy gesture. Which just leaves Jaron. Yes. This has the feel of the outlandish and unorthodox—and that describes Jaron to a T."

Michael smiled as he replaced the cell phone in his pocket. "And if you're a gift from Jaron, the bridal gown is definitely a prank. Jaron is far too footloose and fancy-free himself to seriously suggest marriage to another bachelor. Right?''

The sleeping bride did not respond. If this incomparable creature wanted to warm his arm tonight at the celebrations, and perhaps later his bed, who was he to play Scrooge?

He rested his hand on her shoulder and gave it a gentle shake.

"Time to wake up," he said softly.

She stirred not an eyelash.

Michael put a little more emphasis in his shake and the volume of his voice. "The parties are already in full swing. You don't want to miss them, do you?''

She continued to lie as still as a statue.

A disturbing thought occurred to Michael. He leaned closer, until he was almost nose-to-nose with her. The subtle, winsome fragrance of sweet herbs and amber mixed with woman rose up to greet him. He could detect not even a trace of alcohol. At least she had not passed out from too much holiday cheer.

He leaned back on his heel. A quick glance out to the well-lit parking lot of the institute revealed that the only car there was his own.

Michael rose to check the glass doors. They were unlocked. Still, whoever had dropped her off had to have had a key to the front doors in order for her to have been carried inside. Unless the guard had forgotten to lock the doors when he left?

Michael discarded the possibility. She had to have been brought here by his friend. This had to be a prank. Nothing else made any sense. He returned to the sleeping bride.

"Do you realize if you're faking this sleep, your heartbeat will give you away?" he warned.

The lovely vision before him still did not stir. Michael gave her a moment more to reconsider before leaning down to rest his ear between the gentle swell of her breasts.

Her sweet fragrance filled him. She felt warm and soft and way too good. It took a moment for him to control the rapid rise of his own heartbeat before he could listen to hers. It was steady, slumberously slow. She was asleep, all right. He drew back until he could once again see her eyes moving beneath her closed lids. Not just asleep. She definitely was dreaming.

He was growing more perplexed by the moment. Why had she fallen into such a deep sleep? Was she experiencing a side effect from some medication?

Whatever the reason, Michael knew, he couldn't leave her lying on the cold marble floor. He wove his arms carefully beneath the satin folds of her dress and picked her up. She curled her body into his with a soft murmur, a small smile drawing back her lips. Her eyes continued to move beneath her closed lids. She was still fast asleep, and still dreaming.

She was also a warm and totally enticing armful. He couldn't resist holding her soft body close, cradling her head against his shoulder. Her thick, silky bangs fanned his neck like seductive feathers.

Michael carried her across the rotunda, through the door to his wing, down its corridors, and finally to his private apartment, at the back. Once there, he punched in the key code to unlock the door. He swept her inside, flipped on the light and headed for the couch.

He laid her gently on its soft cushions and knelt beside her. Her veil was so long it swept the floor. He worked the rosebud crown free of her hair and withdrew its elaborate folds from around her head. Then he tossed the assembly onto a nearby chair.

Her hair tumbled across the teal-blue couch cushions in thick, loose, fiery waves. He ran his fingers lightly across the flaming strands, fascinated by their crackling beauty. They were cool and silky to the touch. But when he drew back his hand, it felt strangely hot from the contact.

His eyes returned to her face. The brighter light of the room cloaked her cheeks in a fair blush and set an enticing shine across her lips. She was absolutely captivating. He suddenly couldn't wait to know the color of her eyes, the sound of her voice, the feel of her smile.

"If you've swallowed a potion that put you to sleep," Michael whispered, "that qualifies you as a true Sleeping Beauty. Maybe all this situation calls for is a kiss to awaken you."

It was a tempting thought. And the moment it came to Michael, he found himself succumbing to its temptation. He sought her hand, lightly pressing his middle fingers to the pulse point in her wrist. Then he leaned down to brush his lips lightly over hers.

She tasted as sweetly insubstantial as whipped cream, and as coolly mysterious as her unexpected appearance on his doorstep in the dead of night. He drew back quickly, all too aware of the increasing beat of his heart.

He studied her carefully, noting that there was no change in the steady, sluggish pace of her pulse. Her breathing was still slow and even. Her eyes still moved beneath their closed lids.

She was still dreaming.

It looked like this Sleeping Beauty was going to need a more arousing kiss, if he hoped to wake her.

There was an element of the unfathomable and forbidden about that thought that Michael was finding entirely too enchanting and intoxicating a blend to resist.

He didn't.

He pressed his mouth to hers more firmly, eagerly claiming its soft curves and contours. She tasted warm and sweet, and so wonderfully giving. He quickened the tender friction, focusing all his attention on her soft lips. A sensuous heat radiated into him from the delicate fusion of their mouths.

Michael could feel his breath thickening as his body responded to the intimacy of the contact. With the tip of his tongue, he caressed the sensitive skin at the edges of her lips with bolder and bolder strokes, until he could feel them parting.

When the warmth of her breath was suddenly, exquisitely mixing with his own, her pulse quickened. His went wild.

He forced himself to hold back, reminding himself that she

was still fast asleep, still unaware of him. He was determined to make her aware of him—completely and totally aware. He removed his hand from hers, concentrating on touching her only through his kiss.

He pressed the warm wetness of his tongue against the enticing slit of her parted lips. He slipped inside to taste the sleek porcelain smoothness of her teeth before dipping into the warm, deep softness of her mouth. Her flavor filled him like a hot cinnamon cider.

He sensed her body softening and lifting subtly toward him. He felt the vibration of the low sound deep in her throat. It was the last warning he got before her mouth came alive beneath his own and her arms circled around his back.

His Sleeping Beauty was not just awakening, she was responding.

Her arms embraced him hard as she kissed him back with a sweet eagerness that nearly took his breath away. Michael's stiff amazement came and went in a heartbeat. In the next heartbeat, he'd wound his arms around her and crushed her breasts to his chest, molding her to him.

Eagerly he deepened the kiss, sinking into the heated softness of her mouth, absorbing the tang of desire on her tongue, feeling the incredible heat of it invade his body in a crashing wave.

Michael was totally unprepared for the pure, unrestrained desire that jolted through him. Shock, disbelief and delight all crowded into his head. And pushed every other coherent thought right out of it.

BRIANA COULD FEEL HERSELF on the brink of awakening from the most delicious dream. She tried to resist the pull of reality as she clung to her dream lover's ardent kiss.

And what a kiss! His mouth was insatiably demanding as it devoured her own. His hands felt like heated irons on her back and waist as he crushed her willing body to a warm, hard male chest. His arms held her so tightly she had to gasp for breath. He felt so real—so wonderfully real.

Then she inhaled his scent—a rich mix of expensive balsam and clean, heated male skin. She had never smelled anything so arousing or so erotic before. And that was when she knew. This was way too real to be a dream.

She came awake with a start. And found herself being kissed—really kissed—as she had never been kissed before. It was hot and sweet and pure seduction. And insanity.

Briana grasped broad shoulders that felt like huge boulders and pushed, trying to break off the kiss.

As hard as he had been holding her, he instantly relaxed the fierceness of his embrace. She drew back to look into the face of her all-too-real dream lover.

And wondered if she was still dreaming.

For he was as handsome as hell. His blond hair shimmered beneath the light like thick, moonlit sand. His clean, bold features were tanned to a light bronze. His eyes were as deep a blue as midnight and filled with a frank and enthusiastic heat—a heat that seemed to suck every hard-won breath right out of Briana's laboring lungs.

"Who are you?" she asked, knowing her voice was hardly audible enough to qualify as a whisper.

He slowly rose to stand formally before her.

He was tall, very tall, wearing a full-dress tuxedo and the kind of smile that could melt a woman's kneecaps at twenty paces. Even the homeliest of men looked good in a tuxedo. This man looked like some mythical Norse god.

"I'm Michael Sands," he said with a small bow of his head. "And you are?"

His voice had a deep timbre and a rhythmic cadence that rolled into Briana's ears and registered in a warm, seductive streak all the way down to her solar plexus. She was having difficulty catching her breath and absolutely no success in capturing her thoughts.

"Briana Berry," she heard herself say, and wondered why it was impossible to look away from his mesmerizing deep blue eyes.

"Briana," he repeated, and her nerves sparked with excitement, because of the incredible warmth he had managed to put into the sound of her name. And then she remembered the feel of his ardent lips and powerful arms and rock-hard chest, and the heat behind his burning kiss.

Briana shot up to a sitting position, feeling as though she were just now coming fully awake.

"Why were you kissing me?" she asked, more than unsettled to find her voice far below its full volume.

"Because I found it very hard to wake you up by more conventional means."

"You kissed me to wake me up?"

He smiled, not at all apologetically. "It is the proven, time-honored way of waking a Sleeping Beauty."

Briana almost chuckled at that one. This guy didn't just look and sound like a dream. He had a line that could reel a woman's heart right on in. Although why he was using it on her, she had no idea.

She tore her eyes away from his long enough to look around at the strange surroundings in which she found herself. The room was gorgeous—a tribute to art deco, indirect lighting, decorative glass, beautiful gold-leaf sculptures, imaginative furniture shapes in deep, dreamy blues.

A black granite floor reflected up at her like a mirror, adding depth and drama and a sense of the ethereal.

In every direction Briana looked, she saw a rich and eclectic variety of furnishings that fit with a sense of spaciousness and shimmering tranquillity. Altogether, the room struck her as marvelously bold and brimming with sophistication.

Briana's attention swung back to the man who stood before her so elegantly and so at ease in his black tuxedo.

"Where am I?"

"My place."

It fit him, all right. "How did I get here?"

"I carried you in when I found you asleep under my Christmas tree."

"Asleep under your *what?*"

"In point of fact, it was the institute's Christmas tree you were adorning."

"Institute? What institute?"

"The Institute of Dreams, of course. I live here on its grounds. Didn't Jaron tell you?"

"I don't know any Jaron," Briana said. "And I've never heard of the Institute of Dreams."

"How did you get here, then, Briana?"

Good question. How *had* she gotten here? Her mind was blank. A feeling of panic began to lick at the edges of Briana's brain. How could she not know how she'd gotten here?

"Briana, please believe me when I say that it is a pleasure meeting you, under these or any circumstances. But you have to admit that appearing all wrapped up in a wedding dress under a Christmas tree in the middle of the night does smack of a practical joke."

"A wedding dress?" Briana repeated, looking down at herself for the first time, in some astonishment. Dear heaven, she *was* wearing a wedding dress. What was she doing in a wedding dress?

She swung her legs over the side of the couch, fighting with the long white folds that seemed determined to get in her way. She rose to her feet and found herself rocking precariously on a pair of stilts.

She lifted the hem of her floor longth satin gown to reveal three-inch satin heels. At five-nine, she rarely saw the need to wear heels, and she certainly never wore any three inches high.

Disbelief took the rest of her balance. She collapsed back onto the couch.

"Briana, is everything all right?"

She looked over to see a concerned look on Michael's face. If he was playing a part, it was an Oscar-winning performance.

"Is everything all right? Let me give you a hint. I've just

awakened to find myself dressed as a bride and in the arms of a strange man in a strange place."

"*You're* claiming this is a prank?"

"And you're claiming you're not in on this?"

A frown drove into his forehead. "I'm not in on *this*, Briana, whatever *this* is."

The sincerity just poured out of those midnight-blue eyes of his.

Briana knew she should suspect him. He was the one who had been kissing and embracing her wholeheartedly when she awakened. That in itself was highly suspicious behavior. He had to be lying to her.

But her practical, logical core just couldn't buy it. People did things for a reason. What reason would this breathtakingly handsome man have for putting on such a charade with her?

She had no money to tempt a swindler, if that was what he was. And if seduction was his intent, he would have pressed his advantage while he had it. He hadn't. When she pushed out of the kiss, he had released her, accepting her withdrawal without protest.

It just didn't make any sense for him to be lying. But none of the answers he'd given her had made any sense either. It was time she found some that did.

"You say I'm at the Institute of Dreams?"

"Yes."

"And where is this institute?"

"In the southern Nevada desert."

"Near Las Vegas?"

"Vegas is about ninety miles west."

"Ninety miles," she repeated. Well, here at least was a point of reference. She had just come to Las Vegas. Now the only question was, how had she gotten from there to here?

"Briana, are you on some type of medication?"

She looked up to where he stood before her, the epitome of calmness as he asked what he obviously thought was an entirely reasonable question.

"No," she said. "And I'm not an escapee from the local loony bin, either. Are you?"

"Not at the moment." The wattage from his smile was blinding. "I thought perhaps your earlier drowsiness might have been a side effect to some cold or pain capsules."

He came over to the couch and sat next to her. She could feel the warmth of him, smell his rich, sophisticated scent. He gazed directly into her eyes. Her heart skipped a very long beat. But this time there was nothing sexy about his look. On the contrary. It possessed a decidedly clinical air.

"Your pupils are normal," he said after a moment. "The whites of your eyes are clear. Your skin color is good."

He took her hand and consulted the watch on his wrist. She could feel her pulse leap at the touch of his warm, strong fingers against her vein.

Her question came out on a laugh. "Don't tell me you're a doctor?"

"A psychiatrist," he answered absently.

The laugh died in her throat.

"And I suppose you're next going to tell me that the name Institute of Dreams is a euphemism for the local loony bin?"

He waited until he had finished counting her pulse before answering. His eyes once again met hers.

"We don't deal with the delusional here, Briana. Just the dreamers. Your pulse is a little fast, but not out of range."

His thumb strayed across her palm, sending little thrills up her arm. Briana knew that if he tried to take her pulse now, he'd have to go to the moon to find it. This man's touch was absolute seduction. Everything about him was too good to be true.

"Do you have some identification on you?" she asked, quickly slipping her hand away from his.

He pulled a slim wallet out of his tuxedo jacket. He opened it to his Nevada driver's license and held it out for her to see. She studied it carefully. He was Michael David Sands, blond hair, blue eyes, six-four, two hundred pounds. He had turned thirty-three on the seventh of November. He even managed to look wonderful in his driver's-license picture.

"I don't see anything indicating you're a psychiatrist," she said.

He flipped the wallet card holders until he revealed a membership card in the AMA and another in the American Psychiatric Association. They certainly seemed authentic.

"And now for the most important test, Dr. Sands. How many psychiatrists does it take to change a light bulb?"

He smiled at her question. Briana was beginning to wonder if he hadn't slipped her some delicious drug. It was simply impossible to resist that smile.

"If it's a well-insured light bulb, you can be certain a lot of specialists will need to be called in."

"You're a psychiatrist, all right," Briana said, grinning. "Or at the very least a medical doctor. What do you do here at the Institute of Dreams?"

"Run the place," he said casually as he returned his wallet to the inside pocket of his tuxedo jacket. "There are four of us at the institute, each specializing in a different area of dream research. Are you married, Briana?"

His question came out of nowhere, and began an odd throbbing inside her blood. "Why do you ask?"

"Because you're dressed in a wedding gown. I'm trying to find a logical reason for this situation we find ourselves in."

"*We* find ourselves in? You know how you got here."

"But I don't know why a beautiful sleeping bride was left beneath my tree."

Beautiful? Of course, it had to be the clothes she was wearing. Just as men always looked great in tuxedos, women always looked beautiful in bridal gowns. Maybe she should try wearing this one a while longer—like for the rest of her life.

"I'm not married, Michael."

"Engaged?"

"No."

"A significant other anywhere?"

"None."

"Ever married?"

"No."

"Any serious relationships?"

"No."

"How old are you, Briana?"

"Thirty."

"And you've never had any serious romantic relationships?"

His tone and look of surprise clearly said he didn't believe her. It was flattering, as though he thought her some raving beauty who had to have succumbed to the attention of at least one in a league of adoring admirers over the years.

This must be one sensational wedding dress she was wearing.

"I've been saving myself for Prince Charming," she said with a deliberate grin.

"I'm glad," he answered, no returning grin on his lips.

Briana found herself quite shocked to see the sincerity in his blue eyes. And more than hesitant to accept it.

Once upon a time, she had let herself embrace the old adage "Beauty is in the eye of the beholder."

She had since found out that believing in fairy tales could be quite painful. But it was damn hard not to believe this man who both looked and acted like Prince Charming.

"Do you have any identification on you, Briana?"

"In my handbag." She looked around. "Where is my handbag?"

"You didn't have one when I found you at the front doors."

Great. Every woman's nightmare. "I can't have lost my handbag, Michael. Everything is in it. My identification, keys, money, credit cards, everything."

"You may have been robbed."

Briana thought about that possibility for a moment. She laughed at the absurdity of the picture that flashed into her mind.

"I can just see it now. A mugger steals my money and

clothes and then decks me out in a spectacular wedding outfit with a value that no doubt exceeds my entire credit limit.''

He gave her a quizzical look. ''An explanation has to exist somewhere, Briana. Although I have to admit, every logical one eludes me at the moment. What's the last thing you remember?''

''I was at the hotel.''

''Which hotel?''

''The Mirage in Las Vegas. I'm attending a convention there this weekend.''

''*This* weekend?''

''The rates are better during December.''

''What kind of convention is it?''

''For architectural designers. My partner and I own Berry, Willix and Associates in Seattle. I flew in today specifically to attend the convention.''

''Your partner didn't come to Vegas with you?''

''No. Lee's wife is having a baby any day now. He didn't want to take a chance of being out of town when the baby came.''

''Tell me what you did from the moment your plane landed.''

''I took the shuttle bus to the hotel. Checked in. Registered at the convention. Picked up my attendance packet. Got dressed for the opening dinner. I had an hour to kill, so I went for a walk through the hotel mall.''

''I take it you're not a gambler?''

''Never held any interest for me. But the hotel mall has other attractions. The dish of fat-free chocolate yogurt I had in a specialty shop was heavenly. Then I went into a boutique to try on this little black dress I saw in the window. Just for fun. It was way out of my price range. The next thing I knew, I was waking up in your arms…apartment,'' Briana amended quickly.

''You didn't drink anything?''

''I was going to have some wine when I got to the banquet.''

"What time did you walk into that boutique?"

"I'm not sure. Dinner was to begin at seven-thirty. I suppose it might have been a little before seven."

"And I found you here in the rotunda at ten. That's three hours unaccounted-for. Are there any practical jokers among your family or friends?"

"Trust me, Michael. If I knew anyone who would pull something like this on me, I would have murdered them years ago."

"Is there a rejected suitor who perhaps thought he could meet you here in Vegas and sweep you off your feet and into a hasty marriage?"

He looked so serious when he asked that, as if she could really inflame such passions in men.

She laughed. "Hardly."

"Briana, do you have a headache, or any sensitive spots?"

"You think I've hit my head and become delusional?"

"No, I think someone might have struck you on the head and carried you away."

"To this institute? For what purpose?" she asked, the logic behind such a scenario just refusing to take shape in her mind.

"Perhaps leaving you at the institute was not the original intent, but was resorted to because of changing circumstances. I don't mean to alarm you, Briana, but this wouldn't be the first time a beautiful woman was abducted against her will."

A *beautiful* woman?

Briana smiled. "Michael, my head feels fine. But I'm beginning to wonder about yours."

He frowned at her answer. "Would you mind if I looked at your arms?"

"Excuse me?"

"I want to see if someone has injected something into your veins."

The very idea of it sent a cold chill down Briana's back.

"That seems rather ridiculous, doesn't it?"

"As ridiculous as my finding you lying beneath a Christmas tree dressed in a wedding gown?'' Michael asked, his eyebrow arcing ever so gently.

"Point made," Briana said.

She turned her attention to the long satin sleeves that ended at her wrists. She noted with dismay that each was fastened with at least two dozen tiny pearl buttons.

Briana had difficulty disengaging the tiny pearls from their tight loops with only one hand.

"I'll do that for you," Michael said, kneeling beside the couch and taking over the job of unfastening them for her.

What was it about the deep resonance of his voice that vibrated through every cell of her body, as though tuning it?

You are definitely Prince Charming, Michael Sands. First you kiss me awake. Next you call me beautiful. And now you kneel at my feet, ready to perform the slightest of services.

She was all too aware of the seductiveness of his rich balsam scent, the close presence of his powerful body, the light shifting like starlight through his thick sandy hair, his warm fingers brushing against the sensitive skin of her arms.

Last time she felt even a fraction of what she was feeling for Michael, the guy had ended up being married, with three kids.

Briana forcibly reminded herself that as charming as Michael Sands seemed to be, she knew nothing about him.

"Do you live here with your…family?" she asked, trying to sound casual.

His response wasn't casual at all, but direct, and delivered with a brief, emphatic punctuation from his eyes. "If I had been married, Briana, I never would have kissed you."

He sounded so forthright and sincere when he said it, too. She didn't know whether she was a fool to believe him. She suspected she probably was.

He undid the final button on her right sleeve and pulled it back to expose the pale blue vein in the crook of her arm. He gave it a careful scrutiny.

"This one is clear. Let's take a look at the other."

He turned his attention to her left sleeve. He had it half-unfastened when he asked his question. She supposed she should have anticipated it, but she hadn't.

"Why did you kiss me back?"

His eyes were such a beautiful blue as they looked directly into hers. Every time Briana saw the warmth inside them, she could feel her pulse race and her heart sigh with pleasure. How could any woman not want to kiss this man back?

"The kiss fit right into this dream I was having, Michael. I know it sounds strange. I can't really explain it logically, but I was confused for a moment between what was real and what was the dream."

"It doesn't sound strange or illogical at all. Confusing a fading dream with emerging reality is not an uncommon occurrence upon first awakening."

Michael folded back her second sleeve and once again focused his attention on her skin. "This vein is also clear of any recent injections. If you have been drugged, they didn't use the most obvious sites. However, you should still be checked over very thoroughly."

Briana felt a flush start up her neck. "I...uh—"

"Naturally, the examination would have to be done by another doctor," Michael told her, interrupting smoothly as he began to refasten her sleeves. "I'm in no position to perform it with the professional detachment that would be required."

The smile that lifted his lips this time had a delightfully disreputable twist to it. He was definitely and deliberately flirting with her.

She was thrilled and appalled at how much she enjoyed being the recipient of this charming man's attention.

"Really, Michael, I feel fine," Briana said, trying to get a grip on reality. "Great, actually. I don't need a physical exam. What I need to do now is report what has happened to the police. May I use your phone?"

"Of course." Michael rose and retrieved a cordless instrument from off a lacquered black credenza. He handed it to Briana.

"Is there a local police?" she asked.

"The Las Vegas metropolitan police force covers all of Clark County. You realize, of course, that they are going to want to see you in person?"

"In which case, maybe I should just call a taxi and go see them."

"Briana, you'll never get a taxi to come out here. The Institute is not just ninety miles from Vegas. We're ninety miles from *anywhere*. I'll drive you."

"Absolutely not, Michael. You're obviously dressed to go somewhere. I'm not interrupting your evening any more than I already have."

"I had nothing special planned for tonight, Briana."

"Oh, right. You lounge around your apartment in a tuxedo all the time."

He smiled. "The functions I was to attend were far more business obligations than social enjoyments. A couple of phone calls will take care of them. You have to let me drive you. Even if you could get a taxi to come out here, you have no money to pay one with, remember?"

Yes, that, unfortunately, was all too true.

"Besides, you can't just kiss me senseless, Briana, and then leave me without an explanation to this intriguing mystery."

Kiss him senseless? Was that what she had done? She did remember putting a definite enthusiasm into that delicious dream embrace. She swallowed uncomfortably as her neck got hot.

"Maybe I could get the police to come out here."

"Not unless it were a life-threatening emergency. I'm afraid you're stuck with me as chauffeur."

He held out his hand to her and smiled.

Stuck with him? Who among the entire female population of America wouldn't want to be "stuck" with this handsome, charming man?

Briana slipped her hand into his large, warm one and rose to her feet before him.

She had no idea what was going on. But she had no doubts

that whatever had happened to her over the past few hours, at least she had landed under the right Christmas tree.

"YOU REALLY EXPECT ME to swallow this...tale, Ms. Berry?" Sergeant Elena Vierra asked, her dark eyebrows flying up to her prominent widow's peak as she gave Briana and her wedding outfit yet another incredulous once-over.

Michael found the Las Vegas detective sergeant to be a big-shouldered, fortyish woman with a full mouth that jutted forward defiantly, as though ready to attack.

From the moment she saw them approach, Sergeant Vierra had been treating both them and their situation with irritated disbelief.

Vierra had disregarded his credentials, as she had the obvious sincerity with which Briana told her story. She was more than beginning to get on Michael's nerves.

But Briana chuckled good-naturedly in the face of the sergeant's pointed disbelief. She obviously possessed a special type of toughness, the ability to simply stand firm. She spoke slowly, reassuringly, with the ease of conviction.

"I don't blame you for doubting it, Sergeant. I'm sure if I were in your position, I'd be wondering what I had been drinking, too. But I am sober, and very serious. This is no joke. I have lost my purse, my clothes, and three hours out of my life."

Michael watched the hard-nosed woman detective as she stared at Briana. He wasn't certain, but he thought he might actually be seeing a flash of uncertainty cross her dark eyes.

She leaned forward in her chair and reached for the phone on her desk. "You registered at the Mirage for this convention?"

"Yes."

The sergeant hit a button on her speed dialer, then spoke to someone who was obviously a clerk at the desk at the Mirage. She asked several questions about Briana and the convention. Nothing on her face revealed what answers she was getting. When she hung up the phone, she looked directly at Briana.

"The Mirage has no record of your reservation, nor of your checking in. What's more, they don't have a convention for architects at their hotel."

"But they do," Briana insisted. "The hotel's famous erupting volcano was on the front of the brochure announcing the convention. Call my partner. He'll tell you. He was the one who first showed it to me."

"Who is this partner of yours?"

"Lee Willix."

"And the firm you're partners in?"

"Berry, Willix and Associates."

Sergeant Vierra wrote down the telephone number Briana gave for her firm. "Let me see your driver's license, Dr. Sands."

Michael handed it over.

"I'll be back in a minute," Sergeant Vierra said as she rose and walked to the end of the room, where she stepped around a corner and disappeared out of sight.

Michael understood that she had left the room to check out the information she'd been given.

"She doesn't believe me," Briana said, resting back in her chair with a shake of her head.

"The police are taught to be suspicious of anything out of the ordinary, Briana."

She nodded, and the light danced like fireflies through her thick flame hair. Her voice was lovely, thick and mellow, reminding him of autumn honey. Still, he found her eyes to be her most arresting feature. When she first opened them on his couch, he had thought them an enticing teal blue, and a striking contrast to her luscious flame hair.

But as he looked at them now, beneath the harsh fluorescent lights of the police station, he could see that they were actually a pale, clear crystal, absorbing and reflecting back whatever colors were around them.

Michael didn't doubt that Briana was telling the truth about not knowing how she'd come to be at the institute. Everything about her struck him as genuine—completely genuine.

"Michael, I've been thinking. It took us well over an hour to drive into the city from the institute. That means that whoever was behind this bizarre charade had less than two hours to somehow incapacitate me, take my purse and clothes and deck me out in this wedding dress. Does all that seem possible?"

"There could have been more than one person involved."

"But what possible reason could anyone have for such outlandish behavior?"

"Maybe this was meant to be a romantic escapade—like when the South Sea islanders used to kidnap the young maiden who was to become the bride and spirit her away to where the groom waited in seclusion. When your 'playful' kidnappers suddenly realized they had grabbed the wrong woman, they panicked and left you at the nearest dwelling, which in this case just happened to be mine, out in the middle of the desert."

"You should be a scriptwriter," Briana said. "That's certainly a better plotline than those horrible made-for-TV movies where a trusted lover or husband turns out to be a psycho and chases the hapless heroine through the last ten minutes of the program with a sharp knife and a lot of screaming."

"Watched some of those, have you?"

"Too many. Whatever happened to those nice little murder mysteries where the villains were imperfect—not psychotic—and the story emphasized the indomitable sleuth uncovering the clues?"

"You know what they say about a society's fiction, Briana."

"Actually, I have no idea. What do they say?"

"That it's a mirror of its emotional health."

"Now *that's* a frightening thought."

"Take heart. Nearly fifty percent of all paperback novels sold are romances. There are still some sane souls left out there."

Her face broke into an immediate smile, and light danced in her eyes. "Now I *know* you're too good to be true. What planet are you from, Michael Sands?"

He chuckled. "Debra, one of my favorite clients, is an editor at a major publishing house in New York. I've shared a few things about dreaming with her. She's helped to smooth out that rough male-chauvinist-pig edge to my Y chromosone."

Briana's sudden laugh was filled with spontaneity, generosity, and a hearty humor that held not an ounce of pretension.

He could imagine that most people finding themselves in such bizarre circumstances as hers would have become angry, frightened, even hysterical, by now. But she had remained amazingly calm, intelligently examining the situation in logical steps and with a gently humorous air.

Michael had thought her enchanting when she was asleep. Now that she was awake, he found her absolutely fascinating.

He didn't know by what chance fate had brought her into his life. But he had no intention of letting her out of it until he had gotten to the bottom of the mystery that surrounded her.

Sergeant Vierra came pounding back into the room and lumbered over to her desk, plopping heavily into her chair. The moment Michael saw the expression in her dark eyes as she glared at Briana, he knew that whatever news she had brought with her would not be good.

"There's just one problem with your story, Ms. Berry," Sergeant Vierra said. "None of it checks out."

"Excuse me?" Briana said.

"That wasn't the telephone number of a Lee Willix you gave me. It belongs to a Mrs. Eliot. She's never heard of a Lee Willix, or any Willix, for that matter."

"You must have reached a wrong number," Briana said.

"There's also no listing for an architectural firm of Berry, Willix and Associates in Seattle."

"Of course there is," Briana said evenly.

"Look, I don't know what your problem is, lady," Sergeant Vierra said. "And I don't want to know. Get out."

"Hold on a minute, Sergeant—" Michael began.

"No, you hold on, Dr. Sands," Sergeant Vierra said, as she threw his driver's license on the desk in front of him. "Be happy that I was able to verify that *you*, at least, are who you say you are. Otherwise, believe me, I'd have called the guys in white coats to come get you both."

"This is absurd, Sergeant," Michael said, pocketing his license. "Ms. Berry is perfectly sane. She is the victim of a crime. Her purse and personal possessions have been taken. Now, there has to be a logical way to approach this situation."

"Well, here's my logical approach. You take her out of here right now, or I book her and she spends tonight and Christmas in jail for filing a false police report."

"Christmas?" Briana repeated, but the sergeant ignored her as she continued to shoot her angry words at Michael.

"And trust me, Dr. Sands—she'll do the time. No judge or prosecutor is going to come in tomorrow for the bail hearing of a lunatic. Now, am I making myself understood?"

Michael rose, turned to Briana and offered her his hand as she rose. He'd heard enough.

"Perfectly," he said through clenched teeth.

Michael turned and led Briana quickly to the door. And with every step, he fought to keep his anger in check.

"Michael, I don't—"

"It's all right, Briana," Michael told her, eager to be out of the police station and away from the irritating sergeant.

Michael welcomed the sting of the freezing night air against his overheated skin as they walked to his car in the parking lot. But when he realized that Briana was shivering beside him, he took off his tuxedo jacket and wrapped it around her shoulders, quickening his pace to the passenger door.

When they were settled inside, he turned to her.

"I didn't mean to cut you off back there, Briana. But I

tend to get a little hot under the collar when an uninformed person starts yelling 'crazy' at someone or some situation they simply don't choose to take the time to understand.''

''But, Michael, there *is* something crazy here.''

Michael stared at Briana's face, softly lit by the overhead streetlight. What he saw there caused a small warning bell to go off in his brain.

''Briana, what is it? What's wrong?''

''Sergeant Vierra said she'd put me in jail tonight and keep me through Christmas without bail. But how could she? Today's December third. Christmas is more than three weeks away.''

Michael felt his thoughts twisting, skittering, trying to avoid their collision course with the wall of logic that lay dead ahead.

''Briana, tonight is Christmas Eve,'' he said slowly, carefully. ''Christmas is tomorrow.''

He watched his words flash across her face, robbing it of all color. When she spoke again, her voice came out on a hoarse chuckle, its brave humor trying to mask the horror of her words.

''Looks as though I'm not just missing three hours, Michael. I'm missing three *weeks*.''

Chapter Two

Michael's classic pale-cream-and-bronze 1955 Thunderbird convertible flew over the deserted desert highway.

Briana knew it was fortunate that he had the top up. Otherwise, she felt certain, they both would have been pulled out of their seats by the sheer force of the wind whipping past. She had glanced at the speedometer only once. The pointer was quivering past a hundred. She hadn't looked at it again.

She'd never been comfortable with speed, but, oddly, she didn't feel afraid. The way Michael's broad hands held the wheel with such steady ease told her that he was in command of both the car and himself.

She, on the other hand, wasn't even in command of her own memory.

Three weeks out of her life! Gone! Blank! As though they had never been! It was unbelievable. Unthinkable. And yet, undoubtable.

What had happened to her in those three weeks?

And how could she not have known she was missing a part of her life? How could she have awakened feeling so normal? Clearly, she was not. It was a good thing she'd been dumped on the doorstep of a psychiatrist.

She gazed over at Michael's chiseled-stone profile. His mind was clearly elsewhere as he stared unblinkingly ahead at the black desert highway. Since the moment she told him that she was missing not just three hours but three weeks from her life, Michael's demeanor had undergone a definite change.

Briana supposed it was only to be expected. He had to be reassessing his belief in her sanity—a belief that he had so assuredly expressed to Sergeant Vierra less than thirty minutes before. He'd been her stalwart supporter then. Briana wondered what he would say to the good sergeant on that subject now.

Michael moved the car over into the right lane and began to slow down. Briana couldn't see anything beyond the headlights streaking into the black night. Still, she knew that the exit for the Institute of Dreams would not be along for a while.

"Where are we going?" she asked.

"Dr. Fay Wynd lives a few miles from here. Fay's one of my colleagues at the Institute. I'd like her to take a professional look at you."

Briana felt her stomach turn. "By professional look, I suppose you mean psychiatric evaluation?"

"I want Fay to examine you to determine if you were subjected to any physical harm. I believe there's a strong possibility that you were abducted during these three missing weeks in your life."

The implication in Michael's words sent Briana's stomach into a full-fledged cartwheel. She supposed she should have thought of that possibility herself, but she hadn't. Moreover, it wasn't something she wanted to think about.

She reminded herself she needed answers. Michael's suggestion was a sound, logical starting point, no matter how much she loathed it.

She raised no objection when he took the next off-ramp.

Dr. Wynd answered the door in a dressing gown. Briana realized Michael's call to her from the car phone a moment before must have awakened her. Fay was somewhere in her thirties, blond, with a pretty heart-shaped face and warm gray eyes.

And a houseful of out-of-town relatives.

One youngster was sprawled out on the couch. Three more were in sleeping bags on the floor, crowding the presents under the Christmas tree. Fay led Michael and Briana through the minefield of bodies into the kitchen. Once there she closed the door so that they could talk in privacy.

Michael's quick explanation about finding Briana at the Institute and her three-week amnesia brought an amazed look to Fay's face.

She turned to Briana and rested a gentle hand on her arm. Her voice was ultrafeminine, and had care rippling all the way through it. "How do you feel, Briana?"

"Fine. Really. But Michael believes a physical examination is in order."

"He's absolutely right. Come on. It won't take long."

Fay circled her arm in Briana's and led her out of the kitchen and down a long hallway.

"How strange it must have been for you, waking up to find yourself dressed as a bride and missing three weeks out of your life. Do you suppose there's a groom out there somewhere?"

Briana laughed. "Oh, no. Absolutely not."

Fay stopped in front of a closed door at the end of the hallway to take Briana's left hand.

"No ring. Still, a lot can happen in three weeks' time. Briana, are you sure that the thought of a groom brings back no memories?"

"Fay, if I were emotionally involved with someone else, I couldn't feel—"

Briana halted her sentence when she realized what she had been about to admit—that she was having some very romantic feelings for Michael. She substituted a quick modification. "I couldn't feel so free and emotionally unencumbered."

Fay's returning smile was accompanied by a knowing look in her gray eyes. "I wish I had been there to see the Sandman's face when he found a sleeping bride under his tree," she said.

"The Sandman?" Briana repeated.

"It's what we call Michael at the Institute of Dreams."

"Why?"

"Michael's specialty is designing dreams for his clients to enhance their abilities, accomplishments and enjoyment in their waking lives."

"How is it possible to design a dream?" Briana asked.

"You'll have to ask Michael that one. None of the rest of us dabble in his particular brand of dream research."

"The Sandman," Briana mused. "Like in that fanciful song, 'Mr. Sandman, bring me a dream'?"

"Yes, although Michael's a solid scientist and his approach is far from fanciful. His successes are walking around, as famous politicians, movie actors, professional athletes, you name it. Without Michael's feats with his clients, none of us other doctors would have the funds to pursue our research into dreams."

Fay opened the door to a tiny back bedroom that had obviously once been a porch. She switched on a dull ceiling light that barely revealed the small single bed, dresser and nightstand now occupying the space.

"With a houseful of guests, this is where I'm sleeping tonight," Fay explained. "It's not exactly an examination room, but I'll bring in a bright spotlight and my medical bag and see if we can make it do."

"I appreciate your going to this trouble."

"This is no trouble, Briana. Michael's my friend, as well as colleague. I'm pleased to help. There are a couple of stray hangers in the closet over there. I know you'll want to keep that gorgeous wedding gown from getting wrinkled."

"I rather suspected it must be gorgeous," Briana said as Fay began to help her unfasten the sleeves.

"Looks like it was made for you, too. It's a shame this room doesn't have a mirror so that you can see yourself in it. There, that's the last button on those killer sleeves. I'll be back in a couple of minutes."

Briana hung the wedding gown and stepped back to examine it. It was a spectacular peau satin sporting a corsetlike bodice beaded with seed pearls and sequined lace. Its off-the-shoulder neckline was embellished with handmade rum-pink satin roses and celadon leaves. Rosettes and petal-edged satin streamers cascaded down the back onto a sweeping chapel-length train.

No wonder Michael had thought her beautiful in it. Even Cruella De Vil would look enchanting in such a dress.

As Briana continued to undress, she discovered that she was wearing fancy silk panties and bra, and a garter belt with silk stockings. She shook her head, thoroughly bemused.

A beautiful formal wedding dress, and sexy silk lingerie. This was definitely not her normal look.

As she bent over to remove her stockings, a long tendril of hair fell in front of her. She was more than startled to discover its gorgeous flame hue.

She was fingering a long curl wonderingly when Fay returned to the bedroom with both a handheld spotlight and her medical bag in tow.

Briana's face must have shown some of her bewilderment, because Fay's expression and voice immediately expressed concern. "Is something wrong, Briana?"

"I'm a redhead," she said on a disbelieving chuckle.

"Are you telling me you weren't three weeks ago?"

"My hair has always been a mousy brown."

"Let's take a look at the rest of you and see if there are any more interesting changes."

MICHAEL PACED the kitchen floor and drank two cups of coffee while Fay conducted her examination of Briana. When his colleague finally joined him, he was not reassured to see her frown. He schooled his voice into an even tone.

"Well, Fay?"

"This is a very odd case," Fay said, almost to herself. And then she set her medical bag on the kitchen table and stared at it.

Michael's patience was fast disappearing. *"Fay."*

"Oh, sorry, Michael," Fay said, seeming to come out of

her daze as she looked up at him. "I just keep trying to make sense out of the mental puzzle Briana presents. She has absolutely no sense of lost time at all. But the good news is that she's in perfect shape physically. No cuts, bruises, or any sign of physical abuse. It's obvious she hasn't been sexually active in what appears to be quite some time, so I can safely say she hasn't been assaulted in that way."

"Thank you, Fay," Michael said, feeling an enormous weight shifting off his shoulders.

"As you no doubt also observed, she shows no overt signs of having been drugged," Fay continued. "However, I took a blood sample just to be sure. I'll drop it off at the lab for analysis."

"Still, with the Christmas holidays, I doubt we'll get an answer anytime soon," Michael said frowning. He walked over to the sink to rinse out his cup before turning back to her.

"Fay, you did check her over thoroughly? You're sure she's not suffering from a head injury?"

"I'm sure. But there is one physically curious thing that she noticed herself. Her hair color appears to have been changed from brown to red."

"That is...curious."

"Everything about her situation is most curious, Michael. And rather fascinating. How are you going to handle it?"

"If you'd found any physical injury, I'd have driven right back into Las Vegas and called in some favors for a police investigation. But now I have to assume it's emotional trauma that has caused her to lose her memory. Which means—"

"She needs psychiatric help," Fay said, completing Michael's sentence.

"I'd like you to put her up for the night, Fay."

"Michael, those bodies you stepped over on your way to this kitchen are my brother's ever-increasing brood. He and his wife and kids have claimed every available bed, couch and sleeping bag in the house. There is no room left at this inn. Surely you have an extra bed for Briana at your place."

Michael took a deep breath and exhaled it heavily. "I suppose that's where I'll have to take her."

"Why do you look and sound so glum about it? Briana seems sweet, and amazingly cheerful, considering the situation she finds herself in. Not to mention, she's absolutely stunning."

"And she's suffering from an emotional trauma. That puts her out of bounds."

"Oh, I see. Having a hard time keeping our professional distance, are we?"

"I'm not her doctor, Fay, so ethics don't enter into it. However, it would be unconscionable of me to pursue someone in her confused mental state."

Fay's attempt to stifle a smile failed.

"You find this funny?" Michael said, feeling his frustration at the situation lending an uncharacteristic irritation to his tone.

"I'm sorry, but I've never seen the erudite and coolly sophisticated Dr. Michael Sands looking so nonplussed before. It's oddly comforting."

"And why is that?"

"Let's just say that it makes this mere mortal feel a little less flawed. So what are you going to do?"

"Find her competent help."

"What about Jaron?"

"He left town yesterday to spend the holidays with friends in New York."

"Oh, that's right. I forgot. And Nate's not into the psychological-evaluation end of things, so that lets him out."

"How about you, Fay?"

"Sorry, Michael, no time. I'm leaving with my brother and his brood at dawn. We're spending an old-fashioned Christmas at my grandparents' home up in Reno. I won't be back for at least two weeks."

"There has to be someone available."

"During the Christmas holidays? Good luck. Why don't you just break down and treat her yourself?"

"That wouldn't be ethical."

"Why? Are you already emotionally involved with her?"

"Of course not."

The moment the words were out of Michael's mouth, he knew they weren't true. He had feelings for Briana. And they were definitely not the feelings a doctor should have for a patient.

"Well, then, what's the problem?" Fay asked him challengingly. "You know it's not ethical to use that consummate, legendary charm of yours to sweep the lady off her feet. You might as well be useful to her in some way."

"How pragmatically put."

Fay chuckled at his sarcasm. "Look, I've given Briana some everyday clothes to wear, and some personal items that should get her through the next couple of days. If you decide not to treat her, I'll by happy to take her case when I get back."

"I appreciate the offer, Fay, but she needs help now, not in two weeks. You have any suggestions as to where we can get something to eat tonight?"

"Only place I know around here that's open at this hour on Christmas Eve is a Chinese takeout about a mile up the road. The guy who owns it goes by the name of Uncle Chen. Order his Lake Tung-Tin prawns. They're out of this world."

The kitchen door swung open, and Briana walked in. She was wearing a pair of blue jeans and a sweater, both of which were snug, due to Fay's shorter stature and smaller bones.

Seeing just how much more snug made Michael swallow hard.

The idea of having to play the role of her doctor instead of her lover was not at all appealing to him. No, not at all.

What rotten luck.

A lovely dream walked into his life, and he was stuck with having to treat her missing reality.

BRIANA FOLLOWED MICHAEL into the guest bedroom of his spacious apartment at the back of the institute. As with the rest of his place, she found its floor mirrored black granite, its walls etched-glass panels that lent a feeling of endless space and time. He set the suitcase full of borrowed things that Fay had packed for her onto a queen-size bed with a cobalt coverlet edged in rich gold.

"Your private bath is through there," he said, in exactly the same formal tone a hotel bag handler might. "You can bolt the bedroom door from the inside. You'll be perfectly safe."

Briana didn't have any doubts. There was a solid ethical sincerity about Michael that she had sensed from the first. He would never take advantage of this situation.

"You must be tired," he said.

"Considering it's after one in the morning, I'm sure I should be," Briana said. "But, oddly, I'm wide awake. Maybe I slept through the past three weeks, and that's why I feel so refreshed."

Michael looked at her searchingly, but said nothing.

"It was a joke, Michael."

"Of course," he said, an immediate smile drawing back his lips. Briana recognized that smile. It was the kind of re-assuring one a doctor gave a patient. Its lack of personal warmth made her heart sink heavily in her chest.

Clearly, Michael's assessment of her mental state had gone through a radical change.

Great. Just great. She kissed Prince Charming, and *she* turned into the toad.

Briana knew that she had to accept Michael's hospitality tonight. She had no money, and no place else to go. But she wished she was somewhere else—anywhere else. She no longer felt beautiful or desirable when he looked at her.

She faced him, holding firmly on to the remnants of her pride. "Michael, I really appreciate everything you've done for me. You've been…wonderful. I just want you to know that tomorrow I'll call my partner and ask him to wire me some money. Then I'll be out of your hair and on my way."

"Aren't you concerned that Sergeant Vierra wasn't able to get in touch with your partner?"

"Obviously she dialed a wrong number."

"The Mirage didn't show a record of either your reservation or the convention."

"Of course not. Sergeant Vierra didn't know to tell them that it had all happened three weeks ago."

"Even so, it was rather odd of them to just tell the sergeant there was no convention in progress. Why didn't they mention they had one three weeks ago?"

"Well, busy clerks, like busy police sergeants, don't always go out of their way to make that extra effort, do they?"

"No. I suppose they don't."

He said the words hesitantly, almost as though it were hard for him to accept anything she suggested now. Briana felt a sharp pain of disappointment, even sharper than what she had experienced when the warmth left his smile.

She could accept the distance he had put between them. His personal interest in her had always seemed too good to be true, anyway.

But she could not accept the mental distance that came with his thinking her unbalanced. She might be missing a few weeks, but she was not missing her marbles. And she was thinking just as clearly as he.

"Briana, you must realize that you have to have help in order to recapture those lost weeks."

She took a deep breath, infusing her tone with a delicate and deliberate lightness. "Don't worry, Michael. I've been looking after myself for quite some time now. I've sort of gotten the hang of it."

He fastened his eyes on her as he unfastened his tie with a quick flip of his wrist. The movement was so smooth, so perfectly executed and so unexpected that Briana felt her pulse leap. Was anything else coming off?

"While we tackle that Chinese food, you can tell me all about yourself."

The words could have contained a warm, personal meaning. But they didn't. Briana was aware of the new air about Michael, the professional air—polished, refined, pleasant, cool. She knew she was no longer facing the man, but rather the psychiatrist.

Clearly, her only allure for him now was her psychologically interesting lapse of memory. It would be betraying both her honesty and her dignity to trade on it.

She forced her lips into a polite smile. "Michael, no offense, but I have no intention of spending time on your psychoanalytic couch tonight."

"I don't have a psychoanalytic couch. Don't believe in them. But I do believe in comfortable couches. There's one in the living room. There's also a chilled bottle of champagne in the refrigerator. I'll meet you in the first with the second in five minutes, and we'll see if Uncle Chen's special Lake Tung-Tin prawns live up to their reputation."

He headed out the room, not waiting for a response.

"I'm not big on drinking, Michael," she called after him.

He flashed her a brief glance over his shoulder, but did not slow his pace. "Good. It's not that big a bottle."

Briana watched him walk away, unable to think of one single coherent thing else to say.

Surely his suggestion that she have a drink with him wasn't the action of a doctor toward a patient? But if it wasn't, what was it? There had been no personal warmth in his manner.

Michael joined Briana in the living room a few minutes later. He had changed into jeans that hugged his long, lean legs, and a dark blue sweater that matched his midnight eyes. He was carrying the open bottle of champagne. The cartons of Chinese food were already sitting on the coffee table, with chopsticks, forks and napkins beside them.

He flipped a switch, and a glowing fire burst into life in a black diamond hearth. Another flipped switch, and a piano began to play softly. The notes were just loud enough to be a pleasant background to conversation.

Briana had to admit that the setting was one much more conducive to seduction than to analysis. But it didn't seem that either was on Michael's mind. He took the chair across from her and raised his glass for a toast, a polite smile on his lips.

"Merry Christmas, Briana Berry."

She returned the greeting and sipped the champagne. It tasted heavenly—cool and sweet and refreshing. The last time Briana had champagne had been back in June, at a ground-breaking ceremony for one of her clients. She didn't remember it tasting anywhere near this good.

Nor did she remember the company being this good. Even in these more casual clothes, there was nothing casual about Michael Sands's drop-dead-gorgeous good looks.

If anything, he was even handsomer, the sweater revealing the enormous expanse of his shoulders and chest and the muscles in his arms, something his tuxedo had only hinted at.

And yet Briana felt an almost crushing calmness emanating from within that powerful frame. It was as though all his muscles had been completely stilled. And then she saw the deep glow of control in his midnight eyes, and was suddenly struck by the certainty that this man was in total command of himself. His mind, his body, his emotions, everything that defined him, was at the command of his will.

Briana was certain she had never met anyone like Michael Sands. She rather suspected that was because there was no one else like him. She also suspected that if she sat here staring at him for much longer, all these foolish feelings she was having for him would be flashing all over her face.

She refocused her attention on the carton of Uncle Chen's specialty before her. The prawns tasted as though they had been marinated in egg white, then sauteed with broccoli, water chestnuts and mushrooms in a delicate wine sauce. They were heavenly.

"So, who would you be with now if you hadn't found me beneath your tree, Michael?" she tried to ask casually.

"Someone I met at a party, perhaps. Or I might be alone."

"Alone?"

"You find that strange?"

"A little. Why would you be spending Christmas Eve alone?"

"I enjoy being with others, Briana, but I'm not a person who has to seek out other people's company because I'm uncomfortable with my own. Who would you be with tonight if you were back in Washington?"

"The person I'm with every Christmas Eve. My grandmother, Hazel."

"She's special to you?"

"Very. I was three years old when my mother died. Hazel raised me."

"No father?"

"He left my mom and me."

"What about siblings?"

"I had two older brothers, but they both died before I was born. There's just Hazel and me now. So, are your parents the kind who call to badger you to visit them during the holidays?"

"My parents were killed when I was in medical school."

"I'm sorry, Michael."

"There's no reason to be. Talking about it causes me no discomfort."

Briana wondered if Michael was kidding himself. She still felt a soreness of heart when she spoke of her mother's death, and she couldn't even remember her.

"Do you have any brothers or sisters?" she asked.

"I was an only child."

"How did your parents die?"

"In the pursuit of their work. They were geophysicists, dedicated to the field of plate tectonics."

"That has to do with earthquakes, right?" Briana asked.

"Yes. It's a relatively new science that seeks to explain the changes taking place in the earth's crust. My parents were sailing the Atlantic on a research vessel, laying cable in preparation for an experiment. A sudden swell washed them overboard. It was all over quickly. They died together, doing what they wanted to do."

He said that so matter-of-factly. Could it really be true that he felt not even a small pang at the memory of their passing? The possibility did not make Briana comfortable.

"So tell me more about your grandmother," Michael said.

"My grandfather died when she was only twenty. She took over his auto-repair shop and ran it by herself, long before women ever thought of doing such things. She was teaching me how to rebuild carburetors while other grandmothers were teaching their granddaughters how to bake cookies."

"Sounds like she's an original."

"Yes, a wonderful original. While I was growing up, Hazel used to take me to a retrospective theater in town that showed those old cowboy-and-Indian movies. She thought they were cleaner than the stuff in the regular theaters. But when the horses were made to fall down, she'd jump up and shout about how cruel it was and how many horses had been injured and killed while filming those scenes. The other patrons would start yelling at her to shut up and sit down." Briana paused to laugh in remembrance. "I can't tell you how embarrassed I used to be by Hazel's outbursts."

"What would you do?"

"Sink down in my chair and wish I were invisible. It wasn't until years later that I realized how truly brave she had been. She stood up for what she believed was right. And she let nothing and no one shout her down."

"You talk about her as though she's gone, Briana."

"That warmhearted, gutsy lady I knew is gone, in an important way."

"I don't understand."

Briana inhaled deeply before she went on to explain. "I was twenty when she started to get forgetful. Then the confusion came. Finally, she was diagnosed with Alzheimer's."

Briana felt the familiar ache and helplessness clogging her throat. She brought the glass to her lips and finished her champagne.

Michael's voice was suddenly very gentle. "They didn't

know that estrogen could be used to prevent Alzheimer's and minimize its severity at that time, did they?''

Briana shook her head. ''Hazel's decline continued. Four years ago, she could no longer recognize me or take care of herself. I had to put her into a nursing home. It was the hardest thing I've ever had to do.''

Briana stopped as tears threatened at the back of her eyes. She knew she mustn't cry. Hazel had taught her to laugh, not cry. She would not think of her with tears.

''This is the first Christmas Eve I've ever missed being with her,'' Briana continued after a moment.

''You visit her at the nursing home?'' Michael asked.

''I realize she doesn't know me anymore. But I talk to her anyway, about all those other Christmases she made so special because she was there for me. She always used to say that the secret to happiness was so simple—just laugh often and love a lot. I remember that now for both of us.''

The piano notes beat slowly, softly in the background. The muted light seemed to be darkening on the edges of the room. Briana closed her eyes and sent her love to her grandmother.

''You make me wish I had had a Hazel while I was growing up,'' Michael said after a quiet moment.

She opened her eyes to see the sincerity resting within his. Both his comment and his look surprised Briana.

''But you had your parents,'' she heard herself say.

''No. They had their careers.''

''They didn't raise you?''

''Their interests were not on child rearing.''

''Who was there for you?''

''An assortment of paid caretakers—some actual carers, other merely takers. They came and went so fast I remember very few of their names or faces. Time for some more champagne.''

She was surprised to see her glass was empty. As he refilled it, she thought about his words. She understood now that his parents hadn't been there for him. And that was why their deaths hadn't saddened him. The realization saddened her.

"It doesn't bother me, Briana. Don't let it bother you."

She shook her head, wondering how he had known what she was thinking. "So, they taught you to read minds as part of the psychiatric curriculum, I suppose?"

He leaned back in his chair and smiled.

"Sadness clouds the crystal clarity of your eyes."

His voice was deep velvet, the heat in his smile melting. Briana's heart sighed with a sharp, sweet longing. She told herself she was just feeling the champagne. She picked up the fortune cookie at the edge of her plate, cracked it open and focused her attention on the message inside.

Dreams can come true, it said.

Unfortunately, she found it far from sobering.

"What does it say?" Michael asked.

"Nothing important. So why don't you believe in psychoanalysis?" she asked, crumbling the piece of paper as she tried for a safer subject.

"The patient has to do all the talking, the exposing, the trusting, the risking," Michael said. "Which leaves the analyst with all the power. Any relationship between two people that is so severely one-sided is psychologically dangerous. Which is why so many patients end up angry at their analyst and sicker than when they started their so-called therapy."

"I've never experienced psychoanalysis personally, but I certainly can't fault the logic of your argument. What type of therapy do you use?"

"I don't have patients, so I don't use therapy. But if I did, it would be dream analysis. For it is only in dreams that the patient can learn to take control."

"You're talking real dreams, not daydreams?"

Michael came forward in his chair, leaning his elbows on his knees. His voice suddenly became deeper, the light in his eyes more intense.

"Daydreams are just another aspect of night dreams, Briana. Both tap into the unexplored continent on the other side of consciousness. Wild. Beautiful. Full of unadulterated natural resources. The source of incredible power.''

Briana wondered whether Michael had explored that continent, tapped into that incredible power. Was that why he seemed so different from other men?

"The only dreams I've ever recalled were either frightening nightmares or nonsensical, silly things,'' Briana admitted. "I'm having difficulty envisioning how such abstractions could become empowering.''

"How do you think lumber, nails, concrete and plaster are transformed into a beautiful dwelling?''

"Through the imagination and manipulation of the architect,'' Briana answered, without hesitation.

"And that is how dreams are transformed.''

"Who is the architect?'' she asked, intrigued by the analogy.

"The architect of any dream is the dreamer herself.''

"Then why do so many of my recalled dreams seem to be so negative?''

"We bring to dreams our feelings about the waking world. Two-thirds of most people's waking world is unpleasant. So it's no surprise that two-thirds of dreams are also unpleasant.''

"Two-thirds?'' Briana repeated. "That seems high.''

"Personal logs have been kept by literally thousands of people representing a cross section of society.''

"What kind of logs?''

"Volunteers recorded their thoughts each hour and evaluated them as pleasant or unpleasant. Then they spent the night in a sleep lab, where they evaluated their dreams in a like manner. We found human beings have a curious propensity to dwell on the disagreeable without even being aware of it.''

"Why?''

"I believe it's based on an inborn survival mechanism. Even a baby's attention will be drawn to the most frightening thing in its environment. We are wired to be on the lookout for whatever might come along to menace us.''

Briana laughed. ''Sounds like a healthy reaction to me.''

''If you're walking through a jungle where a tiger might be lurking. But constantly looking for threats in our more civilized world becomes an unhealthy habit. You stop noticing the beauty around you.''

''Are you saying that even if these volunteers were looking out at a beautiful scene of nature, they were still trapped in an internal world of worry?''

''That's exactly what I'm saying.''

''I never realized we were a species that lived our worries instead of our lives.''

''Well put. And what was also fascinating to discover was that when the individuals in the studies were foolish enough to watch the TV news or terrifying movies, their unpleasant days and dreams rose to nearly a hundred percent.''

''Did they realize what effect these things were having on them?''

''No. The pattern of worry and the tendency to let our minds dwell on the horrific are so ingrained that they go unnoticed and unanalyzed and, therefore, unchanged.''

''So we don't even know we're doing it to ourselves.''

''But the good news is that by learning to create pleasant dreams, we can also learn to create a more pleasant waking life.''

''How do you create pleasant dreams?''

''Same way you create everything else. With the right materials—desire, determination, and the power of imagination.''

''Fay called you the Sandman, Michael. She said you *design* dreams for people.''

''I can, when they are trying to achieve a particular goal in life. But for most people, their own dreams hold the secret to attaining whatever they could desire. You were dreaming when I found you tonight. It seemed to be a very pleasant dream. What do you remember of it?"

"Nothing, really. It faded fast when you awakened me."

"But you said earlier that the reason you kissed me back was because you thought the kiss was happening in the dream."

"Yes, I remember."

"Who were you kissing in that dream?"

"I don't know."

"But you wanted to kiss who it was?"

"I feel sure I did. But now it's so fuzzy."

"That's...regrettable."

Michael did look disappointed. Briana had the sudden suspicion that their entire conversation had been leading up to this.

He'd said he didn't believe in psychoanalysis. He hadn't said he wasn't going to suggest another way to treat her.

"Michael, tell me. Were you hoping to diagnose the reason for my missing weeks by getting me to pay attention to my dream?"

"It was worth a try. Dreams as compelling as the one you were having are often the secret to understanding what we're missing in our waking lives."

"When I return to Washington, I'm sure I'll recapture my missing memories."

"I doubt you'll be able to reclaim them on your own. You've suffered an emotional trauma."

"You believe my emotions are preventing me from remembering?"

"Briana, it's the only explanation left after physical trauma has been ruled out. Something happened during the last three weeks that you don't want to remember. And in every way it can, your mind is going to keep you from remembering it."

He was the expert on this stuff, of course. But it was still hard to accept. She didn't feel as if anything terrible had happened to unhinge her. She didn't feel unhinged at all.

"The weeks are gone," he said, "but the memories are still in your mind. Unfortunately, there is no question but that they'll be painful ones."

The seriousness in his voice gave her a chill.

"Hey, you're looking at a gal who's been body-waxed," she countered with a nervous chuckle. "I can handle pain."

He smiled, but his focus was not deterred. "Briana, it's extremely important to get the memories back and deal with them as soon as possible."

"What happens if I don't?"

"Suppressed memories are like rattlesnakes hiding under rocks. Sooner or later they'll come slithering out and strike."

It was a disturbingly vivid image. Briana rose quickly to her feet. This was beginning to feel too much like therapy.

"Thank you for the champagne and conversation, Michael. I'm sure you're a great doctor. I just don't want you to be mine."

He rose to stand before her. She was once again forcibly aware of the considerable height and breadth of him, and the sense of large-scale power leashed within his formidable frame. And the contrasting, heart-stopping gentleness in his eyes.

He took her hand in his, surprising her completely when he brushed a kiss across her knuckles. "Good night, Briana. I'm glad you don't want me as your doctor. I sure as hell don't want you as my patient."

And with that far-less-than-professional proclamation, Michael turned and strode from the room.

Briana stood absolutely still for several seconds as her heart pounded and every single inch of her skin tingled.

He *did* think her beautiful. She had felt it in the claiming of his hand, in his kiss across her fingers, in the sudden glow of his blue eyes before he turned away.

It was the nicest Christmas present a man had ever given her. That it had come from Michael Sands made it perfect.

Briana was still in a daze when she picked up her shoes and padded her way into the guest bedroom.

She didn't know whether it was the lateness of the hour or the two glasses of champagne catching up with her, but the moment her head hit the pillow, she went out.

If she had any dreams, she was not aware of them.

The next thing she knew, she was opening her eyes to morning pouring in from above. A skylight sat directly over the bed. At first she felt disoriented as she looked around at the strange bedroom. And then memories of the night before came flooding through her thoughts.

Three weeks gone! It seemed unbelievable in the stark light of day. But her surroundings were evidence to the truth.

She glanced at the clock on the nightstand. It was seven-thirty. She had gotten to bed very late. She was still very tired.

But she knew she couldn't afford to go back to sleep. She had a lot to do today. First, there was Lee to call. He must be getting very concerned, after no word from her for weeks. Unless the baby had come to claim his attention? She hoped so. She wouldn't want to have worried him.

She also hoped the nursing home would be taking calls today. It had been three weeks since she visited Hazel. The staff kept saying her grandmother wasn't aware of anything. But Briana kept hoping there might still be a spark left.

And, lastly, she had to say goodbye to Michael.

Briana felt an ache of regret at that last thought. She swung her legs off the bed and into her borrowed slippers. She padded into the bathroom and turned on the shower full blast. As soon as it was warm, she threw off her nightclothes and stepped beneath the strong spray.

She let the water pound the grogginess out of her brain. By the time she had shampooed her hair and scrubbed the rest of her body, she felt that all vestiges of sleep had slipped away. She reached for a towel and blotted the water off her skin.

Now all she needed was to brush her teeth and hair and get dressed and she'd be ready to face the world, maybe even her three missing weeks of it.

At least that was what she told herself.

But the instant she glanced into the mirror, she knew she'd been wrong. Dead wrong.

Chapter Three

Michael looked forward to his dreams as eagerly as he looked forward to the waking world. For he had discovered what few would ever know—and still fewer would ever achieve. He had discovered how to be conscious in his dreams.

"Waking up" in a dream had led Michael to some extraordinary experiences. He had walked through walls, perfected skills, soared past stars in the night sky, watched the birth of a sun, created colors beyond the spectrum of light and music beyond the scales. He could do anything he wanted to in his dreams.

But tonight, all he had wanted to do was make love to Briana.

Michael had worked hard to integrate his dreaming life with his waking one. To behave in his dreams in a manner inconsistent with the image he held of himself would be tantamount to putting his very sense of self in jeopardy. Which was why he had fought indulging his desires in his dreams tonight.

He had never had to fight his dreams before. It disturbed him deeply. Michael was a man in full control of his actions. But not even he was in full control of his dreams.

He wanted Briana. It was a good thing that she was leaving today. If she couldn't immediately get a plane to Washington, he'd make sure she had a hotel room in Las Vegas for however long she needed it.

He needed her safely on her way back home, so that he could safely work on controlling his dreams tonight. For he strongly suspected that she would be back in each and every one of them.

He glanced at the clock on the nightstand. It was after seven-thirty.

He rose from his bed and quickly washed, shaved and dressed. He headed for the kitchen to make himself some much-needed coffee.

The water gurgled and spit as the rich aroma of the ground beans filled the room. Outside the window, the winter sun was stretching across the horizon in a saffron haze. The desert terrain spread beneath it in patches of ivory and oatmeal. Night clouds unraveled in silken threads of plum and puce.

Michael never tired of this view.

Here in the heart of the high desert, he had found a quiet, subtle, unhurried beauty unlike any other, anywhere. Here he had found the perfect place to dream.

He had just poured himself a cup of the rich-smelling coffee when he heard the noise behind him. He whirled around, thinking it was way too early for Briana to be up. But there she was, stepping into the kitchen.

He froze in place, the cup in his hand suspended halfway to his lips as he stared at her. She had been an arousing enough apparition in the dark night. Beholding her by day made him feel a little dizzy, as if he'd stared at the desert sun too long.

Her hair was liquid fire, long and wet from her shower. Her skin was pure white desert light, and her eyes were that porcelain blue that he'd seen only once before, when he watched a winter sunset dip into the warm waters of Lake Mead.

She was wearing a blue terry-cloth bathrobe that hugged her slim body and ended high on her thighs. Her legs and feet were bare.

He rather suspected that the rest of her, beneath that robe, was bare, as well.

He wanted to act nonchalant, wish her good-morning, offer her a cup of coffee. But her unexpected arrival and attire after a night of dream denial made his brain go numb.

"Michael, I have something odd to tell you," she said, stepping forward. "I think you'd better sit down. Matter of fact, I think I'd better sit down."

She moved over to the table and pulled out a chair. The instant Michael saw that her hands were shaking, he snapped out of his mental daze.

He set his cup on the counter and came over to hold out the chair for her. She smiled up at him weakly as she murmured her thanks.

"Would you care for some coffee, Briana?"

"Care for it? I'd marry it and have its children."

Her humor seemed almost desperate. The sound of it sent a small warning tremor through Michael.

He'd witnessed her standing up to the unfathomable the night before with both strength and considerable stubbornness.

He saw neither of those emotions in her eyes this morning.

Michael filled a second cup with coffee as he tried to keep the foreboding from filling him. He brought it to Briana, and as he sat across from her, he watched her stir in milk and sugar before she took a hefty swallow. Her hands were still shaking.

"You've remembered something?" he prodded, keeping his voice even, mentally preparing himself for whatever it might be that had shaken her.

She set the cup carefully down and stared directly at him.

"Michael, I called my partner, Lee Willix, a little while ago. A Mrs. Eliot answered the phone. She doesn't know a Lee Willix. She says she's had that number for years."

"So you remembered the number wrong. These things happen."

She shook her head. "Not to me. I also called information. There is no Lee Willix listed. There is no Berry, Willix and Associates listed, either. And I spoke to the nursing home.

They say they have no record of a Hazel Doud in residence. My grandmother isn't there, Michael. I can't...find her.''

The sudden, devastatingly lost look in her lovely eyes made his heart lurch.

"It's all right," Michael said quickly. "As I told you last night, you've suffered an emotional trauma. You're confused about things. With time, with help—"

"That's not all."

Yes, there was something else clouding her eyes. Something that went way beyond confusion. "Go on," Michael said, in a voice that he made sure was perfectly even.

She laughed—not a merry sound, a lost sound. "I'm afraid to tell you. It sounds so...absurd."

Michael laid his hand over hers and smiled at her. "Briana, you never have to be afraid to tell me anything. Believe me, I've heard it all. We psychiatrists live on the very edge of absurdity."

Her eyes met his and steadied. "Michael, this isn't my face."

The smile slid off Michael's lips. He had thought he had prepared himself. But he had not been prepared to hear this.

"You're speaking metaphorically, Briana?" he asked, hopefully.

"No, literally. The face you're looking at is not my face, Michael. The first time I saw this face was when I woke up this morning and looked in the mirror. I'm not just missing three weeks. I'm missing my face."

She paused to laugh, with no mirth at all.

"You said you lived on the edge of absurdity? Well, it looks like I've just dropped off it."

"SHE'S A NUTCASE, all right," Nate said as he leaned back in his chair and plopped his feet on the edge of the desk in the computer room at the institute.

Michael let out a frustrated breath. "Thank you so much for that helpful contribution."

"Either that or she's been lying to you, Michael. Would you rather believe that?"

Michael rose from his chair behind the screen and paced out into the middle of the room, his friend's words mercilessly ringing through his ears.

After a moment, Michael turned back to face him. "Nate, she's not lying to me. And she's not a nutcase."

"Then what is she?"

"I don't know."

"Well, here's what I know, buddy. We've been on the phones and computers for hours, trying to find someone or something to substantiate that story she handed you, and we've come up with nothing. You want to hear it all again?"

"No."

"Maybe you need to. The Mirage did not have an architectural design convention three weeks ago. There is no Berry, Willix and Associates in Seattle. No grandmother Hazel Doud in a Silverdale nursing home. No Briana Berry in DMV records in Washington. No partner, Lee Willix, in those DMV records either. And when I searched the Internet for architectural designers in Washington State, neither Briana Berry nor Lee Willix were listed. Michael, the names, the numbers, nothing checks out. And to top it off, she tells you her face isn't hers. What more do you need to convince yourself you're dealing with someone who's lost it?"

"She hasn't lost it, Nate. Briana Berry is as sane as you or I."

"Okay, I'll bite. How do you know?"

"Because she still has her sense of humor."

"Since when did a sense of humor become the definition for sanity, *Doctor?*"

"Nate, anybody who can laugh and make jokes when she discovers the world she knows doesn't exist has a deep core of sanity inside her. She'd have to. Humor is the first emotion to go on the road to madness."

"All right then, answer me this, Michael. How can she be sane and yet not be in touch with reality?"

"I admit the situation doesn't lend itself to logic. But there is a sense beyond logic, Nate. That sense is what brought the Institute of Dreams into reality. That sense is the gut feeling that tells us something's right, even when that something doesn't fit in with what is accepted as the current 'truth' or 'logic.'"

Nate stared up at Michael, a frown pulling together his dark eyebrows. "Are you sure it's a feeling in your gut, and not another part of your anatomy, that's telling you the lady is sane?"

"Meaning?"

"You know what I mean, Michael. Are you attracted to this woman?"

"A man would have to be dead *not* to be attracted to this woman."

"Then you definitely can't treat her."

"I don't want to treat her. And she doesn't want me to treat her."

"Good. It's unanimous."

"There's just one problem."

"What?"

"You have another psychiatrist to recommend?"

"Me? You know I wouldn't trust most psychologists or psychiatrists with the emotional health of my goldfish, much less another human being. What about a colleague you trust?"

"I was on the phone trying to get in touch with every one I know this morning, while you were on your way over. It's no use, Nate. None of the doctors I have any confidence in are available until after the holidays."

"Can't you just leave it alone until then?"

"Briana needs help now. She's dealing with this exceptionally well, but everyone has a limit. And unless I can get her some answers quickly, she'll soon be reaching hers. Consider. No one and nothing she remembers is real. How long do you think you could remain sane under such circumstances?"

"So you're saying you have to treat her? You have no choice?"

"There's always a choice. I can turn my back on her. But what kind of a doctor and man would that make me?"

"Prudent."

"Come again?"

"Michael, have you ever handled a case like hers before?"

"I've never even *heard* of a case like hers before."

"Which is my point. Your practice, even before you founded the institute, was geared toward enhancing mental health, not trying to reclaim it. Have you considered you may not be able to help her?"

"The nice thing about specializing in dreams, Nate, is that through them you can help anyone with anything."

"Spoken like the eternal optimist you are, Michael. So, did you call me over here on Christmas to act as an expert for checking her background through the computer databases, or as a sounding board for a decision you had already made?"

Michael smiled. "Both, of course."

Nate shook his head. "You expected me to try to talk you out of this?"

"I hoped you could."

"Hoped?"

"I'm not blind to the fact that I'm far closer to...this situation than is comfortable. There was always the possibility that you could come up with a viable alternative to my treating her."

"I may think of one yet," Nate said, rising. "Stay close to the phone."

"I'll pick it up on the first ring."

Nate studied Michael's face. "You weren't kidding. You *really don't* want to treat her."

"I'd rather be put in a straitjacket and locked in a padded cell."

Nate shook his head. "Maybe you should be, if you like her that much and still treat her. Which reminds me, our Christmas present to you left the party last night with a widower from Alamo who has a ranch, two kids and apparently a hankering to get hitched. Seems as though it was love at first sight. Laura told me to thank you for not showing up.''

Michael smiled. ''Tell her she's welcome. Hope you two have a great Christmas, Nate.''

''Unfortunately, it's not going to be all that great,'' Nate said. ''We're having dinner at Uncle Everett's.''

''Our old nemesis Everett Thaw? Ah, yes. I keep forgetting he's part of your family now that you and Laura have gotten married.''

Nate headed for the door. ''I wish I could forget it.''

''At least he's stopped trying to infiltrate the institute with his spies. Could be he's finally given up on the idea that he's going to get his hands on his late wife's legacy to us.''

Nate reached the door and turned around, his hand on the knob. ''And then again, it could be that Everett Thaw is still mired in that slick primordial ooze the rest of us climbed out of a billion or so years ago.''

Michael chuckled.

Nate opened the door, his expression taking on a somber look as he gazed back at Michael. ''Buddy, be careful. That wasn't a Christmas present left beneath your tree last night. That was a ticking bomb.''

Nate was out the door before Michael could respond. It was just as well. He had no idea how he could respond. For Nate was right.

The moment Briana awakened in his arms and returned his kiss, the fuse had been lit. And he knew that if he didn't want all that dynamite exploding in his face, he must never, ever, take her back into his arms again.

''BUT LAST NIGHT you told me you didn't want to be my doctor,'' Briana said to Michael, very surprised to hear his offer of help.

''I want you to be well,'' Michael responded.

Briana didn't miss the equivocation in his words. Or their

professional delivery and phraseology. It sounded almost as though he didn't think anyone else would take her case.

Maybe no one else would.

Nothing about her life had proved to exist. There was no Grandmother Hazel, no partner Lee, no architectural firm, not one scrap of evidence that anything she remembered was real.

Not even her face.

She understood now why Michael had looked at her with such warmth when he kissed her awake the night before. This face she was wearing was absolutely fabulous. Not in her wildest imagination had she ever seen herself looking this good.

At least, if she had to lose her mind, she had lost that homely mug of hers along with it.

Dear God, her face was gone! Everything was gone! As often as she said it, she couldn't make herself believe it was true.

And yet a part of her had accepted it—a part that sent her nerves screaming inside her body in panic and outrage. She took a deep breath, trying to calm them, trying to hold on to a thin rim of reality while the earth tilted and the ground disappeared from beneath her feet.

She had called everywhere. There was not one available airline seat on any plane to Washington for a couple of days, even if she had the money to pay for it. She needed help. And Michael was offering his.

"So, Dr. Sands, if I wait another day before availing myself of your professional services, do I get the benefit of an after-Christmas sale?"

A small smile drew back his lips. "Actually, you got lucky, Ms. Berry. My hourly rate is always its lowest for treatment started on Christmas Day."

"Slow time of year, huh?"

"Got to do what I can to beat the competition."

She didn't know if it was the man or the doctor who was indulging in this light banter with her. To either, or both, she sent a silent thank-you. Humor was the only scaffolding she had left to support what remained of her sanity.

She took another deep breath, trying to summon up some conviction for the words she was about to say.

"Michael, sane or not, I still know who I am."

"I'm glad, Briana. Hold on to that knowledge."

Her words rushed out on a breath filled with incredulity. "You believe me?"

"I never thought you were lying to me."

"Despite the fact that nothing about the life and people I described to you appear to exist?"

"You're real, Briana. That's good enough for me."

Her relief broke through on a hearty laugh. "Michael Sands, you may be the one who needs his head examined."

He laughed with her, surprising her anew. "I've no doubt I do."

The sound of his laughter filled Briana with an odd sense of rightness—as though the world might actually find its proper axis again.

Or was she kidding herself? Could it be that he was simply responding to this beautiful face she was now wearing?

She had seen what the power of a woman's physical beauty could do. Men would make almost any allowance for such a woman.

"Michael, you should know what I really look like," she said, determined to have honesty between them if nothing else.

"All right. What do you really look like, Briana?"

"I have a Cyrano nose, a lantern jaw, and no cheekbones or chin to speak of. My hair isn't really this gorgeous flame color. It's the proverbial mousy brown. I also generally weigh about five pounds more."

He seemed remarkably unaffected by her confession. "Anything else?"

"Michael, I don't think you're getting it. I'm not pretty at all. I'm quite plain."

"Briana, when you look in the mirror, what do you see?"

"I may be crazy, but I'm not blind. The face I'm wearing now looks like one of those gorgeous airbrushed ones that grace the covers of fashion magazines."

"How do you feel when you look at it?"

"Like Santa Claus answered all those letters I've been writing to him since I was six."

"Briana, the reasons for your not recognizing your face are undoubtedly related to your reasons for not remembering the last three weeks. Don't worry about what you look like on the outside right now. Think about how you feel on the inside."

"I feel like Alice when she fell into the rabbit hole. The world doesn't make sense to me anymore. Nothing I know is out there. Where is Hazel, Michael? Why can't I find her? What's happened to her?"

"We've checked everywhere we could to locate her," he said calmly. "If there is something else, somewhere else that you can think of our checking, we'll do it. Is there?"

"No."

"Then do you believe that you have done all you can?"

"Yes. But I'm still worried."

"Remember our discussion of last night? People who fill their moments worrying about things over which they have no control live very unpleasant lives."

"But my thoughts keep turning to her."

"Then we need to find something else to occupy them."

He rose and held out his hand.

She slipped her hand inside his large one. Michael drew her gently to her feet. His hold on both her eyes and hand was wonderfully steady.

"It was too dark last night for you to see the Institute of Dreams properly. Would you like to see it now?"

She nodded, falling into step beside him, aware that he was deliberately slipping his hand out of hers. Still, there was a lovely, comforting warmth left in its wake.

"I don't believe in insisting on an unnatural formality between doctor and patient," Michael said. "That just erects walls to understanding. But I do believe in ethical, professional behavior. You will be absolutely safe here.''

Briana knew exactly what he was telling her. He was her doctor now. And, as her doctor, he would be making no personal advances toward her. A wall might not be between them, but he had definitely drawn a line.

She realized it had to be this way—that he had to be this way. He was being true to both his profession and himself.

Briana found the Institute of Dreams to be an enormous building full of gleaming white marble walls and floors. In sharp contrast to the richness of Michael's art deco apartment, its interior was clean-lined, ultramodern, with four large wings radiating out of a huge glass-domed central rotunda. Each wing was marked by a phase of the moon inscribed above its door.

Michael led Briana down the long, spotless white hallways of the wings. Feeding off them were sleep labs, libraries, lounges, conversation centers, computer hubs and many offices, all deserted on this Christmas day.

Briana was struck by the calmness of it, certain that the impression of unhurried relaxation would still pervade it even when it was filled with people.

Michael walked her through his wing last. A full moon adorned its entryway. Briana stopped to read aloud the words etched into the golden plaque that hung beside the door to his private office.

'''Discover Your Dreams and Discover Yourself.'''

"Do you mean that literally, Michael?"

"Yes. I believe that to really know ourselves we first have to know our dreams."

"Is that what you do for your patients—help them to discover themselves in their dreams?"

"I haven't had a patient since I started the institute. But it is partially what I do for my clients."

"The ones who are successful politicians, entertainers?"

"Yes, some use what they learn in their dreams to attain such ends, or to enhance their abilities in those fields. The confidence that comes with knowing who you are is tremendously empowering. With it, you can achieve a great deal.''

He leaned in front of her to open the door, bringing that rich scent of balsam with him.

"What have you achieved with yours?" she asked.

"Everything I want," his deep, mesmerizing voice answered.

His office had that same spacious, calm feeling that pervaded the rest of the building—as though the quiet expanse of the desert had been coaxed indoors.

"So, what do you think of the institute?" Michael asked.

"It's very impressive, Michael."

"Only...?" he invited, appearing to be perfectly aware of the qualification she had so carefully kept out of her words.

"Except for the spectacular rotunda reaching for the sky, I get the impression of a blank, white canvas, lacking that splash of color that would give it focus."

"And that is exactly why the institute was designed the way it was, Briana. It is the canvas. The insightful dreams that take place here are those splashes of color, the events that give it meaning and focus."

"People have insightful dreams here?"

"People have insightful dreams everywhere. Still, there is something about the stillness of this high desert and the isolation at the institute that seem particularly suited to encouraging the unconscious to come forth and introduce itself."

"Is that how you define an insightful dream?"

"I try not to limit an insightful dream by trying to define it. All dreams have the capacity to be insightful if the dreamer cares enough to delve deeply into them. You'll spend tonight in my sleep lab, Briana. Tomorrow we'll work on the dreams we discover."

"And in the meantime?"

"In the meantime, it will be best not to fill your mind with worry. It helps not at all. And it hurts. As your doctor, I'm prescribing some sun and exercise. Do you like to swim?"

"Very much. But I haven't done it in a while. Is there a pool nearby?"

"Right in our backyard. Come on, I'll show you."

They stepped out into a lovely day. The temperature was in the sixties, with a light breeze and a bright yellow sun and a view that went on forever. Briana discovered to her delight that the institute sat atop a high, flat, enormous mesa, surrounded by the towering Virgin Mountains, a deep violet valley, and pale ribbon strips of cyan, carrot and cocoa in a parchment sky.

The open spaces between the building's four wings were shaped like pie wedges. Michael pointed out a gazebo in one wedge with white wrought iron and stained-glass globes, twinkling in the winter light like a Fabergé egg.

Another pie wedge contained a large circular pad with a helicopter. The third a parking lot.

In the final pie-wedge sat an Olympic-size pool. Its blue water was shaded beneath a cream canopy and flanked by a row of swaying palms.

Michael led the way to the pool through a carefully pruned landscape of jade and piñon pines. Briana looked out at the glowing day and expansive view around her.

"I have to admit there's something special about the wide-open spaces and warmth of the desert. This time of year, where I live in Washington, the ground's covered in snow and ice and the sky's heavy with clouds that block out the light. I can't believe this is Christmas and I'm standing in this incredible sunlight."

"What do you like about living in Washington?"

"The way its towering trees scrub the air until it's sparkling-clean. And the way a new season suddenly touches you."

"How does a season suddenly touch you, Briana?"

"With the jubilant cries of the geese as they wing over the waterways, heading north to herald in the spring. Or with the scent of heavenly summer warmth from a hundred-year-old cedar tree anchored firmly in the rich earth of a forest. Or with the sight of an autumn dawn showering the chilly air with leaves of red and gold and amber light. Or when the enticing heat of a rare winter sunshine warms my skin as I trudge knee-deep through snow.''

"You do seem to know the seasons in Washington State quite well.''

She turned to him. "You've been there?''

"Several years ago. I can't attest to what it's like in summer and fall, but the rarity of sunlight in winter and that noisy arrowhead formation of geese following the waterways into Canada in spring are events I remember well.''

"So you accept the fact that I live there.''

"Or else you've read a lot of travel brochures,'' he said with a smile. "I don't want you to tire your muscles out when you swim. Just give them some gentle exercise. Concentrate on enjoying yourself. And do your best to dwell on the beauty of the day, not the darkness of worries.''

"Is that your prescription for good dreams?''

"For a good life in general. Regular physical activity also has a beneficial effect on dream recall.''

"My physical activity isn't all that regular,'' Briana admitted. "Life just always seems to be too busy to fit it in.''

"You'll be fitting it in as long as you're here. Doctor's orders. That pink-striped cabana on the opposite end of the pool has an assortment of women's bathing suits. You should find one that fits.''

Briana followed Michael's pointing finger to the dressing room and nodded.

"When you're finished swimming, you can change back into your things and meet me in the apartment.''

"You're not going to join me in the pool?''

"I'll take my swim later. After you're done, I'll see what I can do about putting together some kind of Christmas dinner for us. You don't happen to cook, by any chance?''

"No, just an architect. But I know how to use a microwave, if you need any help.''

"Have you always wanted to be an architect?" Michael asked, a quizzical look in his eyes.

"Astronaut was my first choice," she replied. "I saw my husband and myself living on a distant planet, giving birth to our brood of little astronauts. I probably read too much Isaac Asimov."

"When did you change your focus to earthly structures?"

"When I started to notice that all the spaceships I envisioned had sunken tubs and skylights and I was having more fun designing them than fantasizing about taking off in them."

"What design would you say the institute reflects?" he asked, his questions taking on a more focused direction.

"Frank Lloyd Wright meets Boeing Aircraft?"

Michael chuckled.

"It's a complex of strong shapes blended to stand up to the sun and cast striking shadows," Briana answered more seriously. "It reminds me of no one school of design, but rather seems to be a great white bird of architectural sophistication that has momentarily landed on this flat desert mesa in order to better enjoy the view."

"How is its dome-shaped ceiling in the rotunda portion achieved?"

"The hemispheric shape is constructed on the principle of an arch, where the downward forces are transferred outward to the walls that support its weight."

"And now for the most important test, Ms. Berry. How many architects does it take to change a light bulb?"

She smiled. "Just one. But now that I've taken a closer look at that light bulb, I can see that the beam supporting its socket will have to be replaced. Looks as though the job will cost at least triple my original estimate and will take at least three times as long to complete."

"You're an architect, all right. Or at the very least a building contractor."

They grinned at each other before Briana turned and

walked toward the cabana. She didn't know how Michael had done it, but she already felt a whole lot better.

She suspected that all he had really done was be Michael Sands. It felt good being around a man who didn't let worry control him. A man who saw silver linings, not clouds. A man who appreciated the moment. A man who lived what he believed.

A woman could be herself with such a man. No, a woman could be the *best of herself* with such a man.

When Briana carefully waded into the water a few moments later, she was delighted to find it warm. She knew she was out of condition and expected to soon be out of breath as she kicked off from the side. But after three laps, her muscles weren't at all tired and she still had wind and stamina.

This was incredible. Not only did she have a new and improved face, she also had a new and improved pair of lungs and muscles.

What next? Einstein's I.Q.?

"OUR MICHAEL SANDS found a bride beneath his Christmas tree?" Laura Lacen Quinn asked as she smiled across the table at her husband of two months.

Nathaniel Quinn grinned back as he speared a piece of turkey with his fork.

"Her unexpected appearance at the institute was the reason that our fearless leader ended up a no-show at the party last night."

Laura chuckled, thoroughly delighted with the thought. And thoroughly captivated by her husband's smile. She knew she would never, could never, get tired of it. Or of seeing the way his dark hair curled errantly over the collar of his white dress shirt. Or the way the warmth in his gold-dust eyes poured through her like liquid sunshine.

She loved Nathaniel Quinn with a passion that seemed to get deeper and more intense with each passing day. She was so filled and overflowing with happiness that she wanted everyone she liked to experience the joy that such a love could bring.

Which was why she had tried so diligently to match Michael Sands to every one of her attractive, unattached women friends.

All to no avail, of course. The suave and sophisticated Dr. Michael Sands had proved impervious to every feminine persuasion. He was not marriage material, he kept insisting. Which was why Laura was so tickled by the idea of someone sending him a bride.

Whoever was behind this prank obviously had a marvelous sense of humor.

"Who did it, Nate?" Laura asked.

Nate shrugged his shoulders. "Michael doesn't know."

"The bride won't say?" Laura chuckled delightedly once again. "Good for her."

"I think it's more the bride doesn't know," Nate said more seriously. "It appears she's...unbalanced."

"Oh," Laura said, disappointed to have what had seemed to be a merry tale end on a sad note.

"Unbalanced?" Everett repeated the word, his voice rising to an odd pitch. "What do you mean, unbalanced? What did she say?"

Laura looked over at her uncle's pudgy face, and was more than surprised to see the pinpoints of interest in his light eyes. Everett seldom took an interest in things that didn't fatten his pocketbook, his social standing or his stomach.

"The woman has become Michael's patient, Everett," Nate answered Laura's uncle. "It would be unethical of me to discuss the specifics of the case."

"Patient?" Everett repeated at the top of his voice. "Michael Sands made this bride his *patient?*"

"Everett, what's wrong with you?" Laura asked. "Why are you getting so upset?"

"Upset? I'm not getting upset," Everett said, his cheeks belying his protestation as they turned the same color as the cranberry on his plate. "I just want to know why Michael

Sands thinks he has the right to involve the institute in this business!''

"Thinks he has the right?" Nate repeated.

"He shouldn't have done that!" Everett shouted. "What does he know about this woman, or where she came from? She could be anyone, from anywhere!"

"Everett, what are you talking about?" Laura asked, getting more and more alarmed at her uncle's odd outburst and anger.

"What do you mean, what am I talking about? Could I be any plainer? Sands is overstepping his authority!"

"Michael Sands is the founder, chairman of the board *and* the chief stockholder in the Institute of Dreams," Nate said, his voice not quite its normal calm. "Just whose head is he supposed to be going over?"

"Naturally *you'd* come to his defense, Quinn."

"Michael doesn't need defending," Laura said. "He hasn't done anything wrong. Everett, you're seriously overreacting to this situation."

"Overreacting?" Everett repeated, that odd strident pitch still riding his voice. "We'll just see who's overreacting. Sands is going to get the institute into trouble one of these days! You mark my words!"

"Everett, what has gotten into you?" Laura asked, her exasperation coming through.

"I don't want to talk about this anymore!" he said, his voice almost a shout. "I've said all I'm going to say. Now let me eat my dinner in peace!"

Laura watched as Everett's rounded shoulders hunched around his head, as though he were a turtle suddenly trying to retreat into his shell. He began to ruthlessly cut his turkey breast into tiny little pieces.

Laura looked across the table to see if Nate understood anything that Everett had just been ranting about. It was clear from Nate's expression that he didn't have any more of a clue than she did. But Nate's shoulder shrug was a signal to Laura that he'd just as soon let the subject drop.

Laura understood. Nate hated engaging in pointless conversations with her Uncle Everett. Which for the most part meant *any* conversation with her Uncle Everett.

But as they finished their Christmas dinner in silence, Laura couldn't help wonder what was eating at her uncle.

Could it be that he was behind the mysterious bride appearing beneath Michael's tree? Had Everett sent her to the institute to spy?

Laura would have sworn that Everett had given up on that silly business back in September, when he tried unsuccessfully to use *her* as his spy.

But there was no denying that he was acting very strange tonight. Very strange. And if that wasn't guilt written all over his pudgy face, then she was Santa Claus.

What was Everett up to now?

Chapter Four

The single bed in the sleep lab was fairly comfortable, but Briana looked at the black mask Michael held dubiously.

"It's feather-light," he assured. "The latest technology. You'll hardly know you're wearing it."

"What's its purpose?"

"There are tiny computer chips buried in the fibers. They'll record your brain waves so I'll know when you're asleep. The ones across your eyes will let me know when they start moving. That's called rapid eye movement or REM sleep. It's the time when dramatic dreams take place."

"What do you mean by dramatic?"

"We dream through most of the night. But the dreams that accompany REM sleep are those in which the subconscious reveals itself in the most theatrical way."

"Dressed in costumes, wearing wigs?" Briana said, chuckling at the image, not really meaning to be serious.

"Sometimes in elaborate disguises," Michael said, very seriously. "And sometimes stripped to the bare essentials. Briana, as soon as my instruments tell me a REM dream is over, I will be awakening you and asking you questions about it."

"How will you awaken me?"

"By calling your name. I'll remain in the control room. There's a two-way microphone built into the nightstand. I'll talk to you through it."

"And after I tell you about my dream?"

"Then you can go back to sleep. Until I wake you after the next one. You should have at least three REM dreams tonight."

"What if I don't have any dreams?"

"You will. We all do. Most of us simply don't remember them. Tonight you will."

She could feel his fingers brushing lightly against her temples as he fitted the mask into place. She could feel the warmth of him, smell his scent. Her pulse took a small leap. The sudden blackness was absolute.

"Michael, if you're monitoring my sleep all night, when are you going to get any shut-eye?"

"I'll take a nap tomorrow. Now relax and stop worrying, Briana. Concentrate on telling yourself you're going to have an insightful dream."

"You can get one by willing yourself to have it?"

"Always feel free to ask your unconscious for what you want when you dream. And don't be surprised when you get it."

She heard his footsteps recede out of the sleeping cubicle.

He was what she'd really like to dream about tonight. Not that there would be anything insightful about such a dream. She already knew how she felt. She would love to be back in Michael's arms, melting into his kiss. Briana sighed as she turned onto her side.

The words from that silly fortune cookie came back to her, *Dreams can come true.*

She wondered how Michael would respond if he woke her tonight after a REM episode, expecting some insightful dream recitation, only to hear her tell him of how she'd been tearing off his tuxedo and jumping him on his own couch?

She chuckled at the thought.

Here she was facing a world without a familiar thing in it, and all she could fantasize about was the doctor she had met on awakening into it. No doubt about it. She was bonkers.

MICHAEL WATCHED the displays on his control panel, feeding in from the sleep cubicle, monitoring Briana's brain waves and eye movement states. He knew he had more than an hour to wait before he could expect her to enter REM sleep.

He eagerly awaited her dreams. The thought that she was just missing three weeks had been one thing. But she wasn't just missing time, she was missing her identity.

The woman she thought she was didn't exist. And yet, whoever she was, she was more real to him than any woman he had ever known.

He remembered her telling him about her grandmother as they sipped champagne on Christmas Eve. Briana's bitter-sweet memories of her grandmother had brought her alive for Michael. Whether Hazel was real, he didn't know. But he did know that she was real to Briana.

And yet, Briana's beauty was not real to her. Michael knew beautiful women walked around with an antenna, that unconscious air of understanding that all eyes would be on them. It was in their walk, the way they held their shoulders, the knowing smile on their lips, the artfulness of their makeup and dress, the covert glances to judge their effect on others.

Briana had no such antenna, no such air, no such awareness at all that she was beautiful. And that was astounding, particularly considering how astoundingly beautiful she was.

Whatever had happened to strip her of her memories had also stripped her of the knowledge of her beauty. Completely. Even her unconscious knowledge.

If this was a fantasy she had created in her mind, it defied all logic. Which was the most mysterious part of all. Because Briana herself seemed quite logical.

Michael remembered telling Nate that very morning that the nice thing about dreams was that by paying attention to them, anyone could be helped with anything.

He couldn't wait for Briana's dreams to solve her mystery.

Briana's REM state began precisely ninety-two minutes after she had fallen asleep. The dream wasn't a long one, lasting only ten minutes. When the REM state was over, Michael switched on the microphone to her cubicle.

"Briana?"

He called her name several more times before he saw her brain wave pattern changing to wakefulness and then heard her voice saying groggily, "Michael?"

"You were dreaming, Briana. Sink back into the dream. Tell me where you were."

Her words were soft, slightly slurred. "I was in this elaborate bedroom suite. The furniture was very ornate, ponderous."

"Who was with you?"

"Two women. One was older, in her sixties, I believe. She was elegantly dressed. The other seemed younger—fifty, maybe. She was well dressed, too, but not quite as elegantly as the older woman."

"Who were these women?"

"I seemed to know them, Michael, but I don't know who they were, if that makes any sense."

"Perfect dream sense. Go on."

"The two women were upset at me. It had something to do with this dress the older woman had handed me. It smelled terribly unhappy—like lavender."

"You could smell the dress in your dream?" Michael asked, more than surprised.

"Yes."

"Was the dress a lavender color?"

"No, it was white."

"And you're sure it smelled like lavender?"

"Yes."

"Why did the scent of lavender on the dress make you think of something terribly unhappy?"

"I don't know. It just did."

"What happened next?"

"The women were angry because I wouldn't wear the dress. I felt upset, too. The more we argued, the more their voices sounded like barking dogs. I finally couldn't stand it anymore. I ran from the room. That was when the dream ended.''

"Go back to sleep now, Briana."

Michael turned off his microphone. He watched the monitor until Briana's brain waves indicated she had returned to sleep. He checked the recorder to make sure he had captured Briana's account of her dream and then leaned back in his chair, waiting for the next one.

The first dream hadn't made much sense to him. But he knew that was normal. Most dreams didn't make sense to outsiders. The only person who could really interpret a dream was the dreamer. Tomorrow they'd discuss all her dreams and she'd decipher their meanings.

Michael yawned sleepily.

Normally, when he spent a night in the sleep lab control booth, he had planned ahead and caught a nap the afternoon before. Or at least a good sleep the night before.

Tonight he had had neither. And he was feeling it. Still, he was determined to keep awake and alert.

Michael had frequently witnessed a sort of beginner's luck associated with those first attempts a person made to get in touch with their dreaming mind. The first night often yielded astounding results.

This was Briana's first night. It was absolutely necessary that he capture her every dream.

He rested his head against the back of his chair and closed his eyes, relaxing his muscles, putting himself in a meditative state that would allow him to become instantly alert with the start of Briana's next REM dream.

She awakened more easily after the second dream, and responded quicker to his questions.

"I was at the top of this awkwardly winding staircase with a deep red carpet, part of a procession. On the walls to my left were all these old family portraits."

"Your family?"

"No. Someone else's. The house was not mine. Thankfully."

"Thankfully?"

Briana laughed. "It was an enormous stone structure with several dozen rooms, a crenellated roofline, a central square tower, a totally enclosed Tudor-Gothic fortress that looked like it belonged on an eighteenth-century Scottish hillside."

"Is that where you were? In eighteenth-century Scotland?"

"No. It was contemporary time. The tuxedos and pierced ears on the men were proof of that. Although how a hunky guy who has to shave twice a day just to look marginally civilized could ever think pierced ears are sexy is beyond me."

"The men in your dream were wearing tuxedos?" Michael asked.

"They were ushers. A full orchestra was playing the wedding march. The maid of honor and the bridesmaids had on deep red dresses with white sashes."

Michael felt every muscle in his body snapping to full attention. He carefully kept his rising emotions out of his voice. "Were you in this procession or watching it, Briana?"

"I seemed to be behind it. Only I turned around, and when I turned back, the bridesmaids and ushers were gone."

"Were you still at the top of the stairs?"

"Yes, but the stairs were different, steeper, and it was the older woman who stood with her back to me, the one who had tried to give me the dress that smelled of lavender."

"In your earlier dream?"

"Yes. She was dressed differently, not nearly so fine."

"Go on."

"The woman was cleaning the stairs with this old canister-style vacuum. The cord was looping around her ankles. She didn't seem to be noticing."

"What happened?"

"I called out to warn her. But she didn't hear me, because the vacuum was making so much noise. She tripped on the cord and began tumbling down the stairs."

"What did you do?"

"I watched her fall to the bottom. I wanted to go down to

her, but I was afraid. I tried to climb on the banister so that I could slide down. But the banister was too high, and I couldn't reach it. I didn't know what to do, and I was so scared. I started screaming something.''

"What, Briana?"

"I don't know. The dream ended. It made no sense."

"It will, Briana. Go back to sleep now. Your next dream is going to be even more important than your first two."

Briana didn't know whether Michael was just giving her a suggestion so that she would have an important dream or whether he knew something she didn't. But she sank quickly back into sleep, suddenly quite sure she would have that more important dream.

When it came, it brought her fast awake, sitting upright in her bed, her palms perspiring, her heart pounding. She tore off the sleeping mask.

"Michael?" she called.

"Yes, Briana, I'm here. You've just brought yourself out of this last dream. What's wrong?"

"I was back at the wedding, Michael."

"The same wedding in your earlier dream?"

"Yes. I recognized it. The same house. The same full orchestra playing the wedding march. The same procession of bridesmaids and ushers."

"Briana, were you the bride in this wedding?"

Briana took a very deep breath, willing her heart to steady. "Yes."

"Describe everything you remember."

"We marched through the house outside to an elegant formal English garden sitting right in the center of the house's inner courtyard. There were thousands of pure white rosebuds, mixed with bloodred ones, adorning a series of arches. We walked under them."

"Go on."

"A minister and groom waited beneath a single pure white baby rose altar arch at the end of the garden."

"For you?"

"Yes. I marched up a clover-carpeted path to stand by the groom. He was big, with brown hair. I tried to see his face, but the bridal veil was suddenly too thick. The minister was asking me if I would love and honor him. And then he said the words 'until death do you part,' and I answered, 'I will,' only I was vehemently shaking my head no."

"You didn't want to marry this man?"

"I don't know what I wanted."

"What happened next?"

"I shut my eyes tightly for a moment, and when I opened them again to face the minister, he had disappeared, and suddenly I found myself in this elegant ballroom, being whirled around to an old-fashioned waltz. And I knew I was at the wedding reception."

"Who were you dancing with?"

"I couldn't see his face."

"Was it the groom?"

"I think it might have been. I was looking around as my partner whirled me over the floor. I saw a smiling man in the crowd on the sidelines of the ballroom."

"Who was the smiling man?"

"I don't know. He had black hair. I saw his features only in profile. He was talking with someone who didn't seem to be responding. Then the person he was talking to suddenly turned toward me. He or she was wearing this hockey player's mask, with nothing but black holes where there should have been eyes and a mouth. I didn't want to look at it."

"What did you do?"

"The music was suddenly playing too loudly. My dancing partner was holding me too tightly. I pulled away from him and ran out of the room. And then I was outside again, in the English garden, underneath the wedding arch. The minister was smiling and telling the groom it was time to kiss me. I felt his lips on mine, and the dream ended."

"On a happy note, it seems. You've spent a very productive night, Briana. Your dreams have exceeded even my expectations. They are detailed and very unusual."

"More unusual than you know."

"What do you mean?"

"I didn't just have that dream this morning, Michael. I was having that same dream last night when you awakened me. When I kissed you back, it was because I thought I was kissing my new husband, the husband of my dreams."

SERGEANT ELENA VIERRA was not happy. Matter of fact, she was livid.

It had taken *four years* for her to finally get enough seniority to have the holidays off and spend them with her kids. And what happened? At the very last minute, two of the force came down with the flu, and she got stuck with holiday duty anyway.

And on top of that, she had a terrible case of PMS.

She always snickered when she heard the experts talk about overtestosteroned men and the damage their raging hormones could do. She'd match it with the rage of a woman with a full-blown case of PMS any day.

She felt like shooting someone. And if she had to write up one more stupid, petty complaint with paper and pen because the fools who had put in the computers hadn't had the foresight to keep even one damn typewriter for the times they went down, she *was* going to shoot someone.

"Sergeant Vierra," a male voice called, cold and clipped, the voice of a man who was used to barking out orders.

The sound was akin to a nail scraping across Elena's already irritated chalkboard ears. Maybe this would be the petty complainant she ended up shooting.

She looked up to see a big, broad man of about forty, with glossy brown hair and green eyes. He was very good-looking, and the lines of hard living on his face told her he'd been taking full advantage of it. He reminded Elena of her husband, the one she'd finally booted out after supporting him and his gambling habit for ten years, the one who had made her immune to good-looking men.

Although this one appeared to have some money. He was wearing a handmade silk suit and a platinum Rolex.

Elena rose to face him. She was five-eleven. She judged the man to be six-four and packing at least two hundred and forty pounds on his beefy frame.

Big, handsome, loaded.

In her twenty years on the Las Vegas police force, Elena had seen only one other to match him. And she'd seen him less than two days before. Maybe it was the holiday season that brought out these gorgeous guys.

"And who are you?" she asked.

"H. Sheldon Ayton the Third," he said, and the sound of old money just rippled through the words.

Elena gestured to a chair in front of her desk.

"How can I help you, Mr. Ayton?" she asked, sitting down again. It was a polite platitude that she mouthed but didn't mean.

"My wife is missing," Ayton said as he sat.

Domestic quarrel, Vierra thought. *God, I hate these. Why couldn't it have been another "the Christmas lights on my neighbor's house are so bright they're keeping me awake" complaint?*

"How long has she been missing?" Elena asked aloud.

"Since Christmas Eve."

Elena reached into her desk drawer for the missing-persons report form, once again quietly cursing the powers that be that had left her without even a typewriter to take down the information.

"Your wife's full name?" she asked.

"Natalie Newcastle Ayton."

Vierra wrote. "Date of birth?"

"February 4, 1967."

"Address?"

"Eighteen-eighty-four Ayton Court, Hamish Mountain."

The words brought Elena forward so fast that her shin slammed into the edge of her metal desk. She ignored the pain, her eyes flying to the man's face.

"*Hamish Mountain?*" she repeated with a voice made scratchy with surprise.

"Yes." The confirmation almost hissed through Sheldon Ayton's teeth. He wasn't comfortable with her recognition.

Elena wasn't surprised. Hamish Ayton had been one of the richest profligates Las Vegas had ever seen—and they'd seen some doozies. Nevada's favorable tax laws had had him building warehouses all over the place. Then the word had gone out that Hamish was storing illegal stuff in some of them. Before they could drag his tail into court, however, he had bitten the dust.

Quite literally. Hamish's body had been found next to one of his warehouses far out in the desert, dead by dehydration, lying next to his Rolls Royce, also dead by dehydration.

There were some who said that his nervous silent business partners had "fixed" Hamish's car to keep him from squealing on them when he was busted. But the undercover cops who were investigating Hamish had figured his hauteur fit right in with driving out into the desert all alone and without water.

His death was labeled an accident by arrogance and closed.

Elena had heard Hamish had a son. She'd also heard he'd been quick to get rid of his father's illegal sideline.

And now here he was. Sitting across from her. Well, Sheldon Ayton might not have followed in his father's footsteps, but there was an unmistakable arrogance about him that sure did.

"I thought your family had moved away from this area after the death of your father?" Elena asked as she reclaimed her presence of mind.

"We're back," Sheldon Ayton said coolly. "Now, about my missing wife..."

"Did you and your wife have a disagreement of any kind before she turned up missing?"

"No."

"When was the last time you saw your wife?"

"At approximately seven o'clock on Christmas Eve."

"And where were you?"

"At our home."

"You've checked with family members and friends?"

"Yes."

"Hospitals?"

"Yes."

"Did your wife have any enemies?"

"No."

"What about you?"

"None."

No enemies? Hamish Ayton's son? A rich man who looked like this and was used to getting his own way? Right.

"Mr. Ayton, I assume you have received no ransom note or calls of extortion?"

"None."

"Please describe for me everything you remember about the last time you saw your wife, including everything that you said to her and she said to you."

"We had just finished dancing. Nat said it was time for her to change out of her wedding dress."

"Wedding dress?" Elena repeated.

"Yes."

"Wait a minute. Am I understanding you correctly? This was *your* wedding reception that your wife disappeared from?"

"Yes."

"On Christmas Eve?"

"Yes. She went upstairs to change out of her wedding dress. No one has seen her since."

A bride missing in her wedding dress on Christmas Eve. Elena was getting a bad feeling about this. A really bad feeling.

"Do you have a recent picture of your wife?"

His hand slid into his jacket pocket and came out with a three-by-five shot. He handed it to Elena.

Natalie Newcastle Ayton was a picture, all right. Her hair

was pure flame, her skin was snow, her features were perfection.

Just as Elena remembered them.

"Mr. Ayton, I believe I might be able to help you locate your missing bride," Elena said carefully.

He came forward in his chair, his large hand clasping the edge of her desk. "You know where she is?"

"I believe I do. But I'm not sure finding her is your biggest problem at the moment."

MICHAEL WALKED into the kitchen and stopped in surprise when he saw Briana standing in front of the stove, expertly folding over a fluffy omelet chock-full of cheese and vegetables.

He leaned his shoulder against the doorjamb and crossed his arms over his chest.

"I thought you said you weren't a cook."

She flashed him a glance over her shoulder. "This omelet just seemed to throw itself together."

Looked to Michael like it had had a lot of help.

"I feel really hungry this morning," she said. "Must have been the swimming yesterday. Have a seat. Breakfast is about to be served."

Michael pulled up a chair and dug in. The omelet melted in his mouth. The biscuits she had whipped up from scratch were warm, right out of the oven, and as light and tasty as any from a bakery. Dessert was grilled apple slices dripping with a rich cinnamon sauce and full of chopped nuts and raisins.

He had left her for twenty minutes and she had come up with this. He didn't know of any other woman who described herself as a noncook and then whipped up homemade biscuits and put together an imaginative breakfast from the spare assortment in his kitchen pantry and refrigerator.

Less than forty-eight hours ago, he'd been bragging to Nate that no woman held any more surprises for him. And then he had awakened Briana Berry with a kiss and she'd presented him with one surprise after another. He wondered how many more she had in store for him.

When they had finished eating and were sipping their coffee, he leaned back in his chair and broached the subject he knew was foremost in both of their minds.

"Briana, how do you feel about your dreams last night?"

Her hands were suddenly tense as they circled her coffee cup.

"They made little sense, like most dreams I've had. Although I have to admit your waking me helped me to recall their details much better."

"Why do you think you dreamed about being a bride in an elaborate wedding?"

"When you found me asleep under your tree, I was in that elaborate bridal gown. I probably dreamed about being in a wedding in order to explain why you found me dressed that way."

"Then why were you having that same dream when I woke you the first time, before you knew how you were dressed?"

She had the grace to laugh. "That's a good question."

"Do you have an answer for it?"

She rose, collected the dishes from the table. "You're going to keep asking me questions until I come up with the answers, aren't you?"

"You're the only one who can decipher your dreams, Briana."

Her hands kept stacking and restacking the dishes, as though she couldn't get them in the right order for carrying. Michael watched her, wondering if she was aware of what she was doing.

He suspected she was probably too busy trying to mentally stack and restack the elements in her dreams, as a way to understand—or maybe avoid understanding—their meanings.

"You know something about my last dream, don't you?" she finally asked.

"I have a suspicion, yes."

"What suspicion, Michael?"

He finished his coffee and rose. "I'll help you load the dishwasher, and then we'll talk about it."

When the dishwasher began its cycle, Michael led the way out of the kitchen to the outside porch.

The air was cool and sweet, the sun warm. It was another perfect day. Michael rested his hip against the porch's high wrought-iron railing as he turned to face Briana.

"I suspect the same thing you suspect, Briana. The dreams you had last night were important. And parts of them fit into the waking facts as we know them."

"You think some of the events in those dreams might be...real events," she said, not looking relieved to have put into words what he knew she had been thinking all along.

"It's the logical conclusion," he offered gently. "You were the bride at a wedding ceremony in these last two dreams. You were dressed as a bride when I found you. When I awakened you, you thought you were kissing your new husband."

Briana seemed to be having difficulty swallowing as she grasped the railing and her eyes roamed restlessly over the fat plum mountains rising around her.

"But if these were more than dreams—if these were memories—then I was getting married."

"It's hard to come up with any other logical explanation to fit the facts and the events in your dreams."

"Who did I marry?"

"You saw him in your dream."

"I didn't know that man in my dream, Michael."

"Just as you don't know your own face, Briana?"

He watched as the reminder once again clouded the lovely crystal clarity of her eyes. She frowned and let out a small sigh of frustration.

"I can't just take the events in these dreams at face value. They are so far removed from the life and people I remember."

"There may be a way to get proof, one way or another."

"How?"

"You were still in your wedding gown when you turned up under my Christmas tree. If some of the images in your dreams are actual waking memories, then it stands to reason that the ceremony took place somewhere in southern Nevada. Do you remember what time of day it was when you walked toward that altar to exchange those dream vows?"

She closed her eyes for a moment, as though trying to recreate the scene in her mind.

"The shadows were long from the trees," she said after a moment. "The sun was low in the sky." She opened her eyes. "I believe the sun was just about to set."

"Sunset is right around four-forty at this time of year. Let's assume the ceremony concluded then. All the outside pictures would have been quickly taken by the photographer or photographers before the light faded."

"Photographers? Plural?"

"You described an elaborate ceremony replete with a full orchestra playing the wedding march. I hardly think the family would have relied on a single photographer to capture the event."

"Michael, it *was* all so lavish, so elegant. I can't believe it was real. What would *I* have been doing at such an elaborate, expensive ceremony?"

"What were you doing in such an elaborate, expensive wedding gown when I found you?"

She laughed, and he realized that she was doing her best to cling to her lifeline of humor. "What, indeed? But that mansion, Michael. Surely that had to have been a figment of my dreaming mind?"

"You tell me, Briana."

"I can't imagine anyone building such an impractical place in this day and age, and certainly not in the desert."

"We should be able to find out."

"How?"

"Assume for the moment that the elements in the final segment of the dream were accurately depicted. Did the reception take place at the home where you had the wedding?"

"I don't know."

"What do you think or feel about it? Your first impression, Briana. Did the reception take place at the home where the wedding was?"

"The ballroom had a Gothic feel to it. Yes. I think the reception was there."

"All right. If the outdoor pictures were concluded by four-forty, next would come the indoor ones with the wedding party and the family. That would have taken at least another hour."

"You sound as though you've been to a lot of weddings."

"You're looking at a seasoned best man. There would be the ceremony surrounding the cake-cutting. The opening of presents. The toasts. A formal sit-down dinner. Dancing. I would estimate you left that house no sooner than seven o'clock on Christmas Eve."

"And you found me at the institute at ten. So you're thinking I must have been no further than three hours away?"

"That's exactly what I'm thinking, Briana. Let's look at a map of the area."

Michael led the way to his office. Once there, he retrieved a large aerial map from a drawer and spread it out on his desk. He did some mental calculations and then drew a circle around the institute representing a three-hour drive in all directions.

"This circles encompasses a big chunk of Arizona and Utah, as well as Nevada," he said. "Still, it shouldn't take too long to fly over it and check it out."

"Fly?" Briana said beside him.

"The helicopter is outside, fueled up, ready to go. We can do a sweep of the area I've outlined on the map. Ever been up in a helicopter before?"

"No. At least not before the last three weeks. Who knows what I've been doing during them?"

BRIANA FOUND the flight exhilarating. The sudden lift that shifted her stomach to her soles. The forward thrust that pushed an invisible hand against her chest. Michael flew as he drove, flat out, full throttle, and in full control. The earth whizzed by beneath them.

"I'm familiar with the area that is within the immediate vicinity of the institute," his voice said through the headphones in her ears. "I also know what lies west toward Las Vegas and beyond. I'll concentrate on the other areas."

Michael set a heading for the northwest and pointed out various landmarks as they flew by. Lake Mead was a glistening blue jewel beneath them. A little farther along was an area Michael called the Valley of Fire. It flashed by in impossible shades all the way from claret to cinnabar.

They flew over the Moapa River Indian Reservation, a national wildlife range where wild horses ran the golden hills, a small town named Alamo, a large valley called Meadow.

And it was all lovely.

Briana had always thought of desert terrain as sand and sagebrush. Now she knew it was quite varied and quite beautiful. And, when seen from the vantage point of a helicopter, quite spectacular.

She was so engrossed in the passing scenery that she forgot why they were on this ride.

Until suddenly, out in the middle of nowhere, sitting on a mountain top, there it was: crenellated roofline, central square tower, the Tudor-Gothic horror house of her dreams. Briana could not believe her eyes.

"That's it!" she said, pointing.

"I see it," Michael said, heading the helicopter toward the fortress. He dipped down, hovering over it. Briana could clearly make out the elaborate English garden in its center. It was just as she had remembered it. A chill shot up her spine.

She could feel Michael's eyes shifting to her face. "Shall we land and knock at the door?" he asked.

"No, no!" It wasn't until after the words were out of her mouth that Briana realized she had shouted them.

An unreasoning dread had overcome her. The last thing in the world she wanted to do was get closer to that place.

Michael took the chopper up quickly and headed away from the mountain fortress. Briana no longer noticed the changing terrain beneath her. She was too caught up with the waves of unfocused dread washing through her.

She hadn't really believed it until now. Not any of it. But it was rather too real to discount anymore.

"Briana, are you all right?" Michael's voice asked through the headphones.

She laughed, because she was afraid that if she didn't, she might just start screaming.

"Oh, I'm great, Michael. I've just found out that the only thing that's real in my life is a crazy dream."

Chapter Five

"The house belongs to a Mrs. Gytha Ayton," Michael told Briana. "She and her husband, Hamish, bought the desert mountain and had the house built on its top about ten years ago. Money, apparently, was no object. It's loosely fashioned after the Dalmeny House, the famous family estate of Lord and Lady Rosebery of Scotland. Only this desert rendition has the English garden in its central courtyard."

"How did you find out all this?" Briana asked.

"I called a friend who works over in the county assessor's office. He looked it up in the public record."

"So you couldn't find me in any public records, but you can find that monstrosity from my dream." She paused to laugh. "Damn, don't you just hate it when that happens?"

Michael was aware of the fact that Briana's humor had begun to sound a bit frayed around the edges. And no wonder. That she could maintain any humor at all in this situation continued to both amaze and impress him.

"Does Gytha Ayton's name sound familiar, Briana?"

"No."

"How did you feel when you saw the house?"

"That the architect should be in a padded cell. It's crazy to put that fortress on the top of a desert mountain. The water they have to be using just to keep the English garden so green is probably sufficient to serve a small city."

She leaned back in her chair with a forced laugh.

"Here I'm holding on to a life and face that don't exist, and I have the nerve to call someone else crazy!"

Michael didn't miss the unhappiness clouding her eyes. He would have liked to hold her, comfort her. But, as her doctor, he could not. Besides, he was afraid that if she was ever back in his arms, comfort wouldn't be all he'd offer.

"Briana, do you realize you were most likely married in that English garden?"

"Then why don't I remember any of it, Michael?"

"Your dreams last night remembered. All shared similar people or events. I believe your unconscious did that deliberately, to let you know that the dreams were linked. They are, in essence, different aspects of the same dream."

"And you believe this dream was made up of real events and real people I've been with in the last three weeks."

"You've seen the house, Briana. What do you think?"

She leaned her elbows on the desktop and rubbed her temples with the tips of her fingers.

"You said before that I went through some kind of emotional trauma that made me forget the last three weeks. How do I find out what it was?"

"By studying your dreams."

"But this all seems so damn bizarre."

"Look, Briana, I know you probably feel so lost now that you're afraid to make a move in any direction—even the direction that may lead you to the truth."

"The truth is in Washington State, Michael. It's not in a Tudor-Gothic mansion in the desert. And it's my homely face. It's not this fabulous one."

"I do understand, Briana."

She laughed. "I don't see how you could, since I sure don't."

"There's a story one of my professors told in graduate school. It takes place in ancient times. Five strangers from different parts of the country and different walks of life all traveled to see this great wise man. None of the men knew one another. They were each granted a private audience with the wise man. Each told the wise man of his terrible trouble, a trouble so bad that it had made his life intolerable.''

''What were these troubles?'' Briana asked.

''Only each man and the wise man knew. After listening to all their troubles, the wise man called the men together into one room. He told them that he sympathized with their woes, but that it was within his power to help only one of them. Each man begged the wise man to remove his trouble. Each swore his had to be the worst, and he could not go on living with it.''

''What did the wise man do?''

''He told the men there was a way in which he could help them all. He instructed them to sit in a circle and take off one of their shoes. Then he told them to place the shoe in the center of the circle. When they had done that, he told them that he would clap three times, and whatever man's shoe they reached for would be the new trouble they would assume. Their old trouble would be passed to the man who got their shoe.''

''What happened?''

''At the third clap the men lunged forward and feverishly grabbed—for their own shoe.''

Briana nodded. ''I can believe it. What we know may be scary enough to make us quake in our shoes, but it's still preferable to stepping into the unknown.''

Michael rested his hand on hers. ''It's easier to take that first step into the unknown when you have someone with you.''

She looked straight at him. There was a deep trust in her crystal eyes, and a steady light of warmth that he welcomed as a doctor and was doing his best to ignore as a man.

''I don't want to go back to that house,'' she said. ''Not until I know what happened to me there.''

''I agree you shouldn't—mustn't—go there until you have prepared yourself to face it.''

He removed his hand from hers. He knew he should not be touching her in any way, for any reason. But he also knew that the times he touched her, she had needed to be touched. He was responding to her needs instinctively, with a gut feeling that went beyond professional ethics and logic—and every scrap of common sense he possessed.

The soft sound of an old-fashioned bell chime echoed through the room.

"What was that?" Briana asked.

"The institute's doorbell. When there's no guard on duty, the chime is transmitted into the offices, just in case we're expecting someone."

"Are you?"

"No. The institute is closed until after the New Year."

"Fay knows we're here. Could it be her?"

Michael swung to his feet. "She's in Reno with her family. Besides, she'd use her key. As would Nathaniel Quinn, if it were he."

"Maybe it's an intrepid Girl Scout selling cookies."

Briana's attempt at light humor brought a smile to Michael's lips. Despite everything, she could still joke. Where there was laughter, there was always hope. He walked over to the intercom and pushed the button to talk.

"Yes?"

"I'm looking for Dr. Michael Sands," a woman's voice said.

There was something familiar about that voice. "And you are?" Michael asked.

"Sergeant Elena Vierra, Las Vegas police."

A warning shot up Michael's spine.

"I'll be there in a minute, Sergeant," he said evenly, before shutting off the microphone and turning back to Briana.

Briana rose to face him. "Well, unless it's all your outstanding speeding tickets, Michael, she's here about me."

He saw the worry clouding her eyes.

"I'll see what it's all about," he promised.

"I'd best go with you."

"It might be better if you stay out of sight until I hear what she has to say."

"Sergeant Vierra is going to ask you if you know where I am, isn't she?"

"More than likely."

"What are you going to tell her?"

"Depends on what she tells me."

"Michael, I need to hear what she has to say."

"All right, Briana. I'll bring Sergeant Vierra back here. Wait in the bathroom there and leave the door ajar. That way, you can hear what she says without her knowing you're there."

Briana nodded.

Michael left the office and headed for the rotunda and the entrance, where Sergeant Vierra waited. When he opened the institute's door, he found a large man with glossy brown hair and wary eyes standing beside the sergeant.

The man wasn't wearing the clothes or the look of a policeman. He exuded a different type of authority—the kind that came with birth and privilege and the new red Ferrari sitting beside the police car in the parking lot.

Michael led the way into his office and beckoned them to chairs.

"So, Sergeant, what brings you out here?" he asked as he seated himself behind his desk.

"Dr. Sands, this is H. Sheldon Ayton the Third," Vierra said.

Ayton. Michael's nerves went on immediate alert. He exchanged a guarded glance with the man sitting across from him.

"Dr. Sands."

There was a cold crispness to Ayton's voice that Michael recognized. He'd rubbed shoulders often enough with the rich and famous to know when a man so favorably endowed had let it go to his head.

Michael could feel Sergeant Vierra's eyes on his face. He knew she was looking for a sign that Michael had recognized the Ayton name. Michael gave her none.

When he redirected his glance to hers, he found more than the usual irritation in her eyes.

"Dr. Sands, Mr. Ayton is looking for his bride, who disappeared on Christmas Eve from the wedding reception at their home."

If Sergeant Vierra had hoped to catch Michael off guard with that statement, she was going to be disappointed again. He had prepared himself to hear something like this. He stared at her blandly, as though waiting for a further explanation.

A very quiet, uncomfortable moment passed.

"Damn it, Sands, where is she?" Ayton demanded finally, coming forward in his chair, his impatience obviously getting the better of him.

"Where is who?" Michael asked as he calmly gazed into the man's angry eyes.

"My wife, of course! We know she was with you on Christmas Eve. What have you done with her?"

"You're mistaken. I do not know a Mrs. Ayton."

"Her maiden name was Newcastle," Sergeant Vierra supplied. "Natalie Newcastle."

"I don't know a Natalie Newcastle, either."

Sergeant Vierra stood up and handed a photo to Michael.

"You know *her*, don't you?" Vierra asked him challengingly.

Michael studied the photo. It was a good likeness, posed in a studio by someone who knew what he was doing. The lady's personality shone through her lovely crystalline eyes.

"Yes, I know her," Michael admitted.

"That woman is my wife," Sheldon Ayton said, grabbing back the photo.

"Can you prove it?"

Sheldon shot to his feet. "This is ridiculous. Where is she? I demand to see her!"

Michael remained seated and relaxed as he gazed at the big man who towered menacingly over his desk.

"Your demand means nothing to me."

"Do you know who I am?"

"Yes. You're a man who is going to get thrown out of my office if you don't start acting civilized."

Ayton's face darkened. "I don't have to take this!"

"Calm down, Mr. Ayton," Vierra said as she rose to lay a hand on his arm. "Let me handle this."

She turned to Michael. "Dr. Sands, you and the woman in this picture were in the precinct on Christmas Eve, weren't you?"

"Yes, and you ordered us to leave."

Vierra's cheeks ribboned red at the reminder. "Look, the woman was talking craz— She was obviously confused about her identity. Mr. Ayton has shown me his marriage license and I've checked out his story. I'm convinced the woman you were with is his wife."

"Just as you were convinced she belonged in jail through Christmas?"

"What?" Sheldon demanded as his eyes flew to the sergeant's face.

"A temporary misunderstanding," the sergeant said quickly, not looking at Ayton. "Dr. Sands, this is the woman's husband. He has the right to see her. Where is she?"

"If she wants to see him, she'll no doubt get in touch."

Sheldon exploded. "Damn it, Sands! You know where she is! If you don't tell me this instant, I'll…I'll…"

Michael rose slowly to face the dark-faced, sputtering man. Sheldon Ayton was big and broad and far too ego-inflated to have bothered learning self-control. If he didn't rein himself in, and soon, he was going to regret it.

"You'll what, Mr. Ayton?" Michael asked coolly.

Sergeant Vierra seemed to sense that she had a volatile situation on her hands. She stepped slightly in front of Sheldon Ayton as she leaned over the desk.

"Look, Dr. Sands, Mr. Ayton has been worried sick about his missing bride, looking everywhere for her. Surely, you can understand the kind of stress he's been under, and make allowances for any emotional outbreaks."

"How dare you apologize for me!" Sheldon roared.

"She's my wife, damn it! And he knows where she is! Hell, he's probably drugged her and is hiding her in this place! I'm going to get a court order to have it torn apart!"

"You'd be wasting your time," Briana said suddenly, as she stepped into the room.

Michael tensed, anticipating another outburst from Ayton.

It never came. Sheldon Ayton underwent an astounding metamorphosis the second he turned and saw Briana. The angry light switched off in his eyes. The tension visibly shook out of the shoulders of his suit jacket. It was like watching an attack hound lower its hackles and suddenly become a lapdog. He loped over to Briana, wrapped his arms around her, picked her up off her feet and showered her face with wet kisses.

And that was when Michael's hackles began to rise.

"Wait, wait, no!" Briana cried.

Michael was out and around his desk in a heartbeat. He wasn't sure what he would have done to Sheldon Ayton if the man hadn't set Briana back on her feet, but he suspected it would have been something exceptionally physical and exceptionally painful.

"Natalie, darling, what's wrong?" Sheldon asked, nothing but bewilderment pouring out of his tone.

Briana firmly extricated herself from his bear hug.

"Well, for one, my name isn't Natalie. For two, I'm not your darling. Mr. Ayton, you appear to have me confused with someone else."

"Confused you with— I don't believe what I'm hearing! Nat, it's Shel. *Your* husband. I've been looking everywhere for you!"

"Not for me."

Sheldon Ayton exhaled a heavy breath. "The sergeant said you were confused. But I didn't realize— Darling, you *must* remember."

"No, I don't. I'm sorry."

"So it's really true." Sheldon wrapped an arm around Briana's shoulders and brought her close to his side. "You've lost your memory. No wonder I didn't hear from you! I couldn't believe you'd just disappear without a word. I thought some degenerate had taken you. When the sergeant told me you seemed okay, I didn't believe it.''

''Mr. Ayton, please,'' Briana said as she slipped out from his embrace once again.

''Natalie, how can you push me away? How can you be all right and still not know me? This is incredible! I can't accept it. You hear about these things happening. But you never think it could happen to someone you love.''

''Mr. Ayton—'' Briana began.

''Please, darling, it's Shel. Call me Shel. We'll get your memory back. Don't worry. I'll get you the best help that money can buy. You'll be your old self again soon. I promise. Come. I'm taking you home.''

Sheldon wrapped his arm around Briana once again and started moving her toward the door. She halted and pushed herself out of his embrace.

''Look, Mr. Ayton, you seem most sincere. And I won't deny that I haven't exactly been myself for the last few days. But—''

''Darling, you have amnesia. It's okay. I understand now.''

''No, Mr. Ayton, you do not understand. I do not have amnesia. I know exactly who I am. My name is Briana Berry. And until I can sort out what has been going on, I'm staying right here.''

''Staying here?'' Sheldon's eyes darted to Michael. Michael could see his fur rise and his teeth bare as the man became the attack hound again. ''With him? No way, Nat. You're coming home with me. You're *my* wife!''

Briana retreated to the edge of Michael's desk. ''I am not your wife. I don't even know you. Please stop grabbing me.''

A muscle twitched in Ayton's jaw. His voice became harsh and concentrated. ''Nat, you're ill. You belong at home with me, where I can take care of you.''

''I belong where I feel comfortable. Dr. Sands has very graciously agreed to take me on as his patient to help me sort things out. I've put myself in his hands, and I intend to stay there. I'm not going off with a stranger."

"Stranger? You prefer this...this...quack to me, your own husband? I won't have it!"

Sheldon started toward Briana again. Only this time he suddenly found Michael blocking his way. Like a brick wall.

Michael faced the man squarely. They were close to the same height and breadth. He was ready to use reason or a hard right to the jaw, whatever it took.

He could see that knowledge registering in Sheldon Ayton's very unhappy eyes. Ayton looked over at the sergeant. "I'm taking my wife out of here, and I expect your support."

"She has the right to make her own decisions, Mr. Ayton," Sergeant Vierra said. "She's your wife, not your property. You can't coerce her into going with you."

"But she's not mentally competent! You heard her. She doesn't even know who she is!"

"Mental competency is out of my bailiwick. Legally, she's free to do as she pleases."

"We'll just see about that!" Sheldon Ayton swung around and stomped toward the door.

He stopped there and turned toward Briana, his eyes blazing. "You'll come with me, Nat, one way or another!" he shouted before slamming the door behind him.

The reverberation shook the walls.

Sergeant Vierra pulled a folded piece of paper out of her breast pocket and handed it to Briana.

"This is the copy of the marriage license. I've seen a tape of the wedding. I've even talked to the minister who performed the ceremony. Word of advice, Mrs. Ayton. Judges tend to listen to a man with mountains of money who wants his 'confused' wife transferred to the care of a doctor back at the old homestead. *Comprende?*"

Sergeant Vierra didn't wait for an answer.

Briana turned to Michael the instant Vierra had closed the door behind her.

"Sergeant Vierra was warning me that Ayton's going to get a court order to take me away."

"Not if I have anything to say about it," Michael said, picking up the phone.

He punched in the home number of a very good friend who just happened to be the best attorney in Nevada.

"Keith, it's Michael. I need a marriage annulled."

"What are the grounds?"

"The bride was incapable of making a reasonable decision."

"Hell, Michael, isn't that the definition for being in love?"

"Funny, Keith. What are our chances?"

"If the lady was incapable of assenting due to a want of understanding, it should be a shoo-in."

"How soon can you get this through?"

"I can file the petition for annulment today."

"Good. Now I need a stay order from a judge keeping the husband from trying to exert legal control over his wife until the annulment goes through."

"What kind of control?"

"If I don't miss my guess, he's going to try to have her examined by a court psychiatrist and declared legally insane."

"All under his right as husband, huh? So he marries this lady who's not of sound mind, and now he wants to commit her because her elevator doesn't make it to the top floor. Oh, boy, this guy is playing with a loaded deck."

"Can you deal him out of the game?"

"We'd best go to Judge Manuela Soares on this one. She really hates men who try to control women. I'll get the papers drawn up and call over to the courthouse for her schedule. Damn, I forgot it's Christmas week. I hope Soares is in today."

"What do you need from me?"

"You and the lady in my office in about an hour."

"We'll be landing on your rooftop, just like Santa Claus."

"Good. For a present, I want a big check."

"I'll tie a bow around it," Michael said as he hung up the phone. He turned to see the clouding of Briana's eyes.

"It's all right," he assured. "I don't care if he is your husband. I won't let him take you against your will. I promise."

"Sergeant Vierra says he's rich, Michael. He could make trouble for you."

"He'll be sorry if he tries. Stop worrying. I'm not."

She smiled. "But then, you never do. Thank you."

Michael basked in the warmth that she put into that smile far longer than he knew he should.

He hadn't known just how strong his feelings for Briana had become until that moment when Sheldon Ayton put his arms around her and showered her face with kisses.

The jealousy had been a sudden wind of white heat sweeping through Michael. He had wanted nothing more at that moment than to beat Sheldon Ayton into a bloody pulp.

He could barely believe the force of his feelings. This was not a good sign. No, not good at all.

Briana had gotten to him, fast and deep. And he hadn't even seen it coming.

"Michael, you're shaking your head. Why?"

He looked over at her. "I would have sworn there wasn't a woman alive who could present me with any more surprises."

She laughed, took it lightly, just as she continued to struggle to take in this untenable situation.

"I didn't mean to be this surprising, Michael, believe me. So what do we do next?"

"Did the name Natalie Newcastle sound familiar?" he asked.

"No."

"Did Sheldon Ayton look familiar?"

"Yes."

"You've seen him before?"

"He was the groom in the dream wedding."

"But when you met him today, he felt like a stranger?"

"Yes...and no. When he rushed over to pick me up and kiss me, I had the strangest sensation. It was like I was in the audience in a movie theater, and he was an actor who had stepped out of the movie screen to come over and embrace me."

"You don't ever remember having been embraced or kissed by Sheldon Ayton before?"

"No. Never."

"Did you find it...pleasant?"

"Not at all. He may mean well, Michael. His actions and anger may even be somewhat understandable, if what he says is true and somehow I met and married him during these last three missing weeks of my life. But it's impossible to think of myself married to that man. Absolutely impossible."

Michael was relieved to hear it. And he knew it wasn't the doctor in him that was feeling that relief.

"Michael, it's also becoming rather impossible for me to continue accepting your help without any compensation."

Yes, he knew that had to be eating at her, given her sense of independence.

"You needn't be concerned, Briana. I have that all figured out."

"Have you?"

"I intend for you to pay me back, even if it means making me a member of your architectural design firm when this is all over. We'll call it Berry, Willix, Sands and Associates."

"And if there is no architectural design firm, Michael?"

He heard the uncharacteristic hesitation in her voice. With all the cold uncertainty she had to deal with, Michael knew she didn't need any more.

"Of course there is, Briana. Although if we don't find this Willix guy, I'm all for voting his share out."

Her laughter burst forth like a blossoming flower. "Psychotics build castles in the air, schizophrenics live in them, and it looks like Dr. Michael Sands remodels them."

"I know a good real estate investment when I see it. Come on, Briana. Let's go get you annulled from a man you don't remember in a name that isn't yours. Then we'll tackle some of the weird stuff.''

"THANK THE LORD you found Natalie and she's okay!" Carlie Taureau said as she smiled up at her new son-in-law.

"She's not okay," Sheldon Ayton said. "She's crazy!"

Carlie felt the jolt of his words at the same time she saw the dark, angry flush on his face.

"Crazy? Shel, what are you talking about?"

"She doesn't know me!" Sheldon shouted as he stomped in front of her, spilling the Scotch he had just poured into a tumbler onto a priceless Persian carpet. "Just outright refused to come home with me! My own wife!"

"Don't tell me you two had a fight?" Carlie asked.

"We didn't have a fight! We were just married. We didn't have time for a honeymoon, much less a fight!"

Carlie didn't believe Sheldon Ayton for a minute. Of course they had had a fight. He was notoriously short-tempered and bad-mannered, although he was always on his best behavior with Natalie. Still, Carlie had always wondered if it wouldn't be just a matter of time before he forgot himself.

And as for Natalie...well, she was sweet, but she was no man's doormat.

Carlie sometimes thought it was a miracle that she had gotten the two of them together in the first place.

She also knew that if she was to challenge her new son-in-law on the matter of the argument, he would continue to deny it. Sheldon Ayton was a very wealthy, handsome man, and until his marriage to her daughter, he'd been one of the five most eligible bachelors in the world.

And, as such, he thought himself above criticism—and just about everything and everyone else.

Carlie leaned forward on the settee, setting down her cup of tea. This would take delicacy and diplomacy and a boosting of the male ego, all talents bred into her Southern female soul. She put as much polite confusion into her tone as she could.

"Why, this just makes no sense at all, Shel. Natalie adores the ground you walk on. What would ever possess her to leave her own wedding reception and then refuse to come home? There has to be an explanation."

"Yeah, Shel," Rory Taureau said as he walked over to the liquor cabinet, his limp quite pronounced today. "My sister always has a good reason for what she does. A very good reason."

Rory's tone was sarcastic and biting. Carlie didn't know what the problem was between her son and her son-in-law, but they had been at each other's throats from the day they met.

"Now, Rory, I know you're a mite upset," Carlie said. "We all are. But do let's try to remain understanding of Shel's feelings."

Her son turned to face her, a wicked grin drawing back his lips, a grin that very much resembled his late daddy's devilish and far-too-charming one. "Oh, I am understanding of Shel's feelings, Mama. Quite understanding."

Carlie sighed. Rory was a handful. Always ready for a fight. Or for a loving. Just like his daddy. What a troublesome mix, the Irish-Cajun man! And what an exciting one.

She turned her attention back to her son-in-law.

"What could be the explanation for Natalie's odd behavior, Shel?"

"Nat doesn't know me!" Sheldon said, his words bitten off in frustration and anger.

"You sure the problem isn't she's gotten to know you a little too well?" Rory taunted.

"Shut up, Taureau!" Sheldon spit out the words.

"Natalie is obviously not herself," Carlie said quickly. "Where is she, Shel?"

"She's with this damn doctor at this damn institute."

"Doctor? Institute?" Carlie parroted, her voice rising along with her sudden jump in blood pressure. "Shel, are you saying she's at a *psychiatric* institute?"

"No, no. It's some kind of dream institute about a hundred

miles from here. The police knew all along she was there. Apparently she's been there since Christmas Eve.''

Carlie let out a relieved breath.

"How did she get a hundred miles away?" Rory demanded.

"How do I know?" Sheldon yelled. "I was busy with my mother's needs! I thought my bride was safe in her family's hands! No one bothered to tell me she was missing!"

"We thought Natalie was with you at the hospital, waiting for word about your mama," Carlie said.

"Yeah," Rory said. "Brides generally stay by their groom's side on their wedding eve. Unless, of course, they realize they've made a big mistake."

"One more word out of you, Taureau—" Sheldon began.

"Rory, Shel, come on," Carlie said quickly, trying to soothe that odd anger that always erupted between them. "This has been a very difficult last couple of days for us all. Please, let's not make it worse by attacking one another."

Rory turned toward the bourbon decanter sitting on the corner credenza and poured himself a shot. He downed it in one gulp. Sheldon continued to nurse his Scotch on the rocks.

Carlie would have given anything for a drink herself. But she knew she couldn't. Not now.

At least not until this mess was sorted through. What kind of argument could have caused Natalie to bolt like this?

"So what reason did Natalie give for not coming home with you?" Carlie asked, in as gentle a tone as she could manage.

"I told you, she doesn't remember who I am!" Sheldon shouted, his impatience clearly rising at what he obviously considered to be an unforgivable reminder.

"Doesn't *remember* who you are?" Carlie repeated. "Wait a minute, Shel. Are you saying that Natalie has *amnesia?*"

"Of course that's what I'm saying! It's what I've been saying! Hasn't anyone been listening?"

Carlie swallowed and tried to compose herself. She hadn't understood the seriousness of the situation until now. She told herself to keep a cool head, get the facts, then figure out what in the hell to do about them.

"My sister doesn't remember who you are?" Rory asked, his voice wiped clean of its sarcasm for once.

"Natalie doesn't even remember who *she* is!" Sheldon yelled back. "She thinks she's someone called Briana Something."

Carlie felt Sheldon's words strike like a blow.

"She said she never even heard of a Natalie Newcastle," Shel lamented before throwing back the rest of his Scotch. "I don't know what in the hell has happened to her. She refused to come home with me. And that damn quack at the institute stood in my way when I tried to take her."

"You tried to take *my* sister by *force?*" Rory yelled, his face instantly flushing, as he limped over to stand in front of Sheldon. "You should be glad I wasn't there."

"And if you had been there?" Sheldon's voice baited him.

Sheldon was four inches taller than Rory, and a bull of a man. But Rory's six-foot frame was far more densely muscular, and he worked out hard every day to keep it that way. That, coupled with his skills as an ex-prizefighter gave Carlie no doubt as to what would happen if Rory and Sheldon ever came to blows. Even with his limp, Rory could still move fast when he wanted to. And his fists were nothing less than lethal weapons.

Carlie didn't intend for her daughter to become a widow or for her son to become a murderer. She quickly got to her feet and clasped Shel's arm, the reckless one that looked as if it were ready to make a swing at her son's jaw.

"Rory, that's enough! Shel, please. We have to think of what to do about Natalie."

Rory eyed Sheldon a moment more before turning and heading back toward the bourbon. Carlie felt Shel's muscles relaxing in his forearm. She released her hold.

Carlie let the ensuing quiet separate the men further as her thoughts whirled and she tried to make sense out of the disturbing news about her daughter.

"What are you planning to do, Shel?" she finally asked.

"I told my damn lawyers that if they don't figure a way to get her out of that damn dream institute, they're all fired," Sheldon said after a moment.

Carlie forced herself to take a deep breath and let it out slowly.

"Shel, why don't you go on back to the hospital and be with your mama? I'll go see Natalie and find out what's going on."

"And what will that help?"

"Maybe I can bring her to her senses, bring her home to you."

Sheldon studied Carlie's face for a moment. She was used to men looking at her with appreciation, but Sheldon's green eyes held only cool assessment. His scrutiny made her distinctly uncomfortable, just as it always did. He was a cold man. Natalie was the only one who had ever brought warmth to his eyes.

"Shel, she's my daughter. Let me handle this."

"How can you? She's forgotten who she is."

"Then I'll just have to help her to remember, won't I?"

Carlie saw something that actually looked like gratitude light Sheldon's eyes.

It once more amazed her how hard love had hit Sheldon Ayton. When that gentler side of him came out, he was almost tolerable.

"I'll go with you, Mama," Rory said.

Carlie turned to her son. Although normally she would have welcomed his company, she did not want him in on this particular meeting with Natalie.

"You've had too much to drink, Rory. You know Nat doesn't approve. It'll upset her. Stay here. I won't be long."

"Mama, you know I should be there."

"Not this time, Rory."

Rory was clearly not pleased to be left behind. He turned back to the liquor cabinet and the bourbon.

His drinking had gotten way out of hand over the past few

months. Carlie suspected it was because he hadn't been able to find a new profession now that boxing was behind him. She was going to have to insist he do something about his drinking soon.

But she couldn't worry about that now. Now she had far more serious business to handle.

She had to bring Natalie back.

One more time.

Chapter Six

Briana felt her tolerance for the uncertainty of her situation rapidly disappearing as the helicopter hovered above its pad back at the institute.

The legal maneuvers Michael had put in motion to protect her that morning had made it quite clear just how precarious her position was. She had had to admit to being Natalie Newcastle in order to swear that she wasn't Natalie Newcastle and hadn't been of sound mind when she married Sheldon Ayton, a man she didn't remember marrying at all.

The situation would be absolutely hilarious, if it wasn't so absolutely dangerous.

Until she could prove who she was, anyone could appear at the door at any time saying almost anything, and she wouldn't know whether to believe them. Or whether she could disprove it.

As soon as Michael had switched off the engine, she turned to him.

"I need to know what went on in those missing weeks, and why I've forgotten them. You said the answers are in my dreams?"

"Yes."

"Let's start looking for them. Do we do this in the lab?"

"We can do it anywhere you feel comfortable. The tape and tape machine are portable."

Briana stared out the windshield for a moment, in thought.

"Somewhere outside, then. What's it like sitting over there in the gazebo?"

"Like being inside a rainbow."

"Then by all means, let's go there," she said, unfastening her safety harness.

"I'll get the tape and machine and be back in a minute," Michael said.

Briana entered the gazebo and found that Michael hadn't exaggerated. Sitting inside it was like being inside a rainbow. The leaded-glass roof caught the sunlight and acted like a dozen prisms, each separating the colored light onto the curved marble benches in perfect swatches of red, orange, yellow, green, blue and violet.

It was pleasantly warm, the glass capturing heat, as well as light. Briana took off her sweater and rolled up her sleeves.

Michael joined her a few moments later.

She watched as he sat across from her, beneath a yellow swatch. His tanned skin took on a tawny glow. His moonlit sand hair was streaked with molten gold.

Despite the growing chaos in her life, she was amazed at how oddly happy and balanced she felt every time she looked at the solid, sane strength of him. When he boldly stepped between her and Sheldon Ayton, physically preventing the man from getting to her, all of Briana's insides had gone hot and weak.

Heaven help her, she had it bad. She kept trying to remind herself that she was Michael's patient. All his kindness, all his protection, all of it, came from the doctor, not the man. But she couldn't help remembering that first night, when he'd kissed her awake. And later, when he'd brushed a kiss across her knuckles and looked at her with that glow in his eyes.

He hadn't been the doctor then.

Briana sat across from him under a cool blue light shaft, her legs curled beneath her, as she tried to talk some sense into herself.

She was a woman with memories of a life and face that

didn't exist. A crazy dream made up her reality. A stranger insisted he was her husband.

He probably was.

And as if all that weren't enough, from the moment Michael became her doctor, she had felt the uncrossable line that he had drawn between them. She had no doubt that he would continue to be unfailingly understanding, protective, kind, warm, funny—in other words, himself.

But he would never cross the line to her side.

He held up a small tape recorder for her to see.

"As I replay the recorded memory of your dream, Briana, I want you to close your eyes and concentrate on the images. Often additional details and even meanings that weren't initially apparent will come to you. Are you ready?"

Briana nodded, sobered by her thoughts and more than a little depressed by them.

Michael pushed the button on the tape recorder so that Briana's first dream would replay.

I was in this elaborate bedroom suite, her taped voice said. Briana closed her eyes and tried to picture it as her taped voice described it. *The furniture was very ornate, ponderous.*

She heard a click when Michael stopped the tape. "Can you picture that bedroom suite now, Briana?"

She kept her eyes closed, concentrating on the images that were filling her mind. "Yes. The bed was a four-poster, the coverlet a heavy rouge brocade that matched the drapes."

"Was it in the same house in which you were married in your dreams?"

"I think so. I know the same style of heavy rococo furniture was everywhere in that house."

"Is there anything else you can tell me about that room?"

"No. That's all I see."

"Okay. We'll go on now." Briana heard the click as Michael pushed the play button to restart the tape.

Who was with you? Michael's recorded voice asked.

Two women. One was older, in her sixties, I believe. She was elegantly dressed. The other seemed younger, fifty maybe.

She was well dressed, too, but not quite as elegantly as the older woman.

Who were these women?

I seemed to know them, Michael, but I don't know who they were, if that makes any sense.

Michael stopped the tape again. "Can you picture those two women now?"

"Only vaguely."

"Do you know who they are?"

"No."

"How did you feel toward these women?"

"I felt as though I knew the younger of the women. The older woman felt almost like a stranger. I wasn't at all comfortable in her presence."

"Is there anything else you can tell me about these women?"

Briana let her mind free-flow over the fuzzy faces of the women in her mind's eye. "No. That's it."

"Okay, we'll go on." Michael restarted the tape again.

The two women were upset at me. It had something to do with this dress the older woman had handed me. It smelled terribly unhappy—like lavender.

You could smell the dress in your dream?

Yes.

Was the dress a lavender color?

No, it was white.

And you're sure it smelled like lavender?

Yes.

Why did the scent of lavender on the dress make you think of something terribly unhappy?

I don't know. It just did.

What happened next?

The women were angry because I wouldn't wear the dress. I felt upset, too. The more we argued, the more their voices sounded like barking dogs. I finally couldn't stand it anymore. I ran from the room. That was when the dream ended.

Michael once again stopped the tape. "Can you see that dress in your mind's eye, Briana?"

"Yes, it's a wedding dress. I didn't realize it before, but I can clearly see now that it's an old-fashioned wedding dress."

"Is there anything else that's clearer now?"

"The dress belonged to the older woman. She wanted to have it altered for me, but I didn't want to wear it. I didn't like its smell."

"The lavender smell."

"Yes. It had been wrapped in lavender sachets."

"And the lavender smell made you unhappy."

"Yes."

"Why?"

"I've absolutely no idea."

"It's very unusual to remember a smell in a normal dream, Briana, unless that smell is in the room you're sleeping in."

"There's no scent of lavender in the sleep lab, is there?"

"No, which tells me that it is important to the meaning in your dream."

Briana opened her eyes. "Michael, is any of this helping?"

"We know some things we didn't know before. This argument over the dress took place in one of the bedrooms in the Ayton home. You knew the younger woman. The older woman was almost a stranger."

"Are you thinking they're symbolic representations?"

"Your dream seems to possess few, if any, symbolic representations. I think these are two women with whom you became acquainted during the missing weeks in your life."

Briana let out a deep, frustrated breath. "It's still so hard to accept. Michael, it took me four months to pick out a new car. I just can't believe I met and married Sheldon Ayton in three weeks."

That same bell chime that Briana had heard in Michael's office that morning suddenly echoed through the gazebo. She turned around with a start.

"Could it be Sergeant Vierra again?" she asked.

Michael stood. "The only reason the police would be back is if they were acting on a court order."

"Michael—"

"I have Judge Soares's restraining order right here," he said, patting his breast pocket. "It overrides anything Ayton could have tried to push through today. There's absolutely no cause to worry."

Michael moved over to the intercom.

"Yes?" he said.

"I've come to see Natalie," an unfamiliar woman's voice said.

"There is no Natalie here," Michael responded.

"Then I've come to see Briana Berry."

"Who are you?" he asked.

"Carlie Taureau."

Briana shook her head in response to Michael's inquiring look. The name meant nothing to her.

"Since Briana Berry has apparently forgotten me and Natalie, ask her if she remembers Hazel Doud," the woman said into the intercom.

Briana felt a jumpy, exuberant feeling forming in the middle of her stomach at the mention of her grandmother's name. She shot to her feet.

"Michael, she knows about Hazel!"

"You want to talk with this woman?" Michael asked.

"Yes, definitely yes."

"We'll be there in a moment, Ms. Taureau," he said into the intercom.

Briana had to keep herself from running to the front of the institute, so eager was she to meet with someone who actually knew about her grandmother. Finally, validation of her life was at hand! If Hazel was real, so was Briana Berry.

But as soon as Briana saw the woman standing on the doorstep, her excitement was replaced by an immediate foreboding. She recognized Carlie Taureau as the younger of the two women from her dream.

How could this woman be from her dream and yet be from her real life, as well?

Carlie Taureau was very attractive, with pleasing features and a trim figure. She had Briana's height, deep auburn hair, pale blue eyes. She was beautifully groomed and dressed, a woman who obviously paid close attention to her appearance.

In Briana's dream, she had sensed that Carlie Taureau was around fifty. In the flesh, she barely looked forty.

The moment Michael unlocked and opened the door, Carlie swept in and threw her arms around Briana, surrounding her with a cloud of expensive perfume.

"Oh, Natalie, we've been just wild with worry, honey, thinking the most terrible things! I can't tell you how relieved I was when Sheldon told us he had finally found you and you were all right!"

Briana didn't know how to respond to this woman's sweet Southern accent, or to her generous embrace. She had an odd feeling that there was something else that was very familiar about Carlie Taureau—something she should know.

"Who are 'we'?" Briana asked, stepping gently back and out of the scented circle of the woman's arms. "Who are you?"

Quick tears filled Carlie's pale blue eyes. "Natalie, honey, I'm your mama."

Briana stiffened. She suddenly realized what had looked so familiar about Carlie. This woman's facial features were remarkably similar to her own new, flawless ones.

No! a voice protested, reverberating through her skull.

Acquiring a husband in her missing three weeks had been stretching the envelope enough. There was no way it was going to stretch enough to include a mother.

"My mother died when I was three," Briana said, quietly but firmly.

"No, honey. That was when Briana Berry's mama died and she went to live with her grandmother, Hazel Doud. You only think you're poor little Briana. You're really my sweet Natalie."

Briana shook her head, in both denial and confusion.

"Shall we discuss this matter in a more comfortable setting?" Michael suggested.

He led them to a reception room in his wing with a couple of couches. Carlie sat on the end of one and beckoned to Briana to sit beside her. Briana declined, feeling quite awkward around the woman's open affection. She chose the chair across from her.

"How do you know about Hazel Doud?" Briana asked.

"At some time during your unhappy childhood, you decided to become Briana Berry. Hazel was the grandmother who you created to take care of you. You made her sweet and kind and attentive—everything that you had wanted in a mama, but never had."

"I didn't create Hazel," Briana said, irritated by the woman's words. "She's real, and she's still alive."

"I know you want to believe it, Natalie, but it isn't true."

Briana didn't know what this woman hoped to gain by these absurd proclamations. But she intended to find out. "You said my childhood was unhappy. Why?"

"I wasn't there to care for you, honey. Your daddy employed a succession of nannies, none of whom gave you the love you needed. And your daddy sure didn't. Markam Newcastle never understood anything that had to do with tender feelings."

"I never knew my father," Briana said. "And I've never heard of Markam Newcastle."

"Yes, that's what you insisted then, too. You said you were Briana Berry, a poor little orphan who lived with her grandmother Hazel and didn't have a rich daddy or a houseful of servants at her command."

Briana listened to the woman's words in a kind of incredulous shock. This couldn't be true. It just couldn't.

"Why are you saying these things?" she demanded.

Carlie leaned forward, resting her hand on Briana's knee. "Honey, Briana Berry and Hazel Doud aren't real. They were just people you made up to cushion yourself against a world without any real affection in it. I blame myself for that. If I had been with you—''

''If you are my mother, as you say, why weren't you with me?'' Briana asked challengingly.

Carlie removed her hand from Briana's knee and let out a long, unhappy sigh as she slumped back against the couch.

''Because I was selfish and thought only of myself.''

Her words surprised Briana. ''What do you mean?''

''My mama and daddy were dirt-poor, honey. All I had was my beauty. It took me to the title of Miss Louisiana. First time Markam saw me, I was coming off that stage with a crown on my head. He up and proposed, right there and then.''

The smile that had been growing on Carlie's face disappeared before she went on. ''It's not like I ever loved him. But I thought he would provide me with the financial security that my own mama and daddy had so sorely lacked. And I thought he loved me.''

She laughed—a bitter, unhappy sound. ''What he loved was the idea of owning a beauty queen. He was fifty, I was but eighteen. I was just something pretty to warm his bed at night and be displayed to his friends during the day—much like one of his prize horses.''

Carlie stopped, took a deep breath, her hands clenching. She seemed to be trying to control the bitter memories breaking through. A moment later she continued.

''When I got pregnant with you, Natalie, I thought maybe things would change between your daddy and me. I thought having his child would gentle him some. But it didn't.''

Her light blue eyes met Briana's.

''Your daddy never even came into the nursery to look at you after you were born. He instructed me to make sure you turned into 'something' he could be proud of, just like he instructed the servants in their duties. That's all I was to him. Just another servant.''

She sighed, looked down at her hands. ''I was so young and so lonely.''

Briana was afraid for a moment that the woman might break out in tears. But she didn't. She took a deep breath, got hold of her emotions and continued.

"Then Connor Taureau came to work in Markam's stables. Connor was twenty-two, dark, handsome, and as attentive to me as your daddy was not. I suppose it was inevitable that we would fall in love—and Markam would catch us together.

"I didn't care that my marriage was ending. I didn't even care that Markam was turning me out with nothing but the clothes on my back. But it broke my heart when he got sole custody of you. I never imagined for a moment that he would insist on taking you from me. You weren't even eighteen months old when I lost you, Natalie. I didn't even see you again until you were ten."

"You married Connor Taureau?"

"Yes. We had twenty-two wonderful years together before he died. I knew the first time we were together that there would never be another man for me."

"You said you saw me again when I was ten. Why?"

"The gardener at the Newcastle estate remained friends with Connor. He made it possible for Rory and me to see you at your tenth birthday party."

"Rory? Who's Rory?"

"Your brother, honey, or I guess I should say half brother. Connor was Rory's daddy. I had told Rory all about you. He was just dying to meet his older sister. So we hitched a ride in the gardener's truck and sneaked in to watch you blow out the candles on your cake."

Carlie sighed, shaking her head in remembrance.

"Your daddy had gone out of town on business. You were surrounded with all these kids from your school. And yet you looked so lonely. That was the day you spoke about being this orphan girl, Briana Berry. You said you didn't know Natalie or Markam Newcastle. You said your grandmother Hazel was taking care of you."

"And you claim this all happened on my tenth birthday?" Briana asked, not believing a word of it.

"Yes. It was all my fault, Natalie. I wasn't there for you!"

Briana was very uncomfortable to see the tears welling in Carlie's eyes again.

"Why don't I remember any of this?" Briana asked. "Why do I remember a childhood and adulthood that is totally different from the one you describe as Natalie Newcastle's?"

"Honey, I don't know. I tried to read up on this a few years ago. From what I understand, doctors say split personalities often live parallel lives—their real one and the fantasy one they escape into."

Carlie's eyes were blinking with new tears as she studied Briana's face.

"You've wiped Natalie completely away again, haven't you? Even how you and Shel met, fell in love, your beautiful wedding?"

Briana felt an odd buzzing in her brain at the mention of the wedding. She had no intention of admitting to Carlie that she remembered some of the wedding—at least in her dreams.

She was afraid to admit anything. For if she admitted to any of this incredible story, she was afraid she might have to accept all of it. Briana was not ready to accept anything of the sort.

But to find the truth, she knew she needed to find out more.

"How did I meet Sheldon Ayton?" Briana asked.

"At your box at the Derby."

"The Derby?"

"Kentucky Derby. May third. Your favorite racing event of the year. You've always loved horses. It was a passion that you shared with your daddy."

"So you're saying that Natalie eventually established a normal relationship with her father?"

"I'm not sure the word *normal* would ever describe any relationship your daddy had. But I do believe your fondest memories of him are those when you sat together watching a race, talking about the horses."

"*Memories* of him? Markam Newcastle is dead?"

"Oh, yes. Four years ago. A massive heart attack. It was

sudden, honey. He didn't suffer. Not even I would have wished him a painful death."

Briana searched for, but couldn't find, any feelings for a man of whom she had no memories.

"So Natalie met Sheldon Ayton at the horse races," Briana said. "What then?"

"Then he promptly fell in love with you."

"And she with him?"

"Not right away. You were definitely turned off by his reputation."

"What reputation?"

"Shel is nearing forty. He's been a ladies' man all his life. I've heard it told many a time that there wasn't a woman who he couldn't have."

"I'm not surprised I was turned off," Briana said, thoroughly unimpressed.

"Well, it's to be expected," Carlie added on a defensive note. "Shel is blessed with such substantial wealth and physical attributes. And charm."

"I hadn't noticed," Briana said.

"You didn't see him in his best light, honey. When Shel turns on the charm, well, he is quite irresistible. I suppose that's why your continuing indifference to him drove him a mite crazy. Although you certainly didn't do it to be clever, it was what made him propose. He had to have you. He knew the only way he could was to marry you."

"I can't think why Natalie accepted."

"Can't think why? But, Natalie, Shel is—was—one of the most eligible bachelors in the world! You made a brilliant match."

"Then why did Natalie run away after the ceremony?"

Carlie frowned. "That is a puzzle, honey. Something must have happened. Don't you remember anything?"

"No," Briana insisted. "Who was at the wedding?"

"It wasn't a large affair. Quite modest, really. Just a couple of hundred guests, most of whom were selected by Gytha. She's your mother-in-law, honey. She chose the invitations, decorations, photographers, caterer. Gytha was quite stubborn about the specifics."

"Aren't weddings usually planned by the bride's family?"

Carlie laughed. "Not Ayton weddings. Ayton weddings are controlled by Aytons."

"Christmas Eve seems an odd time for a wedding," Briana said.

"It's a tradition in the Ayton family. Gytha was married on Christmas Eve, and so were apparently all the Ayton brides in recorded history. She was not going to let you and Shel break with tradition."

"And Natalie went along with this?"

Carlie smiled. "You were pretty easygoing about most of it. But you came very near to calling the whole thing off when she started insisting on your wearing her wedding dress."

Briana got a cold chill down her back as the dream argument with the two women over a wedding dress flashed through her mind.

"Did Natalie wear her dress?" Briana asked.

"Oh, no. You said you'd rather stay single." Carlie paused to chuckle. "And you meant it."

"But Natalie didn't stay single."

"Still, no amount of cajoling by Shel or me would change your mind about the dress. You weren't angry about it. But then, you never do get angry. You just draw the line when you've had enough, and you had had enough. You told Gytha Ayton and Shel that either you selected your own wedding dress or there just wasn't going to be a wedding. And you smiled when you said it."

Carlie laughed. "I think it was your smile that made the veins pop out in Gytha's neck. I've never seen such a look like that on anyone's face before. Honey, she was livid, her eyes just spitting sparks."

"Doesn't appear as though Natalie has a very healthy relationship with her mother-in-law."

"Now, you know she wouldn't have been happy with any woman Sheldon selected. Besides, she's so used to deference, and you're not one to give it on demand. But then, why should you? You are a woman of substance, after all.''

"A woman of substance? Are you saying Natalie has money?''

"Oh, you're not rich like an Ayton is rich, of course. Just twenty million or so.''

Just twenty million or so?

"Natalie, doesn't any of this sound familiar to you?''

Briana didn't know what to answer. For the truth was, some of this did fit into her dream.

"Try to remember, honey,'' Carlie said. "You were dancing with Shel. The ballroom was decorated all in white and red. Those are the Aytons' coat-of-arms colors.''

Briana found herself picturing the red dresses with white sashes that had been worn by the bridesmaids in her dream. She remembered dancing with a man. Had it been Sheldon?

"It was no more than a few minutes later that one of the servants found that Mrs. Ayton had fallen,'' Carlie said.

Fallen? Briana felt stunned at Carlie's words, as though she had sustained a blow to the side of her head.

"She's still in a coma,'' Carlie went on. "The doctors don't know if she'll recover. Such a sad business! They found her at the foot of the stairs, just minutes after you had gone up to your room to change out of your wedding gown. The next thing we knew…''

Briana didn't hear the rest of the sentence.

The light in the room began to tunnel. Briana's head spun with images of a woman falling down the stairs as screams filled her head, silent, deafening screams—her screams. Briana felt her muscles knot, her skin go cold.

"Natalie?''

Briana was vaguely aware of Carlie's voice calling out to her, as though from a long distance away.

Then Briana suddenly felt Michael's warm hand on her shoulder and realized that he was standing behind her, standing with her. As nothing else could have at that moment, his touch righted the world once again.

"Do you have some proof that I am Natalie Newcastle?" Briana heard herself ask, evenly and calmly.

Carlie handed Briana the purse she had been carrying. "This is yours, honey. You left it at the Ayton estate when you...disappeared so suddenly."

Briana took the purse from the woman who claimed to be her mother. It was a simple black bag, fine leather, something she might have selected if she ever had the money to afford it.

She opened it. The first thing she saw was the flash of an enormous, brilliant solitaire diamond, at least four carats. It sat in the center of an interlocking set of rings—engagement and wedding. Briana closed the purse again.

"Natalie, come home with me," Carlie's voice coaxed.

"And where is home?" Briana asked.

"The Ayton estate, of course. You're an Ayton now."

"I'm not going there."

"Then I'll take you home to Louisiana until you can become yourself again."

"My home is in Louisiana?"

"Your main house, the one your daddy owned."

"What about Washington State?"

"No, honey. You have no house there. Just the estate in Louisiana and the horse farm in Kentucky and the hilltop in Kauai."

Just, she said.

"And where do you live?" Briana asked.

"In my suite at the estate in Louisiana. But we can go to any one of your places."

"How can I, when I don't remember them or anything about this life you say I've been living?"

"You will, Natalie. Just as soon as I get you home and you feel safe again. Once you feel the love and security around you, you'll be my Natalie again."

Briana could still feel Michael's hand on her shoulder, and its pervading warmth. She had never been more in need of it or more thankful for it than she was now.

"Mrs. Taureau, I'm staying here."

"Here? Why would you want to stay here?"

"Because at the moment the institute is the only place that feels anywhere near like home to me."

Carlie shook her head in disappointment. But she gave no signs of getting up or giving up the fight.

"I brought your traveling trousseau with me, Natalie," she said after a moment. "I thought you'd want to select an outfit so you could look your best when you return to Shel. I hope you'll forgive me if I say that those clothes you're wearing neither fit nor suit your...taste."

"They are on loan from a new friend."

"Well, that was very nice of your new friend, I'm sure. But I'm certain you'll feel more like yourself when you're in some of your own clothes. They're out in the car. Perhaps I could prevail upon Dr. Sands to get them for you now?"

"I'll bring them in on your way out, Mrs. Taureau," Michael said nicely, but formally.

Briana watched a new concern float through Carlie Taureau's light blue eyes as she looked from Briana's face to Michael's hand, on her shoulder.

"Natalie, Shel is not going to understand this."

"Whatever he finds difficult to understand, I'll be happy to explain," Michael said, and the way he said it gave Briana the impression that he would enjoy doing it, too.

As devastatingly convincing as Carlie Taureau's story was, Michael was waiting for proof, too. That heartened Briana more than anything else.

She rose. "Mrs. Taureau—"

"At least call me Carlie, if you can't manage Mama," she said as she, too, rose. "I know that calling me Mama has not always been easy for you."

"Why was it hard for me to call you Mama?"

"Because you always felt I deserted you, honey. If I had not fallen for Connor, I would have been there for you while you were growing. You never would have been so lonely and unhappy as to have to try to be someone else."

There were tears filling Carlie's eyes again.

"The good Lord is only giving me what I deserve," she said, wiping them quickly away.

"Carlie, please don't—" Briana began.

"But you should not be made to suffer, too!" Carlie exclaimed, interrupting her. "Cut off from your husband, your life. Please, let me help you bring back your memories of being Natalie. Let me help you get your life back."

The woman's emotion seemed genuine, and her manner was persuasive. If she was making up this story, her presentation of it was flawless. Still, Briana held firm.

"I need time to think. You've presented me with an identity and history that is nothing like the one I remember. I have to sort out who I am."

"But you can't do this on your own, honey," Carlie said, her voice pleading. "You need help."

"Dr. Sands is here to help me," Briana said.

"But he heads a dream institute. He's not qualified—"

"Dr. Sands is a psychiatrist."

Carlie stepped back in surprise. "Psychiatrist?" she repeated.

"Yes. And, as such, he's eminently qualified to help me. He already has."

As surprised as Carlie had been to hear of Michael's qualifications, she appeared to regroup her thoughts quickly. She took a step toward Briana.

"You need to be around the people who love you."

"At the moment, I need to be around Dr. Sands."

"You're going to just walk away from your mama, your husband, your brother, and put yourself in the hands of a stranger?"

"This may be hard for you to accept, but you're much more of a stranger to me than Dr. Sands. Please listen, and try to understand. I have no memories of you, or Rory or Sheldon Ayton—except for his appearance here earlier today, when he attempted to take me with him against my will."

"Natalie, put yourself in Shel's place! You're his wife.

You'd disappeared from your own wedding reception. He'd been frantic about where you were, if you were all right. Then, when he finally found you, it was with this handsome man—''

"Who is my doctor. And I'm in need of a doctor much more than a husband at the moment," Briana said quickly.

"But you must admit—''

"Sheldon Ayton made no attempt to understand me, Carlie. I hope you will. I have to work this out for myself. Now, I don't mean to be unkind, but I think it's best you go.''

"You're sending your own mama away?''

"If you are my mother, you'll understand why I must. I can't be a daughter or a sister or a wife to anyone until I can be certain who I am to me.''

Carlie Taureau sighed heavily as she turned and headed slowly toward the door. Michael quickly strode in front of her to open it. As she stood in the doorway, Carlie turned back once more to look long and searchingly at Briana.

"Please remember us soon, honey. We all love you very much and are waiting for your return.''

And with that, she disappeared out into the hallway, with Michael as escort.

Briana sank down into the chair, her hands still clutching the purse that she'd been given. She felt as though she had just been engaging in an emotional tug-of-war—Carlie pulling her into Natalie's world, while she fought to hold on to her own.

She dipped her hand inside the purse, drew out the butter-soft billfold. She flipped it open to a Louisiana driver's license with Natalie Newcastle's name and a picture of her face—her new face.

She searched through the rest of the billfold, looking for something, anything, that was familiar.

Nothing was. The half-dozen credit cards all had Natalie Newcastle's name. There was more than five hundred dollars in the wallet.

Beneath a leather flap was a passbook for a money-market

checking account. The balance recorded in a neat script that looked suspiciously like her own showed a hundred thousand dollars and some change.

The last check had been written to Rory Taureau, for five thousand dollars. She put the passbook back in the purse and pulled out a cosmetic case.

There was a lipstick inside, blush, eyeliner, everything with Paris labels. A tiny crystal bottle of golden perfume was inscribed with the name Natalie.

Briana opened the bottle, tipped its top onto her wrist. A sweet, sultry fragrance of herbs and amber filled the air. It was light, sophisticated, lovely.

She found a keyless remote entry transmitter hanging off a gold Mercedes emblem inside the purse. There were other keys, too, no doubt to the estate, the farm, the mountaintop hideaway.

Finally, Briana picked up the rings. She slipped them on the third finger of her left hand.

They fit. Perfectly. She took them off, dropped them back into the purse with a long exhalation.

She had recognized the real Ayton estate from its dream image. She had recognized Sheldon Ayton as the groom at her dream wedding. And now she had recognized Carlie Taureau as one of the women from that dream argument.

But how could the house, or these people, be real? She wasn't Natalie Newcastle, an heiress from Louisiana. She was Briana Berry, a struggling architect from Washington State.

Unless her reality was a dream, and her dream reality?

Briana stood up and walked over to the mirror that hung on the wall in the corner of the reception room and stared at the face reflecting back at her—beautiful, flawless, the face that perfectly matched the one on Natalie Newcastle's driver's license.

The face that wasn't hers.

Briana shut her eyes tightly. But when she opened them again, those perfect features were still there, reflecting back.

What in the hell had happened to her?

Chapter Seven

"'Natalie Newcastle is the sole heir of deceased industrialist Markam Newcastle.'" Michael read the e-mail that had been sent from Dun and Bradstreet and was printing out at that very moment. "She definitely owns that real estate Carlie Taureau mentioned."

"And Carlie?"

"'Carlie Newcastle Taureau, a former Miss Louisiana, married Markam at eighteen, was divorced by him at twenty. Married Connor Taureau the month after the divorce was final. Rory Taureau was born seven months later. Connor Taureau died when a horse kicked him in the head seven years ago.'"

"Anything else?"

"Yes. 'Carlie is the sole owner of Creole Cuisine, a New Orleans restaurant, which has been running in the red for the first two years of its operation.'"

"Carlie didn't mention her restaurant," Briana said.

"She also neglected to mention that when Markam Newcastle died four years ago, Natalie was worth forty million. Now she's worth a paltry twenty-five."

"She spent fifteen million in four years? Sounds like this woman needs to get herself on a budget."

"And this woman, according to Sheldon and Carlie, is you."

"In which case, I'd better pay you now for your professional services, before I blow the rest of the money," Briana said, a nervous chuckle surfacing in her throat for the briefest of moments.

Michael was not fooled by the lightness of Briana's tone, or by her words. He saw the desperation clouding her eyes. He knew that she was having a very difficult time trying to cope with this new information.

The foundation of her sanity was her sense of humor. Sheldon Ayton's and Carlie Taureau's visits had to have begun to break through the floorboards of Briana's certainty about herself. These strangers were the living proof of another life, another reality.

Was Briana a multiple personality? There was no evidence that Briana Berry existed, and quite a lot that Natalie Newcastle did.

Michael realized that this might be what her dreams had been telling her—that there was another personality inside her who had been living another life. But if that was what her dreams were saying, Briana had yet to get their message.

What if she did? What if she stepped out of her Briana Berry persona and into her Natalie Newcastle identity? What if she forgot him as easily and suddenly as she had forgotten Ayton?

The thought shook him. Hard.

He couldn't stand the idea of her forgetting him.

Don't be a fool! The best thing that could happen would be for her to forget you. Then you could start forgetting her.

Michael was determined to listen to the voice of reason. He was determined to do the right thing by her—and himself.

"Briana, if you are a multiple personality, you're going to need the help of a specialist."

"So you're going to dump me on some poor, unsuspecting specialist?"

He could hear the disappointment beneath the forced merriment in her words.

"I thought you didn't want me to be your doctor."

She laughed. "No. I didn't want to be your patient."

Her words didn't make any sense intellectually. But, on an emotional level, Michael understood them perfectly.

And wished he didn't. He had suspected all along that she was as attracted to him as he was to her. And that she, too, had known a doctor-patient relationship would keep them apart.

It certainly should have. And yet every moment, he felt them drawing closer together. He needed to try to put some distance between them. Quickly.

"Briana, I'm no longer qualified to help you."

"Don't my dreams contain the answers?"

"I firmly believe studying your dreams will give you the answers you seek. But if you are a multiple personality, it could be that the personality who is dreaming has to be the one interpreting the dreams. You need a therapist who understands multiples."

"I can see how being a multiple personality could complicate understanding one's dreams. But I just can't believe that there is another person inside me. Michael, I know I'd feel...her." Briana shook her head as the confusion grew in her eyes.

"There's an excellent specialist in multiple personalities in Washington State," Michael said. "His name is Damian Steele."

"At least now, with this money, I can pay for the airline ticket," she said. "Maybe it's not such a bad thing to be a multiple personality, particularly when one of my personalities has this great face and is filthy rich."

He rested his hand on hers, unable to resist the sadness in her eyes, despite her tone.

She smiled at him, with bravery, not humor. "I don't know why I'm fighting it so hard. I probably should go with the flow."

Michael withdrew his hand, keeping his voice even. "And stay married to Sheldon Ayton?"

"I'm not ready to do that much flowing."

"He has money, power and, if Carlie can be believed, apparently charm, when he chooses to exercise it. His feelings for you also seem quite genuine.''

''Michael, you can't be serious! Are you forgetting he tried to forcibly take me out of here? What kind of a man attempts to force a woman to do something against her will? Surely you're not trying to talk me into staying married to him?''

''Just testing the strength of your identity boundaries,'' he said, and knew that hadn't been all he was doing. He had also been testing the strength of her feelings against Ayton. The last thing he wanted was her back with that man.

She looked straight at him and spoke slowly, with the calmness of conviction.

''Michael, I'm Briana Berry. Not Natalie Newcastle. I'm aware that my belief flies in the face of all the evidence and logic. But this goes beyond the confines of evidence and logic. This is *knowing*, despite evidence and logic. I *know* who I am.''

Yes, she certainly did. In spite of everything, she clung to it, too.

Michael was struck anew by how strong she was. Her special type of toughness—the ability to simply stand firm—had not been breached.

If there was a Natalie Newcastle inside her, he wondered if she was as resilient. And then he remembered the picture Sergeant Vierra had shown him of Natalie, the picture that Sheldon Ayton had obviously supplied.

That resilience, that humor, everything he'd seen in Briana, he'd seen in the eyes and the smile in that picture, as well. From that standpoint, the two personalities weren't different at all. How would he feel about Natalie if she was here?

''You have a few days to think about whether you wish to see Dr. Steele,'' Michael said, annoyed with his personal preoccupation. ''Damian's on vacation until late next week.''

''You think I have this other person inside me, don't you?''

''Briana, I know it seems a paradox, but that explanation fits the facts—even the fact that you have such a strong sense of yourself. Each personality would, don't you see?''

She let out a small sigh of disappointment. "No, I don't see. I only know what I feel. I feel like me, just me. Will you at least hang around until I leave for Washington, Michael?"

"Yes." He knew it wasn't wise, but he knew he would, because she needed him to. "We might as well make our time between now and then productive. I suggest we try to get to know Natalie Newcastle better and see if anything about her life reveals insights into your own."

"I must admit, I do like her taste in clothes. The outfits Carlie brought are beautiful."

"How would you like to put one on now and take a trip?"

"A trip? To where?"

"There's only one caterer in Las Vegas who would have been called in to handle a wedding like the one at the Ayton estate. And that's Pettit's Catering. Gene and Ginny Pettit are friends of mine. If they catered an elaborate wedding for Christmas Eve, they are no doubt relaxing at home today. I'll give them a call to let them know we'll be dropping by."

"Why do you want to see the caterers to the wedding?"

"Gene and Ginny are the confidants of high society here in southern Nevada and pretty good judges of character. I'd like to know what they think of the Aytons and the Newcastles. They're only ten minutes away by air."

"This getting places by helicopter has its advantages."

"When time is important—as it invariably is—flying is an absolute necessity out here in the wide expanse of the desert."

GENE AND GINNY PETTIT'S home was a lovely Spanish-style hacienda on several acres, with lots of cool tile and mature trees to offer shade during the hotter months. Briana was anxious as to how the caterers would greet her. She soon saw that she had no reason to be. The moment Ginny Pettit opened the door, she gave both Michael and her a big, welcoming smile.

"Come in, Michael, Natalie," she said, stepping out of the way. "Gene and I can't wait to find out what's up."

Ginny Pettit was around fifty, tiny, with graying brown hair and warm brown eyes. She was quite similar in appearance to her husband, who immediately stepped forward with two glasses of eggnog.

"This is the nonalcoholic version," Gene assured. "I know you're flying. Let's sit in the living room. The fireplace is going."

Briana could immediately feel the warmth coming from the enormous floor-to-ceiling flagstone structure as she stepped into the living room. The sectional couch was a series of mushroom shapes stretching across three walls. The stone floor was covered in hand-woven Navajo rugs of geometric designs. A live piñon pine in a twenty-gallon tub sat in the corner, adorned simply with a single strand of silver garland and a few spare silver bulbs. At the top was a silver star.

The room had a nice feel—simple, spacious, unpretentious.

Briana took a seat on the sofa and sipped the eggnog.

"Michael, if you've stolen Natalie here away from her husband, I'm not blaming you," Gene said as he plopped down next to his wife on the couch. "I've been telling Ginny for months now that she was too good for the guy."

"Months?" Briana repeated, not encouraged to hear yet another report that people had known her as Natalie earlier than three weeks before.

"Ms. Newcastle is suffering from a memory loss," Michael said quickly, by way of explanation. "Gene, Ginny, we need your help and your discretion."

"You have both, of course," Gene said quickly, his face sobering. "But am I getting this right? Are you saying Natalie doesn't know who she is?"

"She has no memory of having ever been Natalie Newcastle," Michael said carefully.

"How awful that must be for you!" Ginny said, with real feeling, as she looked toward Briana.

"Michael, how can we help?" Gene asked.

"We need to know everything you do about the Aytons and the Newcastles. And I don't just mean facts. I want to know your feelings about the people you've been dealing with on this catering job. Please, hold nothing back.''

Briana felt both Gene and Ginny's eyes immediately darting to her.

"Your honest impressions, please," Briana said quickly. "I promise you won't be hurting my feelings. I don't even remember being Natalie. So whatever you say, I can't possibly take it personally.''

She smiled at them in reassurance.

"You were never a moment's trouble, Natalie," Ginny said. "I'll never forget the day you pointed out to your mother-in-law that since she'd hired the best, it was probably only smart to let Gene and me alone so we could get on with doing what needed to be done. I could have hugged you.''

"And your mother-in-law could have strangled you," Gene said, laughing in remembrance. "*'Not in front of the help, Natalie!'* she said, as though Ginny and I were her lackeys. What a royal pitted prune than one is!''

"Can you start from the beginning on this, Gene?" Michael asked.

"Five months ago, Mrs. Gytha Ayton called to say that she was considering Pettit's to cater her son's wedding. She said she expected us at the Hamish Mountain estate at precisely ten the next morning, with our entire selection of hors d'oeuvres and dinners for her to sample. And they'd better be hot.''

"She has such colossal nerve," Ginny said.

"It often goes with a colossal bank account," Gene added.

Michael shook his head. "Obviously, Mrs. Ayton was not familiar with the fact that your chefs are the best in this part of the world, and just how sought-after your catering service is.''

Ginny chuckled. "She soon found out. Tell them what you told Mrs. Ayton, Gene.''

"I told her that for five hundred dollars a plate I would *accept* two reservations from her for a sampling of our selection at our formal dining room in Vegas at two o'clock three weeks from that next Friday. She gasped before hanging up on me."

"Does it really cost five hundred dollars a plate just to sample your food?" Briana asked.

"Generally we don't charge potential customers. And we can accommodate them at a sampling dinner within a week. I just figured Mrs. Ayton should pay for her consummate rudeness. Several hours later, her secretary called back to confirm the two reservations. I suppose it took her that long to learn that any weddings of class in Nevada better be catered by Pettit's."

"Who was at this wedding, Gene?" Michael asked.

"Mostly out-of-towners. Only local faces I saw were the governor's and Senator Frank Mason and his wife, Kathy."

"And that short, balding pudgy man," Ginny said, poking Gene's arm. "What is his name?"

"Oh, yes," Gene said. "I know who you mean. I can't remember his name, either."

"It's all right," Michael said. "I'm sure we can get a wedding guest list if we need to. I take it nothing improved your impression of Mrs. Ayton as you worked on the wedding?"

"It got worse daily," Ginny said. "If it hadn't been for Mrs. Taureau, we probably would have pulled out of the whole mess a month ago."

"What happened?"

"Mrs. Ayton decided to change her mind yet again about the menu. Gene and I were working on two other very large affairs. We'd had our fill of her nonsense. I called and left word with a servant at the estate that we would no longer be doing the catering. Two hours later, Carlie Taureau showed up at our door, begging us to simply ignore everything Mrs. Ayton said and serve what we had planned."

"And you agreed?" Michael asked.

"She had a persuasive manner, and a check for the full amount of our catering bill in advance," Gene said. "It was a hard combination to refuse."

"What did you think of Carlie Taureau?"

"She was okay," Ginny said. "Just too eager to please Mrs. Ayton. I still don't understand how she could let that woman have all the say at her own daughter's wedding."

"That isn't something we see every day," Gene said.

"Every time Natalie suggested something," Ginny said to Michael, "her mother was trying to talk her out of it and insisting the decision be left to the old pitted prune."

"Yeah," Gene said. "Struck me that Carlie Taureau sure seemed eager for Natalie to be marrying Sheldon Ayton, far more eager than Natalie seemed to be."

"Are you saying that Natalie didn't want to marry Sheldon?" Michael asked.

"She seemed fond enough of him," Gene answered carefully. "She just didn't display the kind of excitement that we generally see in a bride-to-be. Mrs. Taureau, on the other hand, was constantly excited—her eagerness for the wedding so obvious and so thick that you *couldn't* have cut through it with the proverbial knife."

"Why do you suppose that was?" Michael asked.

"Mrs. Ayton is worth close to half a billion," Ginny said. "Obviously, Mrs. Taureau wanted her daughter latching on to the heir apparent."

"What kind of money does Sheldon Ayton have?"

"No more than fifty million in his own right."

Briana could have laughed, the way Ginny had said that, as though fifty million dollars were nothing. Of course, next to half a billion, she supposed it was. This was certainly a rarefied society in which the Pettits moved.

"What do you think of Sheldon Ayton?" Michael asked.

"A pompous ass," Gene said without hesitation.

Ginny nodded. "Natalie introduced us to him when he came looking for her one day. Acted like it was beneath him to speak to us mere 'help.' Still, you could tell he was absolutely head over heels in love with Natalie. It was something to see. This big, handsome, autocratic man, with all his money and power, just getting all starry-eyed and unglued around his bride-to-be."

"And how did Mrs. Ayton feel about Natalie?"

"It was clear she didn't think Natalie was good enough for her son. But it was also clear that Natalie was Sheldon's pick. And Natalie was the one subject on which he wouldn't give way."

"Mrs. Ayton didn't like it," Gene said. "She's a woman who is used to having everything her way."

"Everyone in that household kowtowed to her, with the exception of Natalie here," Ginny said. She smiled over at Briana. "You were easygoing with the lot of them, but you never played the suck-up or supplicant to Mrs. Ayton, like her son and the rest."

"Neither did her brother, Rory," Gene added.

"Oh, yeah, Rory Taureau," Ginny said. "I nearly forgot him. We didn't see him that much."

"Tell me what you did see," Michael said.

"Good-looking, bulky," Ginny said. "Few years younger than Natalie. He was a professional boxer once. He limps from some injury. He didn't seem to like the Aytons much."

"How do you know?" Michael asked.

"He'd leave a room every time Mrs. Ayton entered it. Only time I ever saw him with Sheldon, he was taking verbal potshots at his brother-in-law-to-be."

"How did Sheldon take that?"

"Oh, you could tell Sheldon was ticked about it, but was trying to endure it for Natalie's sake. Rory was also guzzling down the bourbon pretty steadily all the time, when his mother wasn't actively preventing it."

"How was he with Natalie?"

"They were always joking," Gene said. "Good-natured stuff. They seemed to get along well, although she definitely didn't approve of his drinking so much."

"What was the wedding day like?"

"A madhouse, like most of them. Both Ginny and I attended, just as we always do, to ensure everything that we are responsible for is done right. Dinner turned out superb, and even the old prune was smiling at the compliments on our cuisine. I was just giving our people instructions on the final beverages and after-dinner liqueurs to be served to the guests when the news that Mrs. Ayton had fallen spread through the ballroom.''

"I saw her, Michael," Ginny said, her voice dropping. "I had just come out of the kitchen, and there she was, lying at the bottom of the stairs, with Sheldon leaning over her, the manservant, Kuen, holding her little whimpering dog in his hands. I knew it was serious. Sheldon was calling out but she wasn't responding.''

"How did they get her to the hospital?''

"The servants made a stretcher out of a table and carried her to Sheldon's helicopter," Gene answered. "He flew her himself to the emergency room in Vegas.''

"Mrs. Ayton's accident put an immediate pall on the festivities, as you might imagine," Ginny said. "Most people left directly afterward.''

"How about you?''

"Gene and I gave our staff instructions to stay as long as any guests did, and then we left, too. I didn't like dealing with the old prune, but I would never have wished anything like this on her. Gene and I called the hospital a little while ago. They say she's still in a coma.''

"Did your people make a video recording of the wedding reception?'' Michael asked.

"Naturally," Gene said. "Do you want to see it? It's still here. We haven't gone back to the office since the reception.''

"I'd appreciate it," Michael said.

Gene got up to get the tape. Ginny turned to Briana.

"Our cameraman dwells primarily on the food and its presentation, so that we have a visual recording of everything served," Ginny cautioned. "He doesn't do much panning of the wedding party and guests.''

Gene came back into the room with a videotape in his hand. He flipped what looked like a light switch. The wall beside him opened to reveal a fully equipped entertainment center.

Gene slipped the tape into a VCR recorder and took the remote control over to the couch to sit next to his wife.

The first scenes were of table after table of a very large and delicious-looking spread of hors d'oeuvres displayed in fine silver and china and crystal.

Briana noticed that although the cameraman primarily concentrated on the food, he also got a few shots of guests tasting the marvelous assortment and smiling appreciatively as they went back for more. Briana recognized Carlie mingling among them. Ginny pointed out a muscular young man with black hair standing next to Carlie, a drink in his hand.

"That's Rory Taureau."

Briana recognized him instantly as the man from one of her dream scenes—the smiling man talking to the person wearing the scary mask. And then a harsh elderly woman's face suddenly filled the screen, and Briana recognized it as belonging to the second woman in her dream argument.

Chills skidded down her spine.

"That's Mrs. Gytha Ayton," Ginny said, confirming Briana's suspicion.

Briana looked closer, to see what Gytha Ayton was holding in the crook of her arm.

"It's a dachshund," Briana said.

"Mrs. Ayton raises them as show dogs," Ginny said. "They're cute as buttons, but excitable. Any noise gets them barking. She's always carrying this one about. He's Napoleon, her prize champion."

The dream argument with the two women played in Briana's mind, and the way their voices had sounded like dogs barking toward the end.

"Are the dog kennels at the Ayton estate?" she asked.

"Along with a full-time dog trainer and handler," Ginny said. "Napoleon stays in Mrs. Ayton's room, though. He even sleeps on her bed."

Briana looked closer at the screen and realized that the clothing was not wedding attire. "When was this footage taken?" she asked.

"At an informal get-together on the afternoon of the rehearsal dinner to welcome those members of the wedding party who had just come from the airport. We provided the refreshments for all events associated with the wedding. What you're looking at is the best man, ushers, maid of honor, bridesmaids—all of them Mrs. Ayton's selection."

"Didn't Natalie have any friends in the wedding party?"

Ginny reached over to hit the pause button on the remote control in her husband's lap before answering Briana's question.

"You told your mother you wanted to have two women in the wedding party who were your friends. When Mrs. Ayton found out that they worked in your mother's restaurant in New Orleans, she nearly had a coronary. The idea was immediately nixed."

"And Natalie gave in to this?"

"Your mother told you that your friends would be far too uncomfortable in the Ayton crowd, and that you'd only be embarrassing them by asking them to be your maid of honor and bridesmaid, since they couldn't possibly afford the clothing or anything else attendant to such positions in such a wedding like this."

"I could have paid for whatever was necessary."

"When you mentioned that to your mother, she told you that you'd be hurting your friends' pride terribly if you offered to do such a thing," Ginny said.

"So I gave in?"

"I think you just wanted to do the right thing, Natalie. You knew your friends. You must have realized your mother was right, that they would be uncomfortable. And you knew it was what she wanted. You two seem very close."

Ginny restarted the videotape. Briana watched the food being served at the rehearsal dinner and the other functions, thinking about Ginny's words about how Natalie had endured her mother-in-law's machinations for her own mother's sake. Would she have done that?

If her grandmother had asked it of her, yes. In a second.

But Hazel would never have asked that of her. Hazel would have wanted her wedding to be what Briana wanted.

The videotape had come to the wedding reception. The spectacular wedding cake had been so large that the cameraman had to step back quite a few feet to get it all in the frame. When he did, he'd captured a lot of the wedding party and guests, as well.

Briana instantly recognized the beautiful wedding dress she had been wearing—and the face of the woman wearing it. Her face. Now. Sheldon Ayton was standing beside her as they cut the cake together.

It was so damn eerie—so damn scary—to think that she was that woman standing next to the groom. That Natalie Newcastle was inside her, a part of her.

"Could you pause the tape right there?" Michael asked.

Gene hit the pause button. Michael rose and moved closer to the screen. "Isn't that Everett Thaw back in the crowd?" he asked, pointing toward a short, pudgy man who was holding up his tie for the scrutiny of a thin, hawk-nosed manservant in the background.

"Everett Thaw!" Ginny said. "Yes, that's the man whose name I was trying to remember earlier. He was asking the Ayton's manservant, Kuen, there for something to take a food stain off his tie. Strange man, that Everett Thaw. Ever since his wife Molly died, one never knows what to expect from him."

"No, one doesn't," Michael agreed.

They watched the tape for nearly an hour more. And all through it, odd feelings of recognition kept surfacing in Briana's mind as Carlie and Rory and Sheldon and Gytha Ayton's faces periodically flashed across the screen.

When it was over, Gene hit the off button.

"Do you remember the last time you saw Natalie that night?" Michael asked him.

Gene shook his head. "I was too busy supervising to pay much attention to anything else."

"What about you, Ginny?" Michael asked. "Do you remember the last time you saw Natalie?"

"It was when she went upstairs to change. I was on my way to the kitchen to make sure there was still plenty of chilled champagne. Natalie was at the bottom of the stairs talking to Rory. She seemed a little upset. I think it was because he was pretty soused by then. Anyway, Sheldon strode up, and he and Rory had a few unpleasant words to say to each other."

"Did you hear what they were?"

"No, I was too far away. But it was clear from the expressions on their faces that it wouldn't have taken much for the two men to come to blows."

"What happened to prevent it?" Michael said.

"Natalie stepped between them—like she normally did—and hustled Sheldon up the stairs with her, leaving Rory at the landing."

"Where did Rory go after that?"

"When I left for the kitchen, he was still standing at the bottom of the stairs."

"And how long after that did you see Mrs. Ayton?"

"It was probably just a couple of minutes later when I came out of the kitchen. Sheldon and Kuen were standing over her at the bottom of the stairs, Napoleon whimpering in Kuen's arms."

"Was Sheldon still in his wedding clothes when he was bent over his mother?" Michael asked.

"Part in, part out, I think."

"And you didn't see Natalie anywhere?"

"No."

"What about Rory Taureau?"

"I don't remember seeing him again. Gene and I left only a few minutes later."

"Thank you, Ginny, Gene," Michael said.

Briana stood and turned to them. "I really appreciate all your help."

"Any friend of Michael's is a friend of ours," Ginny said,

sending Briana a big smile. "I do hope you get your memory back, Natalie. Out of all the people in that crazy household, you were the only one who acted normal. Seems strange for you to be the one to get amnesia."

Gene and Ginny saw Michael and Briana to the door. A few moments later, Michael was handing Briana into the helicopter.

Briana thought about Ginny's words as she buckled up: *You were the only one who acted normal. Seems strange for you to be the one to get amnesia.*

Ginny didn't know the half of how strange it was. Because the truth was, she didn't have amnesia. She knew who she was.

She was just no longer certain of who *else* she might be.

"My ATTORNEYS just sent over these papers," Sheldon said as he pushed a thick brief toward Carlie. The papers slid to a stop in front of her on the edge of the ponderous desk in the equally ponderous study of the Ayton estate.

Carlie barely glanced at the papers. She was irritated that Sheldon had sent a servant to fetch her, and that now that she was here, he didn't even have the presence of mind to offer her a seat.

When it came to even the minimum of social graces, this man was hopeless. She let out an internal sigh as she stepped over to one of the elaborate rococo chairs in front of his desk and gently lowered herself into it. She faced him, sitting straight and smiling pleasantly, determined to maintain her manners, despite the lack of his.

"What is this all about, Shel?" she asked.

Sheldon leaned forward on his elbows, his cold eyes fixed on her. "My lawyers tell me we're going to need your help in order to get Natalie back."

"And how is it that I can be of help, Shel?"

"By signing the petition in front of you. It will permit us to have her examined."

"Examined?"

"That's what I said."

"Natalie is your wife. Why is it that you want me to sign papers to have her examined?"

"My lawyers say that if she is found mentally unsound, it can be argued that she was such when she married me. My legal claim as her husband, in that case, would not stand up in court. But your kinship as her mother would."

"So these papers you want me to sign will force her to be examined by a psychiatrist?"

"By a court psychiatrist. And then she'll be handed over into our hands, to be treated by someone of our choice. His name is Lars Neilssen. He's a longtime friend of the family. I'm flying him in from his clinic in Glasgow. He'll be here first thing Monday."

"You're planning for him to take over her care if the court psychiatrist finds Natalie in need of help?" Carlie asked.

"Not *if*, Carlie. *When*. She's obviously delusional. Once that's been ruled legally, we'll have a clear field to insist on her getting help by who we say, where we say."

Carlie shifted in her chair uncomfortably. "Shel, I can't have Natalie committed."

Sheldon came roaring to his feet and circled around the desk. He towered over Carlie, his voice suddenly booming down at her like a cannon. "You think I want to have her committed? You think I'm taking any pleasure in trying to force her to get help?"

"No, Shel, of course not. But putting her in some clinic—"

"I'm not going to put her in a clinic, Carlie! I'm going to bring her home."

"Home? You mean here?"

"Of course, here! Dr. Neilssen will stay here and treat her. He tells me they have some new drugs now that can do wonders. They will take away all the anxiety, all the pain, get her to listen to reason."

Drugs? Carlie swallowed uncomfortably.

"Pumping Natalie full of drugs is not the way to get her back, Shel. I'm sure if I just spend some time with her I can help her to understand who she is and get her to accept her life again."

"And how are you going to get to spend that time with her? You told me she sent you away."

"I plan to go see her again."

"And what if she won't see you?"

"I'm sure she'll see me."

"And if you're wrong?"

"Then we can think about what to do then. Shel, your mama's accident has canceled all your honeymoon plans, anyway. And the doctors still don't know if she's going to pull through. Surely, you have your hands full enough worrying about her. There's no reason to rush into any hasty decisions about Natalie just yet."

"No reason? Carlie, she's my wife! She belongs with me! Who knows what that guy at that damn dream institute might be doing to her!"

Yes, Carlie had suspected Sheldon would be worrying about that. Dr. Michael Sands was an extremely handsome man. And from what she could see, he was obviously very protective of Natalie. Neither of those facts could have escaped Sheldon's attention.

"Natalie should be beside me," Sheldon said, pacing in agitation. "In my home, my bed. We're married, damn it! I've waited for her for months! I've never waited for a woman before in my life! I'm not waiting for her anymore!"

"Sheldon, you can't force her."

He whipped around toward Carlie. "Force her? Carlie, I worship her! I'd do anything for her! For God's sake, can you really think I'd ever hurt her?"

No, Carlie didn't think he would. At least not intentionally.

"Carlie," he said, his voice losing its frantic tone as he came to kneel next to her chair. "You can't be hoping that Natalie is going to come out of this craziness on her own?"

"I don't—"

"No, of course you don't. Once we get the court to have Natalie put in Dr. Neilssen's care, we'll bring her here, and you can spend that time you want with her. As long as you like. I promise. But if you don't sign the papers, she'll stay out there. And she could get hurt. Do you want her to get hurt, Carlie?''

''No.''

''Then sign the papers. Let's get her back home with us. Where she can be protected and made well. Surrounded by her family, the people who love her. The only people in the world she can really count on.''

Carlie sighed. Yes, about that Sheldon was totally right. There wasn't anyone else in the world who cared for Natalie.

She would be better-off home, wouldn't she?

Of course. She was better-off being made to realize that she was Natalie.

Even if she didn't want to be.

Carlie reached for the papers—and signed on the bottom line.

Chapter Eight

Michael landed the helicopter on the rooftop of the tall Las Vegas building. He helped Briana out and then led the way to the elevator. All around them the skyline was aglow with the billion watts of electricity that lit the city like a gigantic desert Christmas tree every night of the year.

Once they stepped inside the elevator, Michael pressed the button for the Lucky Seasons, the restaurant that occupied the entire tenth floor. He could feel Briana's own special electrical charge zipping through him as he inadvertently brushed the back of her shoulders.

"I'm very confused about this multiple personality business," Briana said, turning to look up at him.

"I'm no authority," Michael admitted as he quickly stepped back from the lovely scent and beckoning warmth of her. "But the evidence seems to suggest that you have been living two very distinct lives—one real, one imaginary. Damian Steele should be able to say definitively if that's what has been happening."

The elevator doors swished open, and Michael led Briana into the elegant restaurant, which was owned and operated by his friend. Whenever he was in town, Michael was certain he'd always find a table here and an excellent meal, despite the lack of a reservation.

The maître d' recognized Michael immediately, smiled

broadly and showed him to his favorite table in a secluded alcove.

Michael and Briana agreed on the evening's specialty—roasted-onion-and-carrot soup, followed by veal rib roast with orange and rosemary, steamed asparagus topped with almond butter, and coconut-coffee parfaits with sesame-caramel sauce.

The food quickly disappeared from both their plates. Michael attributed their good appetites to having just watched the Pettits' tape, so full of tempting dishes.

He watched Briana stir cream into her after-dinner coffee. When she tilted her head, the light from the chandelier sprinkled red sequins through her hair. As she looked up, their gazes met and he felt an unmistakable jolt. Her eyes were jade tonight, matching her outfit.

She was incredibly lovely. Michael didn't have to be touching her skin to feel its smoothness. Somehow the tips of his fingers remembered. Nor did he have to be kissing her to remember her taste. Her sweetness was still on his tongue.

"I can't get used to this, Michael."

"Used to what, Briana?" he asked, scrambling to gather his quickly scattering thoughts.

"Being flown everywhere in a private helicopter. Walking into a five-star restaurant and being immediately seated without reservations."

"Natalie probably wouldn't think a thing of it."

"I'm not Natalie."

Briana leaned over the table toward him, the sincerity in her eyes clear, unblinking. "Michael, I never had the money to go to college. I worked as a word processor during the day and went to trade school at night to learn architectural design. It took me forever to get a job. I was an apprentice at a design firm for five years before it folded. There weren't any other openings anywhere. That's why Lee Willix and I decided to go into partnership, to see if we could make it on our own."

"And you did," Michael said.

"After two years of fourteen-hour days and running in the red. Even then, my foolishness almost had us losing it all."

"I have difficulty imagining you being foolish."

Briana took a small sip of her coffee. Michael knew the frown on her face had nothing to do with its flavor.

"Foolish doesn't begin to describe it," she said after a moment. "Rod was our biggest client. His main office was in Utah. He was living out of a Seattle hotel room. When he asked me out, I assumed he was single. Three weeks into our torrid affair, a birthday card from his wife and three kids arrived for him at our office."

"And you told Rod and his business to take a hike."

"I wanted to, Michael. But if we lost Rod's business, we would have been back in the red. Lee's wife had just gotten pregnant. Lee begged me to find another way to handle it. We really needed the account."

Michael remembered his struggle to get the institute going during its early days. There had been plenty of money to be had—if one was willing to deal with certain people.

Michael hadn't dealt with those people, but he had felt the temptation. He understood Briana's dilemma and knew he could accept any compromise she might have had to make.

"I should have known it was too good to be true," Briana continued. "Rod was rich, handsome. I was living in a fairy tale. I had convinced myself that he saw past my homely face to the person I was inside. What he really saw was a convenient conquest, someone to fool around with while he was away from his wife."

Michael was sad to hear Briana speak of this. He could tell that she had cared for Rod and had been hurt because she did. She struck him as a woman who was always totally open in her feelings and her dealings with others. Like everything else about her, her honesty and forthrightness were most becoming.

"So how did you handle the bastard?" Michael asked, surprised to hear the sudden angry bite in his words.

A twinkle lit her eyes, his only warning. "I asked him to

start calling me Brian. I told him that my doctor had agreed to perform breast-reduction surgery on me, and that I'd already started taking male hormones to prepare me for my new life-style.''

Michael roared at the unexpectedness of her response. Other diners turned toward their table, but he didn't care. He was too delighted and relieved to learn that Briana was not the kind of woman to compromise her ethics—not for money, not even for love.

"I can't wait to hear how Rod took your news," Michael said when he stopped laughing.

"He suddenly found an urgent reason to rush back to Utah," Briana said, her lips dancing into a smile. "He sent his assistant to Seattle to finalize the details on our design contract. The job went through without a hitch, although that assistant eyed me quite strangely for a while."

Michael loved looking at her lips in a smile. The next words were out of his mouth before he had a chance to edit them.

"I don't know what Natalie Newcastle is like, but getting to know Briana Berry is proving to be a real treat."

Her smile grew until it filled her eyes.

God, they were great eyes—intelligent, open, witty, warm, honest.

His logic told him that the experiences she had just related might be all in her mind. Illogically, incredibly, he just didn't care. She was more real than any woman he had ever met.

And he was in more trouble than he had ever imagined.

"I've figured out why you aren't married, Michael."

He reminded himself he was a professional. He could handle this attraction for her. He must handle it.

He tried to sound nonchalant. "Have you?"

"Yep. It's because some femme fatale broke your heart at a young and tender age."

He chuckled as he leaned back.

"I'm right, aren't I?" Briana asked. "What was her name?''

"Mrs. Tigard," Michael said. "She taught seventh grade. She had this exquisite English accent. The first day she read Wordsworth aloud to us, I fell madly in love with her. My rapture lasted until she graded my first composition."

"She failed you?"

"No, she gave me a B. But it was her comment that killed the romance. I'll never forget it. She said that 'with a more mature handling of the subject matter' I could have gotten an A."

"Ouch. The last thing an adolescent boy needs to hear from the older object of his affection is that he lacks maturity."

"It does pack a rather lethal punch."

"And you never again succumbed to this wondrous thing called love?"

Michael detected a new note of seriousness in Briana's question, one that belied her earlier light tone. She really wanted to know. And that was when he knew he wanted to tell her.

"The women I meet are interested in marrying and having a family," Michael said. "I'm convinced a person has to feel passionate about something in order to do it right. Passion clears away all the obstacles to a goal and makes the journey itself joyful. I have no passion for child-rearing."

"Does this have anything to do with the way you were raised?"

"Probably. My parents didn't want to accept the incredible commitment of time and energy needed to raise me. So they left it to others. We all learn by example. It took me a lot of years before I could forgive them for theirs. My job at the institute requires an intensive commitment of time and travel. I'm not repeating my parents' mistake, taking on a job I can't do right."

"You've obviously made the right choice," she said simply.

Michael had been prepared for an argument. Every other woman he shared these feelings with had tried to change his mind, had tried to tell him he would change his mind. But once again Briana had surprised him.

"I thought a woman didn't respect a man who didn't want to become a father?" he asked.

"Life is full of wonderful, exciting, *different* paths. No one should be forced down one that isn't right for him. You know fatherhood is not right for you. I respect that. The men I don't respect are the ones who become fathers and *then* decide they made a mistake."

"Like your father?"

She stared at her coffee cup, circling its top with her fingertip. "He wasn't a bad man. He just didn't understand that families don't all end up with happy sitcom endings."

"You said your brothers died young. Did your father's leaving have anything to do with that?"

"Pretty much everything. He couldn't handle their deaths. Wasn't strong enough. So he just up and left my mother, who was six months pregnant with me. So she lost her husband, as well as her sons."

Michael was amazed at how evenly and calmly Briana had said those words. "Do you hate your father for what he did?"

"No, Hazel wouldn't allow hate in the house. She praised the strength of my mother, her ability to survive and keep going, despite incredible loss. She felt sorry for my father. His failure at being both a husband and father was something she said he'd have to live with for the rest of his life."

"Do you ever think of finding him?"

She shook her head. "I forgave him in my heart long ago. Why should I push myself into his life? I'd only embarrass him and shame him by forcing him to face the child he walked away from."

"You sound incredibly sane for someone who's crazy," Michael said, touched by the bedrock of tolerance she displayed. "I wonder if Natalie Newcastle is as forgiving."

Her eyes clouded as she considered his words. "You talk about Natalie as though she were definitely a part of me. Are you really that sure?"

"You tell me, Briana. We flew over the house that you described in your dream. You met the people. They spoke about events that you described in your dream. If you aren't Natalie Newcastle, what other explanation can there be?"

Briana shook her head on a long exhale. "I don't know. A part of me still can't accept I'm sitting here with you in this lovely restaurant, dressed in this incredibly expensive outfit. Do you know that it was handmade, and that even my bra and panties have the exact same shade of jade ribbon?"

Michael looked into his coffee cup, trying very hard not to picture Briana wearing what she was describing so innocently.

"The dozen outfits that Carlie brought over are all like this," she continued. "Perfectly coordinated. Perfectly fitted. Each with different shoes and handbags to match. I look in the mirror, and I just can't believe what I see. I keep thinking I'm going to be waking up back in Washington any minute now."

"What if you wake up instead to realize you're Natalie Newcastle?" he asked. It was a thought that continued to haunt him.

"If she's inside me, how can I not know? Nothing Carlie or Ginny or Gene has said about her has rung the right memory bell."

"Then maybe we need to try ringing a new one."

"What bell would that be, Michael?"

"Her doorbell. Let's go to Louisiana tomorrow to see this estate of hers. The address is printed out on the Dun and Bradstreet financial report I requested. One of the keys you found in that purse should fit it."

"You think I might remember something of her if I were in her home?"

"It's worth a try. I'm as curious about her as you must be. I'm particularly interested in finding out why Natalie Newcastle would decide she needed to become Briana Berry."

"Carlie implied it was because she felt lonely and unloved as a child."

"I may not be a specialist in the phenomenon of multiple personalities, but I know that it takes an enormous amount of emotional and physical abuse for a child to resort to such a method of escape. I doubt simply feeling lonely and unloved would be sufficient."

"You're saying Natalie was abused."

"If she weren't severely abused, Briana, she would not have had to create another personality into which she had to retreat. Kids who are ignored and lonely may use their imagination to visit fantasy worlds, but they always have a round-trip ticket."

"Did you use your imagination when you were lonely, Michael?"

"Until I got lucky and had my first lucid dream."

"What is a lucid dream?"

"One in which you become conscious."

"Conscious? As in awake?"

"But you're not awake. You're dreaming. And yet, you're conscious of yourself within the dream. I'm still awed by them. I had my first spontaneous lucid dream when I was ten. Ever since then, I have been learning how to lucid-dream at will."

"What was your first lucid dream?"

"It stemmed from a real-life situation. My parents were gone on another scientific expedition that would keep them out of touch for months. They had hired this woman to come into our home to take care of me. She turned out to be a drunk. She moved in her two teenage sons, both of whom were drug addicts. They were hocking my parents' paintings, silver, crystal, TVs, VCRs, stereos, everything to get the money to feed their habit."

"Couldn't you tell someone?"

"They threatened to kill me if I did. I have no doubt they would have."

"What a nightmare."

Michael rested his hand on hers, gave it a quick, reassuring squeeze. "That night I dreamed I was begging my parents to tell me why they kept leaving me and letting people who were cruel have control over me. My parents said they didn't have time to talk about it because they were too busy. And then, suddenly, I became lucid. I knew I was dreaming.''

"How did you know you were dreaming?"

"My father's hat had wet seaweed hanging off of it. My mother's raincoat was wet with salt spray. A part of my mind recognized that if my parents were still off on their ocean voyage, they couldn't be standing in the house, talking to me.''

"What did you do?"

"I decided that since this was my dream, I was going to do something I always wanted to. I walked to the front door, opened it and told my parents to leave, that *I* didn't have time for *them*. When they obeyed me and left, I was filled with this incredible, inexpressible feeling of total freedom. I awoke and knew that the dream had told me what I needed to know.''

"Which was?"

"That I had to stop counting on others to make my life what I wanted it to be. My future was in my hands. That lucid dream was a powerful turning point in my life.''

"What happened with the woman and her sons?"

"I waited until all three of them were passed out one morning. Then I took one of the guns they kept around and started firing it out the window. The noise barely stirred them. I set the gun next to one of them and slipped out to school. The neighbors called the police. When they broke down the door, they found the three of them passed out, with the guns and drugs strewn all around. They were arrested on a number of charges.''

"And you planned all that at ten?"

"And loved doing it. That lucid dream had given me a wonderful sense of control. I knew from then on that my life was going to be great. And it was—it is. I got everything I went for—and more.''

Briana smiled at Michael with so much warmth that his palms began to perspire.

"I thought I was going to feel sad after hearing what you endured as a youngster, Michael. But I don't. I feel heartened. You gave yourself your own happy ending."

Michael had visions of the happy ending he'd like to be having with Briana about now. He once again forcibly reminded himself that he was a doctor and the lovely woman sitting across from him was his patient. Very reluctantly, and with a lot more effort than should have been necessary, he redressed her in his mind and put on his most professional tone.

"The secret is to follow the lead we find in our dreams. And in a lucid one, you can even take a few trips off the beaten path."

"Do you always control a dream when you become lucid in it?"

"Not...always," he admitted, with more than a little discomfort, as he thought of his racy dreams with Briana as the star. "Come on, we'd best get back. We'll have to be up early tomorrow to make the flight to Louisiana."

IT WAS a beautiful December night, filled with a full moon and crisp cool air. Michael dived deep beneath the warm blue waters of the institute's pool and let his body's own buoyancy bring him back up. He was just breaking the surface when he saw Briana.

She was diving into the pool at the other end. He watched as her arms pumped and her feet kicked up a steady spray. Despite the fact that she'd said she hadn't exercised in a while, she seemed to be a strong swimmer. She didn't stop until after five complete laps. An impressive performance.

And then he forgot all about her performance as she stepped out of the pool and into the moonlight.

For she was naked.

And that was the instant Michael knew he was dreaming. She gave her long, wet hair a shake, and the drops danced over her shoulders, her arms, her breasts. He already knew her slim figure was first-rate. But seeing the bare perfection of its glistening pale smoothness had his heart pumping hard.

She hadn't come into his dreams naked before.

He reminded himself that he was her doctor, a professional. He was determined to use this lucid dream to hone his control—so that he could better handle being around her when awake.

Only then she began to walk toward him, and Michael knew he was far from handling anything.

He had never seen a woman move the way Briana moved, with such an elemental sensuality. It carried no calculation, no artifice, just an inborn come-hither grace that was irresistible.

He steadied himself and gave the order firmly.

I'm changing this dream, Briana. Jump back into the pool.

She didn't jump back into the pool. She continued to walk straight toward him, her lovely eyes looking straight at him.

Stay there, Briana. Don't come any closer.

She ignored him and kept right on coming. Her autumn-honey voice filled his head.

Michael, there's no reason to worry.

Stay back, Briana!

But she didn't stay back. She stepped right up to him.

Michael, I was meant for you. And you were meant for me. She raised her arms to circle them around his neck.

Before her dream body could touch his, Michael yanked himself awake. He lay on the crumpled sheets of his bed, sweating and panting and so damn aroused he felt the pain of it. Damn. Why couldn't he ever control his dreams when she was in them?

Michael rose from his bed and grabbed a towel on the way out to the pool. Moderate exercise promoted dream recall. But heavy exercise—the kind that led to physical exhaustion—was often a guarantee of no dream recall.

Which was why Michael dived into the pool and did twenty laps, hard and fast. And then did twenty more.

BRIANA'S FIRST IMPRESSION of the Louisiana estate of Natalie Newcastle was that it was indeed an estate, over one hundred acres of rolling land and more than four-thousand feet of waterfront, all located on the Bogue Chitto River. The bridge that took them across was one of two that led to the property.

Once on the other side, Briana was immediately taken with the beautifully landscaped grounds, the three-acre pond full of ducks and the copious gardens full of hybrid daylilies, azaleas, dogwood, camellias and native hardwoods.

It was green and lush and lovely as it sat beneath a warm, breezy sky of rolling clouds. There was a sense of the past in the mature trees and shrubbery, and a sense of the modern in the large in-ground pool, a seamless expanse of brilliant blue tile.

"What do you think of the house, Briana?" Michael asked.

Briana directed her gaze to the imposing pristine white two-story home.

"It's a mid-nineteenth century vintage, with a mixture of styles. Its door and porch and those classical columns were borrowed from Greek Revival. The bracketed cornice, on the other hand, is definitely Italianate. Both the flattened arch and the jigsaw-cut wood detailing the upstairs porch sport a Gothic Revival influence."

"Spoken just like an architect."

"This wasn't another test?"

"No, I was looking more for a feeling of recognition than a recitation of physical structure."

"Sorry. It doesn't look familiar at all." Briana paused to sift through the keys in her purse. "I hope I don't trigger some security alarm when I try one of these in the lock."

As they walked up the stone steps to the front, Briana saw a head through the drapes near a front window. By the time they had reached the door, it was opening.

"Natalie, you've come home!" a short, sturdy-looking woman called as she swung the door open wide. She was in her late fifties, her mostly gray hair tied at the back of her neck in a neat twist, her light eyes misty with ready emotion.

She wrapped her short, stubby arms around Briana's waist and squeezed her tight.

Briana endured the hug, at a loss about what else to do.

"It is so good to see you, child! Your mama were calling here all frantic-like looking for you two days ago. She told me you disappeared from your wedding reception. I was so worried!"

"It's okay," Briana assured. "I'm okay."

After a moment, the woman let Briana go and reached into her apron for a tissue to dab at her eyes. "When your mama rung me yesterday to say they'd found you and you were safe, she never told me you were coming home."

"It was a spur-of-the-moment decision."

The woman put away her damp tissue and hustled them inside, closing the door.

She paused in the foyer to look up at Briana with concerned eyes. "What nonsense is this I hear about your not knowing your own mama or that new husband of yours?"

"It's true. I don't even know who you are."

The woman shook her gray head, and her eyes grew sad.

"Lord have mercy, child. What has happened to you?"

"I'm Dr. Sands," Michael said as he stepped forward quickly, holding out his hand.

The woman looked Michael up and down before taking his hand for the briefest of shakes.

"Lou-May Lestel."

"How long have you known Natalie Newcastle, Ms. Lestel?" Michael asked.

"It's Lou-May—no Ms. Lestel. I'm the housekeeper here. I were by Carlie's side when she gave birth to this young'n. Come on into the parlor and we'll talk over some coffee and a slice of sweet-potato pie."

The parlor evoked the flavor of a grand Parisian apartment. Eighteenth-century lyre-back chairs set above an enormous French rug fringed in gold braiding. An eighteenth-century musical clock adorned a lacquered Louis XV commode. A parquetry center table was complemented by Louis XVI–style armchairs.

Everything was polished, and gleaming with old Southern money.

Lou-May left them, only to return a few moments later with coffee, smelling strongly of chicory, on a silver serving tray.

"So, what you be a doctor of?" she asked Michael as she proceeded to pour the coffee into beautiful blue-and-gold Frankenthal porcelain cups. She handed a cup each to Briana and Michael and then took the chair across from them.

"I'm trying to retrieve Natalie's memory," Michael answered. "Lou-May, you said that you were here when Natalie was born. How long ago was that?"

"Thirty-one years ago come February. I come to this house with Carlie as her personal maid and companion the year afore."

"Markam Newcastle hired you?" Michael asked.

"No, I were Carlie's personal choice. He thought I were just a maid. He never knew I were Carlie's third cousin on her mama's side. We kept that part 'tween us."

"Why?" Briana asked.

"Markam never would have stood for no wife of his having kin working as servants, less'n they were the out-of-sight-and-out-of-mind kind, which he insisted Carlie's had to be."

"Carlie's parents were also servants?" Michael asked.

"Not actual, but might as well have been, since they had no money, learnin', nor what you'd call social graces. Can you imagine a man telling his wife she had to go visit her kin 'cause they weren't fancy enough to be welcome in her own home?"

Lou-May paused to look at Briana.

"When I seen Markam treating your mama just like she were one of his servants, well, I got right mad and told her to speak out for herself. Trouble were, she be eighteen and Markam be fifty. She didn't know how to stand up to him. She were afraid to, I suppose."

Lou-May took a sip of her coffee as she picked up some pie.

"Tell us about when Natalie was born," Michael said.

"Markam made no secret about the fact that he wanted a son. When Carlie presented him with a daughter, I saw the way Markam looked at her—as though *she'd* done something wrong."

Lou-May sent Briana a mournful look.

"I think that's when Carlie really started to hate him. She didn't do much pretending about it, neither. Markam started to stay away more and more."

Lou-May took a bite of her pie before she went on. "The situation were just ripe for disaster. Then Connor come to take care of a prize stallion that Markam had bought."

Lou-May shook her head. "Carlie were very young and very foolish. I know'd she were lonely, what with Markam being gone most of the time, and treating her more like a brood mare than a wife when he were here. But she didn't have no sense at all, spending so much time over at them stables. I know'd one of Markam's servants were bound to slip a word into his ear about it sooner or later."

Lou-May let out a heartfelt sigh.

"When he found out, Markam were screaming such oaths as could've put hair on a bald man. He got the shotgun and headed on out to the stables. He probably would of killed Connor if I hadn't of gotten there first to warn him to git. When Markam come for your mama, I stood in front of her and told him he'd have to shoot through me. But he told me he weren't about to waste no good ammunition on either of us. He told us both to git."

"You left then, too?" Briana asked.

"Yeah, he kicked out your mama and me and kept you. Your mama couldn't believe it. But I know'd he'd never let her have you. You were his blood, after all."

Lou-May's eyes grew teary. "Your mama were heart-broken to of lost you."

"Did you stay with her?" Briana asked.

"No. Weren't no work for me in these parts, on account of everybody know'd I'd stood up for Carlie against the master of the house. Carlie and Connor couldn't afford to have me do for them. Still, the folks I went to in Mobile were nice enough. And after them, there were other young'ns to raise."

"When did you come back here, Lou-May?" Briana asked.

"Two years ago, Carlie tracked me down. It were just after you come back from your year in Paris with her and Rory. You've no idea how happy I were to see you all growed up into such a beauty. Amazing thing, you turning out so sweet and all, seeing as how you had such a tyrant for a daddy. I've done for half a dozen families over the years. Those autocratic types most often produce either rebellious hellions or sneaky little brats."

"Does the name Briana Berry sound familiar to you, Lou-May?" Briana asked.

"No, can't say that it does."

"You never heard that I called myself by that name when I was little?"

"Nope."

"What about the name Hazel Doud?"

Lou-May shook her head, looking perplexed.

"Did Carlie ever mention to you that she had come to see me here when I was ten?"

"Come to see you? Here? Where did you git such a notion, child?"

"She didn't come to see me when I was ten?" Briana asked again.

"Couldn't. Man like Markam Newcastle don't forgive no woman what betrayed him. He had the court proclaim her an unfit mama. She weren't allowed nowhere near you."

"So when did Natalie and Carlie renew their acquaintance?" Michael asked.

"After Markam died, four years ago. Carlie come to see Natalie. She were determined to git her daughter back, seeing as how Markam weren't in no way of preventing it no more.

Natalie put Carlie up in the servants' quarters. Employed her as a personal secretary to run her errands.''

''I did that to my *mother?*'' Briana said, appalled.

''Now, child, don't you be frettin' about it none. It were just your hurt striking out. Your daddy told you she'd deserted you as a baby. You didn't know he'd separated you. You made it up to your mama later, when you learned the truth. Y'all took off to Europe with Rory, getting reacquainted, like, traveling and buying them beautiful things. You'd give them anything, child. I've never seen a sweeter daughter or sister.''

''But to have initially treated my mother like a servant,'' Briana said. ''It still seems so cruel and vengeful.''

''Your mama don't think so. I never would have even knowed if'n one of the old servants hadn't jabbered on about it afore she left. Carlie's never said one blessed word.''

''Are you certain that Carlie never saw me even once while I was growing up?'' Briana asked. ''You were in Mobile. Could it be it happened and you didn't know?''

''I suppose anything's possible,'' Lou-May said as she popped a piece of pie into her mouth. ''But it just don't seem likely. I were certain Markam'd never let her in his house again. Leastwise, not while he were alive. I'm not happy he's dead, mind you, but I am happy to be back here with you and your mama. The Newcastle estate has always been a beautiful place to be.''

''Would you mind taking us on a tour?'' Michael asked.

''It'd be my pleasure,'' Lou-May said, shoving another wedge of pie into her mouth and quickly swallowing it with a sip of coffee.

She rose to her feet and led the way.

Briana found it to be a lovely old home, the floors polished wood, the attention to detail on the wall panels and the banister to the upstairs quite intricate. The art was muted rural landscape scenes, the furniture reflected various periods of French styles. Briana saw representations of Louis XIV through Louis XVI, and even some French provincial.

She liked the bedroom that was supposed to be hers best of all. The walls were a sunny yellow, the bed and dresser cherrywood, in one of the simpler Louis styles.

Briana stepped through the open doors to the upstairs gallery and leaned over the railing to watch the river roll by.

The sun waltzed in the trees while the breeze strummed the water. As Briana drew the silky air into her lungs, she had a very strong sense of déjà vu.

"This were always your favorite place to be," Lou-May said suddenly from beside her. "Could always find you here, or out lapping the pool."

"This *is* familiar."

Briana suddenly felt Michael beside her.

"How familiar?" his deep voice asked.

"I've stood here before, Michael."

"When?"

"I don't know."

"Were you with someone?"

"I...I don't think so."

"Come inside," he said. "I want to show you something."

Briana stepped back into the bedroom and followed Michael to the dresser. Two pictures in silver frames sat on its top.

One was a candid shot of a smiling, very young-looking Carlie, holding an auburn-haired baby girl of about one in her arms. In the background was the Newcastle house. The second picture was more recent, of Carlie and Natalie, a head-and-shoulders shot. They were wearing identical light blue blouses. The similarity between the two women was remarkable.

"You certainly have growed up to be the spittin' image of your mama," Lou-May said from behind them.

Briana stared at the picture, uncomfortably aware of a growing recognition.

When she had gazed in the mirror that morning, she could have sworn she'd been wearing precisely that same expression.

"When was this taken?" she asked.

"Last year. Your mama insisted. Never did git no pictures of you together while you'd be growin'. Studio photographer took some of you just by yourself, as well. There be extras in the drawer there."

Briana opened it and pulled out several prints. In every shot she recognized an expression, or something else, that seemed familiar.

Her head began to well up with frustration. Where were these familiar feelings coming from? Why couldn't she grasp them and hold on to them long enough to figure them out?

"Are there any pictures of Markam Newcastle?" Michael asked the housekeeper.

"None," Lou-May said.

"That seems odd," Briana said.

"Your mama didn't like keeping them around," Lou-May said.

"Are you saying there isn't even one likeness of Markam Newcastle in this house that used to be his home?" Michael asked.

"We'd throwed them all away, Rory and me. Your mama's orders. She can never be forgettin' that he kept her babe from her. She made sure no picture of that man be anywhere."

"But if he is my father, wasn't it up to me to say if the pictures were to be destroyed?" Briana asked.

"Once your mama gits an idea stuck in her head, it is nigh impossible to git it out. Well, you know'd her, child."

Actually, Briana didn't know her. Did she?

"Burnin' Markam's pictures were the first thing she wanted doin' when she come back from Europe with you," Lou-May continued. "Well, second thing."

"What was the first thing?" Michael asked.

"Gittin' me in to replace them other servants."

"You replaced the servants that Markam Newcastle employed while he was alive?" Michael asked.

"That be them."

"You're taking care of this entire estate by yourself?" Briana asked.

"Oh, my, no, child. I just sees to the housecleaners and gardeners. Make sure they come do what they supposed to. You and your mama always treat me more like one of the family than some servant."

"Who cooks for the family?" Michael asked.

"That'd be Elgin. He's off on his holiday now, seeing as how it'd be only me to make groceries for. He'd be back in a few days, for when your mama and Rory be returnin'. But if you'd be back to stay for a spell, child, I could git him to—"

"No, please, Lou-May," Briana said quickly. "I don't want to upset any plans. And I don't believe Dr. Sands and I will be staying."

Briana looked over at Michael for confirmation, and he nodded.

"Lou-May," he said, "I wonder if you could give me the name and number of any of the housekeepers who were here in Markam Newcastle's time."

"There be just one, Vita Pitts. Don't know her number. I hear tell her sister has a place at New Roads so I expect you can find her there. She did for Markam Newcastle going on forty years."

"Did she retire after his death?"

"No. When Carlie and Natalie come back from their European traveling, Carlie turned Vita out, just as she did the rest of Markam's servants."

"Why would she fire the servants?" Briana asked.

"Because she knew it were one of them who told Markam about her and Connor. She blamed them all for losing you, just as she blamed Markam. I'm the only one else living here now, except, of course, for your brother, Rory, and Elgin. Carlie brought Elgin in from her restaurant in New Orleans."

"I understand that Carlie started that restaurant a couple of years ago," Michael said.

"Natalie gave her the money. Carlie tried makin' that restaurant a go before. Only Rory had that accident, and she had to borrow against the business to cover his medical bills. She ended up losing the restaurant and owing a pile of money."

Lou-May turned to Briana. "You'd always said you'd wished you'd knowed, so you could've been there for your mama and Rory."

"What was wrong with Rory?" Briana asked.

"Broke both his legs in a motorcycle accident. He be a little wild, but a good boy. Carlie be fortunate in her children. Many's a time you've gone to that restaurant of your mama's this last year, even learnin' to cook when it needed doin'. You've a lovin' heart, child."

Briana smiled weakly at Lou-May, not knowing how to accept a compliment for something she didn't remember doing, a compliment she was certain she didn't deserve.

"Do you have the names of any of the other servants that Markam Newcastle kept?" Michael asked.

"Naw. Wouldn't help you none, even if I did. They'd be scattered to the winds by now."

"How did you remember Vita Pitts so well?"

"The way you remember a real bad sore tooth you got once. That woman never took to me nor Carlie. Give us the evil eye since the day we come to the estate. It wouldn't surprise me none if she weren't the one who told Markam about Carlie and Connor, neither."

"Why do you say that?"

"I think the fool be in love with ol' Markam. I knowed she be takin' a portrait of him when she left. One minute it were sticking out the Dumpster where Rory chucked it. Next minute it were sticking out the trunk of her sister's car as they drove off."

"WILL I SEE Natalie Newcastle?" Vita Pitts's voice screeched through the phone in Michael's ear. "Next cold day in hell!"

Michael spoke quickly, before the woman could hang up on him—something he sensed was imminent.

"Ms. Pitts, I'm a doctor. It's imperative that I speak with

you about Ms. Newcastle's upbringing. I believe it has an important bearing on her current mental state. It is most urgent. Please. Will you see me?''

"And what kind of doctor might you be?"

"I'm a psychiatrist."

Unexpected laughter exploded into Michael's ear. "'Bout time. That one be crazy, all right!''

"Why do you say that, Ms. Pitts?" Michael asked.

"You want to come on by, maybe I tell you. But I ain't talking to that woman no more. Don't have to, now I ain't gittin' paid to.''

Michael jotted down Vita Pitts's address, and a few directions, and then hung up the phone. He returned to the coffee shop where Briana was waiting for him.

"Vita Pitts will see me, but not Natalie Newcastle," he said as he slipped into the seat across from Briana.

"I'm not surprised," Briana said. "She's probably still upset about being fired from a job that she held for forty years.''

Michael hadn't sensed that that was the only problem from his brief conversation with the woman over the phone, but he didn't say so. He wanted to get the full story from Vita Pitts before making any comments to Briana.

Michael had come away from their visit to the Newcastle estate with as many questions as when they arrived.

"It's going to take me at least an hour to get out to Ms. Pitts's place, and another hour back, Briana. Plus however long the conversation will be. I suggest we get rooms at a hotel, so you can relax there while I'm gone. I have a pocket recorder with me. I'll tape my conversation with the woman and play it back for you when I return.''

"You think it's really worth going to all this trouble to talk to the housekeeper?" Briana asked.

"Yes," Michael said. "She was there when Natalie was growing up. She'll know how Natalie was treated. I'd also like another viewpoint on the role Markam and Carlie played in their daughter's life.''

"You're not certain we have an accurate one yet?"

"Are you?"

"No," Briana said. "Carlie says she came to see me when I was ten. Lou-May seems positive that Markam would have never let her back in his house. And after hearing about his reaction to her infidelity, I have a tendency to agree. And yet Carlie had to have seen me. How else would she have known about Briana Berry and Hazel Doud?"

"That's an interesting question. Maybe this old house-keeper can help to answer it."

"I certainly hope so, Michael. It seems like every time we talk to someone, it just adds to the confusion. There has to be an answer for all this somewhere. There has to be."

Chapter Nine

Vita Pitts lived in a simple side-gabled hall-and-parlor folk house, two rooms wide and one room deep. She was close to sixty, and on the thin side. She greeted Michael at the door, her apron splashed with tomato sauce and her well-lined face creased with curiosity.

"So, you'd be nasty Natalie's shrink," she said as she stepped back for him to enter. "I always told 'em that she'd be needin' one."

"Whom did you tell?" Michael asked as he followed the woman into a tiny kitchen with a big pot on the stove.

Vita picked up a big ladle and motioned Michael onto one of the hard wooden kitchen chairs.

"Anybody who'd listen."

"Markam Newcastle?" Michael asked.

"Oh, Lordy, no. A body'd have to be touched in the head to be telling *him* anything derogatory about his precious daughter."

"Markam Newcastle was close to Natalie?"

"Treated her like the exalted princess of his kingdom. Were bad enough dealing with him and all his airs. Then he went ahead and made that daughter of his right into his own image."

Michael was getting confused. Not only did this woman show no tender feelings for Markam Newcastle, as Lou-May had implied she would, she was also giving him an entirely different view of Markam Newcastle's relationship with his daughter.

"Ms. Pitts, I wonder if you could start at the beginning," Michael said.

"And where might that be?" Vita asked as she stirred her pot of what Michael imagined must be something pretty wonderful, if the smells filling the kitchen were any indication.

"When Markam brought his bride home," he answered.

Vita laughed. "Fool. Fifty years old and he goes out and buys himself an eighteen-year-old beauty queen for a wife. Then he expects her to be faithful to him!"

"Had Newcastle ever been married before?"

"Nope. Too busy making money and foolin' around."

"What did you think of Carlie?"

"She were a silly, brainless twit. Marries for money, and then acts all surprised-like when it don't turn out to be no romantic fairy tale. Two of 'em ended up gittin' what they gave."

"I understand Markam was disappointed he didn't have a son."

"It were true he didn't cotton to the idea of a daughter at first. Sorta ignored Natalie when she were a babe. But then, so did her mama. She were too busy off in the barn, rolling in the hay with that horse trainer."

"Who took care of Natalie?"

"That maid Carlie brought with her, Lou-May her name. Lou-May were always trying to cover for Carlie, pretending she were out walking or in a bath. Truth be, she were with that Connor Taureau."

"How did Markam find out about them?"

"He come home from business early one day to see Carlie tripping out of the barn wearing hay in her hair, her cheeks all flushed, the top of her blouse all undone. No puzzle as to a what she'd been a-doing. He were hopping mad."

Vita shook her head in remembrance. "Lou-May heard him cussing about killing 'em. She rushed out of the house, yelling for Connor to git and pulling Carlie inside and up the stairs to her room.''

"What were you doing, Ms. Pitts?''

"What ya think? I were staying out of the way. I knowed better than to git in the way of no irate husband with no shotgun.''

"So what happened?'' Michael asked.

"Connor got scarce and Carlie got kicked out on her ear, is what happened. Markam saw to it she be declared an unfit mother when he took her to court on the divorce.''

"Did you think that fair?''

"Weren't my place to be judgin'. Still, I knowed it must of been hard on Carlie losin' her babe.''

"Who raised Natalie?''

"Bunch of nannies.''

"What were their names?''

"Lordy, I couldn't tell you. They come-and-goed pretty quick.''

"Why was that?''

"'Cause Markam Newcastle picked young, pretty girls to take care of his daughter. And then the ol' coot tried to talk them into taking care of himself, as well.''

"He was having affairs with these women?''

"Ones who'd let him. If'n they didn't cooperate, he'd get rid of them, real quick-like. If'n they'd let him, he'd keep them on till he got tired of them or they started talkin' marriage.''

"Was there any reason why he didn't get married again?''

"Money. I hear tell Markam's lawyer claimed he be lucky he caught Carlie messin' 'round. Otherwise he would've owed her.''

"Owed her?'' Michael repeated.

"Alimony. Markam were a real tightfisted man. He don't cotton to no idea of sharing no money with nobody. I knowed it were the reason he never got himself wed again to another one of them beauty queens he were always drooling over.''

"Do you remember ever seeing bruises on Natalie?''

"Bruises? On that pampered child?"

"You're sure she never had a cruel nanny?"

"Don't be talkin' nonsense. Those nannies were always making up to that child, spoilin' her rotten, if truth be told. Most of 'em that give in to Markam Newcastle fancied themselves becoming mistress of his house and a proper mama to his daughter. No cause for 'em to ever mistreat the child."

"What about when Markam sacked them?" Michael asked.

"Markam were a lot of things not to be proud of, but he weren't stupid. He'd have those nannies' things packed and waitin' by the door afore he give 'em the bad news. Then they'd be out and gone, no waiting 'round to git into mischief."

"Did Carlie ever come back to see her child?"

"Not till she were growed."

"You're sure she didn't come back to see Natalie at her tenth birthday party?"

"Nope."

"How can you be so sure?"

"'Cause this were twenty years ago, and this were Louisiana. Markam had the law in his fist. He'd of throwed Carlie in jail, and been right pleased to do it, if'n he caught her showin' her nose around."

"What if Markam wasn't there to catch her?"

"Ho'd of still be told if'n she showed."

"Did Natalie ever have any identity problems?"

"What you mean?"

"Did she ever call herself by a name that wasn't hers, or seem to be living in a fantasy world?"

"Nope. That child had ponies, dolls, clothes, everything that money could buy. She didn't need no fantasy."

"How did Natalie fare with her frequent change of nannies?"

"By five, six years old, you could tell that she knowed what were going on. She'd be all sweet-like to a new nanny that her daddy be interested in. But just as soon as Markam be losing interest in that nanny, Natalie'd know. Next day, she'd turn all nasty-like toward her.''

"And the nanny would be fired?"

"And her daddy would look at Natalie all lovin'-like. Weren't the child's fault, I suppose. She were a-playing to her daddy's tune.''

"He wanted his daughter's displeasure in her nanny to be the reason he could give for letting the nanny go?"

"Yep.''

"Did you ever have the feeling that Markam abused his daughter?"

"He never spanked nor touched her in no improper way, if that's what you'd be askin'.''

"Did he ignore her?"

"Oh, my, no. He doted on her. Except for the times she'd be doing something he didn't like. Then he'd carry on something awful-like, calling her names, telling her that she be acting wild 'cause her mother's tainted blood were bubblin' in her veins.''

"What were these things she did that her father didn't like?"

"Nothing real serious. Just growin'-up stuff.''

"You're certain Markam never struck her?"

"Never laid a hand to her. But he yelled up a storm. He were right strict with her, never allowing her to make no mistakes. Took away her driver's license when she banged up the car at seventeen. Forbade her to date again after she come home drunk when she were nineteen. He were still enforcing a curfew when she were in her twenties, approving or disapproving her friends.''

"Doesn't sound like Markam gave his daughter any trust.''

Vita lifted the lid on the pot, gave it another stir. Then she put it down again as she turned to Michael.

"That be the truth to it. But you could tell he were real proud that she growed up so beautiful. He were always braggin' 'bout it to his friends. He'd buy her just 'bout anything she wanted. Only he never let her have no money of her own to spend. See, that be the way he keep her with him, under his control.''

"How did Natalie respond to being treated this way?''

"She didn't like it no way. She'd fly into rages and order me and the other servants around, just makin' our lives as miserable as he be makin' hers. But she'd never confront him. Guess she knowed she'd lose and he'd just make the controls stricter. He were a tyrant to her, and she were a tyrant to us.''

"Did Natalie love her father?''

"Idolized him and hated him both, I think.''

"What happened when he died?''

"She started goin' through money like it were water. Surprised she got any left for a shrink.''

"How did she spend her money?''

"Gambling, mostly. She and her daddy were always goin' to the horse races.''

"I understand that Carlie came back to the Newcastle estate after Markam's death,'' Michael said.

"Yep, and she were beggin' her daughter to let her stay a spell. So Natalie tells her she can, only she makes her work as her personal secretary. Now, I never much warmed to Carlie none, but I sure did feel sorry for her, the way her own child were treating her.''

"How long did Carlie work as Natalie's personal secretary?''

"Six months. And Natalie be screamin' at her every minute of it, too, even worse than the rest of us. Don't know how her mama took that child's nasty mouth. Carlie be livin' in the smallest room in the servants' quarters. Sometimes at night I'd hear her crying.''

"What about Rory Taureau?'' Michael asked.

"He come out to the estate after the hospital released him. Natalie made him share his mama's room. Mind you, there were a dozen empty bedrooms at the estate. And Rory still was doin' poorly. But Natalie didn't care. That girl weren't nice. No, she weren't nice at all.''

"You said Carlie worked for Natalie for six months. Did their relationship improve during that time?"

"Not as I ever saw. But Natalie and Rory appeared to get along. Leastways after he got on his feet. She'd take him along when she went gambling. Carlie went along, too, but she were made to work."

"What happened to finally change the relationship between Natalie and her mother?"

"Don't rightly know. The three of them were away on one of Natalie's weeklong gambling trips. Next thing I knowed I were getting a call from Carlie saying they'd be off to Europe for a spell and to pack Natalie's things and send them on to this hotel in Paris. They were gone for near on a year. And when they come back, we were throwed out."

"How did it happen?" Michael asked.

"Rory come home day afore Natalie and her mama were to arrive and told us to git. Said Natalie didn't want us around no more 'cause she and her mama were startin' fresh."

"How did you feel about that?"

"How ya think? I'd been doin' for the Newcastles for goin' on forty years. Rory said he were sorry. He said his mama had it in her head that one of us had told ol' Markam about her and Connor. Said Natalie were popping mad 'bout that."

"Did all Markam Newcastle's servants leave that day?"

"All but me. I got no car. Never learned to drive. I called my sister. She said she'd come fetch me the next day."

Vita paused to again lift the lid on the simmering pot and give the brew inside another stir with her ladle. The escaping aroma had Michael's digestive juices going.

"I figured if Natalie come and see me and start a-screamin' at me to git, well then, I'd just a-start screamin' back at her," Vita continued. "But I never saw her the next day, just Rory and Lou-May."

"Did you ever return to the Newcastle estate after that?"

"Never set eyes on it again, and never want to. Truth be told, I were happy to be gone. It were real peaceful-like, that year nasty Natalie were off in Europe. Kind of reminded a body of how pleasant life could be when she weren't around. I weren't lookin' forward to her being back, to being screamed at no more.''

"I understand that when you left you took a painting of Markam Newcastle with you?" Michael asked.

"I never took nothin' that were nobody's," Vita said, her tone turning defensive and her hands going to her hips.

"The painting was seen in the back of the car when you left that day, Ms. Pitts. I understand that you liberated it from a Dumpster. You needn't worry. No one is asking for its return. I would just like to see it, if you don't mind."

"They'd throwed it out," Vita said. "I only took what were throwed out."

"Yes, I know that. It was Rory and Lou-May who threw it out, wasn't it?"

"Uh-huh."

"Why would they do that, do you know?"

"Got no idea. They throwed out all Markam's pictures that day. Even that portrait of him with Natalie."

"Natalie was in that painting, as well?"

"Markam commissioned it for her eighteenth birthday. They posed and posed a lot of days afore it were done. It were a favorite with Markam. He hung it in the livin' room, right above the big fireplace."

"Why did you take the portrait?" Michael asked.

"It were painted twelve years ago by a local artist who'd be gittin' a name for himself now. I've lived too poor most of my life to be one for throwin' away money."

"May I see the painting, Ms. Pitts?"

"Don't got it no more."

"What happened to it?"

"I give it to this man who say he sell it for me."

"Who is this man?"

"Brousseau be his name. He owns this place where they hang the paintings, and folks come in and look at 'em, and if'n they like 'em they buy 'em."

"And Brousseau gets a percentage of the selling price?"

"Twenty-five."

"That's a lot."

"You're telling me. Still, what choice a body got? Don't know nobody who can fork over no two thousand dollar for no painting."

"Is that the price being asked? Two thousand dollars?"

"You be interested?"

"I may be. Where can I find Mr. Brousseau?"

Vita dropped the ladle into the pot on the stove and quickly wiped her hands on her apron. "I'll git his card for you. You just wait right there. Don't go nowhere, now. Won't be no time at all."

Vita was true to her word. She was out of the kitchen and back in seconds, holding out a dog-eared business card. Michael rose as she reentered.

"Address of the gallery be on that card," she said, her face beaming up at him. "It'd be in New Orleans, in one of them fancy sections. Brousseau be having a showin' there tonight. He sent me the notice 'bout it. Goes from eight on to midnight. You could see the painting then."

Vita was obviously eager to be of assistance now that she believed Michael was interested in buying the painting.

"Thank you, Ms. Pitts," Michael said, pocketing the card.

"What ya want with that painting?" she asked.

"It seems to be the last likeness of Markam Newcastle left. If I buy it, I'll be sure to suggest to Mr. Brousseau that he lower the rate of his commission."

"You'd do that?"

"Seems only fair, since you're the one who's sending me to him."

Vita Pitts eyes gleamed. "You just sit yourself level in that chair, Dr. Sands. I'm about to treat you to a taste of the best jambalaya in Louisiana."

WHILE WAITING at the hotel for Michael's return, Briana took a long swim in the pool, relaxed in the sauna and had her hair shampooed in the salon.

She knew she was using the frantic activity to try to fill in the growing sensation of emptiness opening inside her.

For every hour, every minute, every new revelation about Natalie Newcastle's existence, made Briana Berry's seem just that much less real.

She felt as though something had punctured a hole in her and everything that had been her life was slowly leaking out. And now even her sense of herself was in danger of disappearing.

When she finally admitted that the frantic activity wasn't helping, Briana gave it up and went back to her room. She stood in front of the mirror, stared into it. And searched the face that stared back at her.

A face that was beginning to look more and more familiar every time she saw it—more and more as though it were her own.

The shock of that realization sent a chill up her spine.

"Okay," she said, trying to stay calm. "I have your face. I remember being at your wedding, wearing your wedding dress, marrying your man. I even remember standing on the gallery off your bedroom and looking out at a scene that was already there in my mind. So, come on out, Natalie. Let's get acquainted. Might as well, since it looks like we're in this together."

But Natalie Newcastle did not come out. It was Briana's own anguish that filled the eyes staring back at her.

She exhaled heavily, her shoulders slumping as she trudged over to the bed and plopped down.

She had always considered herself to be a person of logic and reason. But she could find no logic or reason in her being Briana Berry in Natalie Newcastle's body.

If her life as Briana Berry had all been in her mind, why couldn't she go back to it? Why couldn't she just will herself to see Hazel again? And Lee? And the spider plant called Oscar that sat on the windowsill in her apartment?

Dear heavens. She had forgotten about Oscar until this very

moment! Who watered a mental houseplant when the personality that had created it went on a vacation into reality?

She was worried about watering a mental houseplant? Yep, she was loopy, all right.

She could feel the beginning of the telltale vibration—the tickle of the internal funny bone. It started in her tummy and worked its way up into her chest—warm and quivery—until it finally exploded through her throat in a rollicking burst of laughter. She rolled on the bed, letting it take her, letting it fill her with its warmth, where only seconds before there had been a cold, stark emptiness.

Hazel had taught her to do this. To always see the humor. To let it support her. To hold on to its joy.

She was certain—absolutely certain—that Hazel was real, even if Briana Berry wasn't.

A knock came at the door. Briana swung her legs over the edge of the bed. She reached for a tissue and dabbed at her eyes.

Another knock echoed through the room.

Her caller was impatient. Briana rose, walked over to the door, looked through the peephole. She felt a jolt when she saw who stood on the other side.

Rory Taureau looked a lot broader than his image on the videotape. He had a craggy face, unruly dark hair, and deep-set dark eyes that stared directly into the peephole at her.

"I have to talk to you," Rory said. "Let me in. It's urgent."

As eager as she was to know why Rory had come to see her, Briana was hesitant to open her door to a stranger.

"Please, Nat," he said, and the words sounded almost desperate.

Briana stared through the peephole a moment more before her curiosity won out over her caution.

As soon as she had swung open the door, Rory Taureau quickly stepped inside. He threw the privacy latch into place and checked through the peephole before turning to survey the room.

"What do you have to drink in this place?" he asked.

"Is that always your first question on entering a room?" Briana asked.

Rory flashed her a smile over his shoulder that was toothy and engaging as he headed for the liquor cabinet. His limp was slight, but definitely noticeable. "Give me a break, Nat. They didn't have any bourbon on the plane. And you know I can't drink anything else."

"I know you're Natalie's brother and that you drink too much," Briana said. "But I know very little else about you—even less than I know about Natalie."

"So you haven't regained your memory?" he said as he bent to unlock the liquor cabinet. "It's probably just as well."

Briana was surprised anew by his comment. "What do you mean?"

"Not before a drink, Nat."

Rory opened the cabinet and pulled out the small bottle of bourbon. He poured it into a glass, added some water, and proceeded to gulp it down.

"Why do you drink so much?" Briana asked.

"Some men have two sound legs beneath them, others have access to a billion dollars. Me, I only have my bourbon."

His words didn't make sense to Briana. Rory Taureau seemed sad in some way, although why Briana should get that impression, she didn't know.

"Since you don't remember, I'll tell you about us, Nat," he said as he refilled his glass with the second small bottle of bourbon from the cabinet.

He fastened his dark eyes on her as a half smile drew back his lips.

"My boxing career came to an abrupt halt three and a half years ago, when my knees went bad. I told myself I'd make it. That it was time to quit, anyway. Then, a year later, I had a bad motorcycle accident. The doctors said I'd never walk again. I wouldn't have made it that time, if you hadn't had me flown to Switzerland and bribed their top surgeon to take me.''

Briana was absolutely startled by the genuine light of affection shining out of Rory's eyes.

"That was two and a half years ago, Nat. It cost you close to two million for the operations, all the specialists, the twenty-four-hour-a-day care that followed to save my legs. Mama was the one who told me about the money. Only reason she knew is she stole a look at the medical bills. You never said a word. Just like you never said a word when you quietly cleared all those past debts from my earlier knee operations.''

Briana was beginning to feel very uncomfortable.

"Rory, I don't remember—''

"I know you don't. That's why I'm telling you. I'm telling you *who* you are. I'm telling you how *I* feel about *who* you are.''

Yes, Briana could see that, even feel that. It was obvious that Rory cared for his sister. A lot.

"You said a moment ago that it was probably just as well that I don't remember being Natalie. Why?''

"Because then you'd be with that bastard,'' Rory said, an angry vehemence snapping through his words.

"You're talking about Sheldon Ayton?''

Rory grabbed his glass and downed the last of its contents. He slammed the tumbler down on the cabinet before taking a couple of steps in her direction.

"Nat, he only wants you because you were the one woman who had the good sense to refuse him! Don't you see? He had to prove that he could have you. That's why he went after you so hard.''

"Rory, you keep talking to me as though I remember him. I don't.''

"All right, I'll tell you about him. He's a controlling bastard, Nat. He's had you followed from the day he met you. He's spied on you, watched you through every move you've made.''

"He did that to Natalie?" Briana asked, appalled.

"He did that to *you! You're* Natalie. Since you spurned him that day at the Derby, he's done his damnedest to find out everything about you, so he could win you. He hired a slew of private investigators. He pretended that he had the same interests as you in order to give you the impression that you had a lot in common. You don't really think Ayton loves piano instrumentals? Unusual architecture? Forests and wild-flowers?"

"How do *you* know what he did, Rory?"

"Because I read the reports his detectives compiled on you. He learned everything about you before he pursued you. That's why he just happened to be a customer in Mama's New Orleans café the times you went there to help out."

"How long have you known this about Ayton?"

"I suspected something was wrong with the guy all along. But I only learned of his spying on you at the wedding re-ception. I overheard Ayton telling the head of his detective agency that he was going to be keeping an eye on you himself from now on, so he wouldn't need him anymore. When Ayton and the detective left, I let myself into the study and rifled Ayton's desk. I found the thick file on you."

"Did you tell Natalie?"

"First chance I got. You were on your way up the stairs to change out of your bridal clothes. You might have believed me if Ayton hadn't come along. He assured you I was just talking crazy because I was drunk."

"Were you drunk?"

Rory's eyes took on an odd bleakness. "Yes."

"Sheldon Ayton knew that you were trying to tell Natalie what he had done?"

"He probably would have hit me to keep me quiet if you hadn't stepped between us. When you turned up missing later, I just figured you had understood enough of what I had told you about him to get away from the bastard before it was too late."

"Did you see Natalie again that night?"

"I didn't think there was any use. Mama found me passed out on the sofa in the parlor later, and told me about the old bag falling down the stairs and being flown to the emergency room. I only wished it had been Sheldon."

"Rory, this isn't the bourbon talking, is it? You're certain that Sheldon had Natalie investigated and followed?"

"How do you think I knew where to find you tonight, Nat? I was in Ayton's study when the fax came in from the detective agency. He called them in again when he realized you were missing. You've been under surveillance at the Institute of Dreams since the second he found you there."

Briana felt a crawling sensation at the back of her neck. Spying on someone was so offensive. That it was done by a man professing to love a woman made it even worse.

"Nat, are you hearing what I'm telling you? Ayton has been told of your every move. He knows all about Sands taking you to that lawyer, and the petition for annulment being filed. And the restraining order."

"Then he knows that I won't be going back to him," Briana said.

"Won't be going back to him?" Rory repeated, his voice rising incredulously. "Nat, you still have no idea of the kind of man you married, do you? Sheldon Ayton isn't going to rest until he has you back in his control."

"How can he?" Briana asked.

"The second you return to Nevada, Ayton is waiting to have you served with a court order. You're to be examined by a court psychiatrist and then forced into the care of some shrink he's flying in from Glasgow."

"He can't do that, Rory. He has no rights as a husband. Are you forgetting the restraining order?"

"The restraining order is against him, not your mama."

Briana felt a sudden apprehension stiffening her muscles. "How does Carlie fit into this?"

"Ayton persuaded her to sign the papers. She's your next of kin. It's legal. It was with her signature that Ayton got a judge to issue the court order."

"Why would Carlie cooperate with Sheldon?"

"A mistaken act of love. She thinks you need help, and Ayton's convinced her he'll get it for you. No doubt Ayton's already identified and paid the court-appointed psychiatrist who is to examine you. He'll say exactly what Ayton wants him to."

"Dr. Sands is my doctor," Briana said confidently. "He won't let Ayton get away with this."

Rory flashed her a look that clearly rated her grasp of the situation at something below zero.

"Just how long do you think this Dr. Sands is going to be allowed to remain your doctor after Ayton's detectives produce evidence that you're been living with him in his apartment at this Institute of Dreams?"

"Rory, it hasn't been like that. I've been in Dr. Sands's guest room. There hasn't been any impropriety—"

"There doesn't have to have been! All it has to do is look that way."

"But—"

"Nat, you will not only be immediately and forcibly removed from Dr. Sands's care, Sands'll be lucky if he doesn't get his license yanked and his institute closed."

Briana tasted panic on her tongue as she started to pace about the room. "No," she said, an ache of frustration in her voice. "All he's been trying to do is help me. Ayton can't do this to him."

"Yes, he can. And make no mistake. He will."

Briana dropped onto the edge of the bed, feeling suddenly like a leaf being blown in the wind of Rory's blustery, scary predictions.

Rory came over to sit next to her. "I sorry, Nat," he said on a long exhale. "I was wrong to listen to Mama. I wanted to tell you my suspicions about the kind of man Ayton was, but she wouldn't let me."

"Why wouldn't she let you? If she loves Natalie, why would she have encouraged her to be with such a man?"

"She does love you, Natalie. Don't ever doubt it. And she

wants the best for you. That's why she picked out a handsome, rich man for you. Only she's blind to what the bastard is. She kept saying that love had changed Sheldon Ayton into something better than he was, and that I had no right to tell you anything against him without proof."

Briana watched as Rory's powerful hands balled into fists.

"But Mama is wrong," he said. "Love doesn't change a man. Love simply makes a man more of what he already was. Ayton doesn't care how he gets you back, or even if you want to go back. All he cares about is that you are once again brought under his control."

A shiver snaked through Briana at Rory's words.

"If I were any kind of a brother, I would have killed him for you days ago!" Rory said, raising his fists.

Briana laid her hands on his fists and lowered them. "No, Rory. Not that way."

His eyes went to her face, a light of hope flickering in their dark depths. "Nat, maybe it's not too late. Ayton's mama is still in that coma. He has to stay in Nevada to see to her. This could be our chance."

"Our chance? For what?"

"To escape," he said, eagerness catching at his words.

"We'll go to Ireland. Both of our passports are up-to-date. There are some of my daddy's kin there who will help hide us."

"Rory—"

"They can keep Ayton from finding you. They should. They've been hiding dissidents from the British for centuries."

He took her hands in his. "Come with me, Nat."

Briana could tell from the look on Rory's face that he had actually sold himself on the possibility of such a scenario working for them.

"Rory, I'm not running off to Ireland."

"Then we'll go anywhere you want. You can't win against a man like Ayton, Nat. His money, his position—he'll use it all to get you back. Come with me, while there's still time. Let me do this for you, as you have done so much for me.''

Rory's affection for Natalie was obviously sincere. Briana didn't want to hurt him. She was trying to think of the right way to refuse his offer when the knock suddenly came at the door.

Rory instantly dropped her hands and jumped to his feet, his fists raised, his stance a fighter's.

''Don't open it, Nat,'' he warned. ''It's Ayton. He's come to get you!''

Chapter Ten

Briana rose to rest a steadying hand on Rory's arm, as she worked to keep herself calm. His fear was far too contagious.

"Take it easy," she said. "I'll see who it is."

Briana walked over to look through the peephole. She felt her heart do a little leap of both relief and happiness when she saw Michael on the other side of the door.

"It's Dr. Sands," she told Rory as she opened the door.

Briana introduced them when Michael stepped inside. At her urging, Rory gave Michael a cryptic rundown on Ayton's spying on Natalie and the legal maneuvers he had planned to get her back when she returned to Nevada.

"I appreciate your telling us about this," Michael said.

Rory was frowning as he took Michael's offered hand. "Ayton is going to do his best to ruin you, Sands."

Briana watched Michael's easy smile. "He's going to fail."

Rory's glance rested on Briana. "He'll try to get her."

"I won't let him," Michael assured.

It wasn't just what Michael said, it was the way that he said it, that had Briana believing him. Whereas Rory was full of gloom and doom, Michael radiated confidence and competence. What a difference there was between the two men.

But then, Briana knew that, compared to Michael, all other men would be found wanting.

As soon as Rory left, Michael closed and locked the door behind him. "Rory Taureau is quite fond of you, Briana."

"Correction—he's quite fond of Natalie," she said. "What do we do about Sheldon and his plans?"

"There's no cause for worry," Michael said as he gently rested his hand on her shoulder. "Ayton can't do anything legally until you return to Nevada. By then, we'll be ready for him."

Briana looked at the strength in his stance, his frame, his face, the steady blue of his eyes. She was struck anew by the capable, confident way he faced everything. She felt her balance returning, as though his presence alone righted the world, making it a safe and sane place to be.

And yet, at the same time, she felt the warmth and nearness of him rocking her world as nothing and no one ever had.

His eyes rested briefly on her face before he dropped his hand from her shoulder and purposely turned toward the door. "I'll be back in a minute," he called over his shoulder.

Once again he'd turned away. The line was still firmly drawn between them. That line he would not cross. Not even if he wanted to.

Did he want to?

Don't ask pointless questions. He's never going to cross that line, no matter what. Get a grip. Show some sense. Forget your foolish heart. Listen to your head.

When Michael knocked softly on her door less than a minute later, Briana had her emotions firmly in hand again. She let him in, surprised to see that he was carrying a full grocery bag.

"We're dining in, I assume?" Briana asked.

"On some of Vita Pitts's homemade jambalaya. I just had it heated up in the hotel kitchen by a very accommodating chef, who supplied a couple of cups of coffee, as well."

Michael drew out the steaming foam cups and set them on the table. He next pulled out a blackened earthenware pot that had obviously spent a lot of time on a stovetop. When he lifted the lid, a mouthwatering aroma filled the room.

"That smells great," Briana said.

"I promise you, it's marvelous. After one taste, I insisted on buying it from Vita."

"Pot and all?"

"She assured me she has a dozen more. This is a better meal than we'd get at a restaurant. She even included some homemade corn bread in the deal."

They sat at the small table. Michael filled their bowls, and between them they finished off the entire contents of the pot, along with the small loaf of corn bread.

Briana leaned back, sighing in appreciation. "It appears you and Vita Pitts got along quite well, for you to come away with that marvelous concoction."

"Actually, I came away with a lot more."

Michael placed the small tape recorder on the table and replayed his conversation with the housekeeper. As Briana listened to her talk about Natalie Newcastle, her confusion grew.

When the taped conversation had ended, Briana was shaking her head. "Rory talked about Natalie as being someone special. And Carlie also spoke of her lovingly. As did Lou-May. Even Ginny and Gene Pettit had nice things to say about her. But the way Vita describes Natalie, she sounds absolutely awful. Were Rory and Carlie and Lou-May and the Pettits trying to be nice about her true character to spare my feelings?"

"I can't speak for Rory, Carlie or Lou-May," Michael said. "But I've known Ginny and Gene Pettit a lot of years. Had they not liked Natalie, they would have toned down their dislike in front of you. But they wouldn't have outright lied and said the nice things they did about her."

"Then I'm more confused than ever. How can Natalie be so different?"

"Perhaps because there are different Natalies."

"I don't follow you, Michael."

"A person who has multiple personalities generally has more than two, Briana."

"Are you saying that there's both a nice Natalie and a nasty Natalie?"

"It's a possibility."

"Terrific," Briana said, forcing a chuckle through her throat, trying to stave off the shock of imagining yet another personality inside her. "Now, I'm not just two people. I'm three! I suppose the good news is that this should qualify me to use the carpool lane on the freeway!"

Michael's hand immediately covered hers. He always seemed to know when things were getting a little too wild for her to handle.

"I'm not saying there is a third personality inside you, Briana. I'm merely offering it as a possible explanation for the facts that we've uncovered so far."

The gentleness of Michael's voice and touch was both wonderfully soothing and wildly intoxicating. Briana had no energy left to fight her feelings for him. She was way past listening to that tiny voice of reason.

She was mad for Michael.

But she would be even madder to let him know it. Because if she did, she knew, she'd be opening herself up to the incomparable hurt of his rejection.

He had told her the rules when he became her doctor.

Even now, she could feel him withdrawing his hand, his warmth. Just as he always did. Just as he always would.

The weight of that knowledge descended full on her chest, sinking deep inside her and taking all her hopes with it.

"You're planning on our going to the gallery showing tonight in New Orleans, aren't you?" Briana asked, trying to make her voice light, despite the heaviness of her heart.

"Yes. I'd like to see that painting."

"What are you hoping to learn from it, Michael?"

"I'm not sure I'll know until I see it. If Vita Pitts can be believed, Natalie did love her father, despite his strictness with her. I think it odd that Natalie would have let her mother and brother throw out all his pictures."

"Maybe her feelings for her father changed dramatically

when Carlie explained to her that Markam had separated Natalie from her mother for all those years?''

"Why did it take a whole year for Natalie to listen to her mother about the circumstances before believing her? Does that seem likely to you?''

"Obviously it doesn't seem likely to you," Briana said. "So, what do you think happened?''

"I don't know, Briana. The more we learn about Natalie, the less I understand her. Something isn't right here. I feel it. But I'll be damned if I know what it is.''

THE NEW ORLEANS GALLERY of Jacques Brousseau was featuring the work of Louisiana artist Jon L. Breen that night. The placard on the glass window said he was an artist known for his female nudes. The popularity of the work was evident from the size of the crowd—elbow to elbow—very few of whom had even availed themselves of the champagne and cheese.

But despite the compelling subject matter of the artist, when Michael walked in with Briana on his arm, he noticed the immediate shift of male eyes in their direction.

He didn't blame them. A walking work of art like Briana—even fully clothed—would always be more arresting than a nude painting hanging on a wall.

As always, Briana seemed totally oblivious to the stares she was receiving. Michael was once again reminded of how unconscious she was of her beauty. And how much more beautiful that made her.

He found Brousseau and asked about the portrait of Markam Newcastle. Brousseau led them to the back wall to which Jon L. Breen's only painting that wasn't a nude had been relegated.

"This portrait thing was just something he did on the side while he was building his skill and his name with his nudes," Brousseau explained. "Still, his incredible talent is quite evident. He captures the soul with a few simple brush strokes.

It's a steal at two bills. We accept Visa, MasterCard and Discover. I'll be up front if you need me.''

And with that, he was gone, leaving Michael and Briana with the painting.

It was large, three feet by five feet. Markam Newcastle was formally posed in an impeccable tuxedo, seated in one of the massive baroque Louis XIV chairs that Michael had seen in the living room of the Newcastle estate. Natalie was standing next to her father, her hand on his shoulder, wearing a floor-length deep emerald gown.

Michael first studied Markam Newcastle's face. For a man in his late sixties, he had not aged well. He had the raw material in his thick white mane and strong facial bone structure. But the hard lines around his cold blue eyes and harsh mouth dominated and diminished every one of his favorable features.

Michael's attention shifted to Natalie Newcastle's face. It was a faithful rendition of her flawless features. Moreover, the artist had managed to put a glow in her white skin and flame hair that reminded Michael of Rembrandt's uncanny ability to make the people in his paintings seem alive.

And yet, as competent as the artist had been, Michael knew instantly that Vita Pitts had been telling him the truth. For in Natalie's eyes and around her perfect mouth was that same hardness that set on her father's features.

And then Michael saw something else—something that set his mind to racing.

Briana stepped back from the painting, frowning hard.

"Until this moment, I thought Natalie to be very much like her mother," Briana said. "But the resemblance I now see to her father in this portrait is unmistakable—and unnerving. Natalie is not a nice person, Michael. She is arrogant and cold and hard. I cringe to think that *she's* inside me."

"She's not, Briana."

Briana looked up into Michael's eyes. They were so deeply blue and warm and sincere. She felt the breath still in her chest.

"How can you know that?" she asked.

"Because *you* could never look like that," he said, with such wonderfully calm conviction that Briana's heart suddenly swelled to fill her chest.

"You can believe that I'm not Natalie, in the face of all the evidence that says I am?"

"Yes, I can. However, I think I should point out to you that not all the evidence says you are. There is one major piece of evidence staring at you right now that says you definitely are not her."

"Michael, what are you talking about?"

"Briana, look at the eyes in this portrait of Natalie Newcastle."

Briana did so, trying to discover what Michael was seeing that she was not.

"Other than the fact that their expression seems so cold and unfeeling, I don't see—"

"Briana, her eyes are light blue. I'm looking at your eyes right now, and they are violet, a shade that matches the color of your gown."

"My eyes are very light, Michael. They have always had a tendency to pick up whatever color I wear."

He smiled into them. "I know."

Michael's words, his smile, everything about him, told Briana that she was missing something. Her eyes darted back to the painting. And then she realized what Michael meant.

"Natalie's dress in the picture is emerald green, and yet her eyes are light blue! Michael, if I had posed for this picture, my eyes would have been green, just like the dress!"

"Exactly. But Natalie's eyes remained a light blue—the same light blue as her father's and her mother's."

"I'm not her," Briana said, on an exhalation of relief so deep that it felt as though it came right out of her soul. "But why do I have her memories, her face?"

"Briana, how would you feel about flying to Washington State tomorrow?"

"To try to find Dr. Steele?"

"No. I was thinking we might try to find Briana Berry."

AFTER the warm, mild temperatures of Nevada and Louisiana, Briana found Washington cold. Light snow greeted them at the SEATAC airport. It got progressively heavier the closer they came to Seattle.

"We always do get our worse weather of the year in the latter half of December," Briana said.

She directed Michael to the appropriate off-ramp and to the fastest side streets. "The firm's offices are just another block up, on Eastlake."

But when they got there, Briana and Michael did not find the architectural firm of Berry, Willix and Associates. They found the Quik-Fix agency, specializing in supplying temporary office workers.

"We send temps to most of the architectural firms in the area," the receptionist said. "But I've never heard of Berry, Willix and Associates. Could you have the name wrong?"

Could she have the name wrong? Briana almost laughed.

"Where do you live?" Michael said as he handed Briana back into the rental car a few minutes later.

"In an apartment seven blocks down and two over. I'll show you the way."

But when Michael drove up to the address Briana had directed him to, all that was there was a parking lot. And beside it was a Chinese restaurant she'd never seen before.

Briana realized that she should be used to finding out that her life didn't exist anywhere but in her mind. But she wasn't. With every new dead end she faced, a futile outrage and impotence washed through her, making her feel weak and defeated.

"Where did you grow up, Briana?" Michael asked.

"Across Puget Sound, in Silverdale."

"We'll take the ferry over."

She supposed they might as well, as long as they were here. But she was fast losing all hope. Very fast.

Briana stood staring out the window of the ferry throughout

the entire trip. The leaden sky dropped low and heavy, releasing its snowy burden in a heavy downpour of white, whirling flakes.

Michael stood beside her, a warm, comforting presence, like a sturdy woodstove keeping back the ice of an emotional winter.

She had always prided herself on the fact that no matter what came along in her life, she faced it standing on her own two feet.

But at this moment, she would have dearly loved to be leaning against that strong, stalwart body next to hers. To be enfolded in those strong arms. To hear the beat of his heart. To feel the heat of his skin.

She was torturing herself imagining these things. But it was a sweet torture.

"There's no use looking for the old A-frame Hazel and I lived in," Briana said as they drove off the ferry a while later. "It was torn down years ago, when a new housing development was put up."

"Where did you go to school?"

"Central Kitsap High, on Bucklin Hill Road in Silverdale. It's been there since before World War II." Briana paused to chuckle. "But with the way things are going, we'll probably find a Christmas-tree farm in its place."

But they didn't find a Christmas-tree farm. Central Kitsap High School actually was where Briana remembered it. She blinked several times, as though she couldn't quite believe it. Despite the fact that it was the Christmas holidays, several cars adorned the parking lot. Michael pulled in beside them.

As they started up the stairs to the entry, Briana read the sign on the placard just outside the door: Give someone the unmatched gift of reading this holiday season. Donate your books! Sponsored by the Literacy Council.

Just inside the doors they found three senior citizens sitting behind a table, wrapping used books and tying them with a bow. One stout woman with round, flushed cheeks and bright, cheery black eyes raised her head to greet them.

"Sorry," she said. "I'm afraid you're too late. We had our final auction last night. These books are earmarked for some housebound folks."

"Actually, we're not here for the auction," Briana said. "We were hoping to get a look at the school's old yearbooks."

"The school isn't open today," the woman said, her cheery black eyes far less cheery now, as she gave both Briana and Michael a closer and more suspicious scrutiny.

"Yes, I realize that," Briana said. "And I can see that you're obviously busy. But if you could take just a moment to show us the yearbooks, we'd be most appreciative. My name is Briana Berry. I used to be a student here. Dr. Sands and I have come all the way from southern Nevada."

The woman's look did not soften.

Michael pulled out his medical identification and held it out for the woman to see. "Ms. Berry and I would like to take this opportunity to make a contribution to the Literacy Council. Do you take personal checks?"

Briana watched the woman's face go from sour to sweet in the blink of an eye. Michael had obviously pressed the right button.

"We take personal checks, cash, and firstborns," she announced with a smile.

Michael wrote out a check and handed it to her. Briana didn't see the amount of it, but when the woman did, her eyebrows shot to her scalp and she shot to her chubby feet.

"The yearbooks are right down the hall," she said quickly. "I'll open the door for you."

She shuffled between them down the hall to the office. "My name's Mrs. Mifflin. I'm the vice president of the Literacy Council. I also teach here at the school. What yearbook are you interested in seeing?"

"1985," Michael said.

"No, 1982," Briana corrected. She felt Michael's eyes immediately swing towards her.

"I thought it would be 1985," he said.

"No, I was graduated in 1982."

"Obviously one of those curve-wreckers," Michael said.

Briana didn't quite understand the connection, but she did understand the smile. She sent one back. Mrs. Mifflin opened the door to the office with the yearbooks and beckoned them inside after her. She circled around a counter and leaned down to pull out the 1982 yearbook off a shelf. She set the yearbook on the counter in front of Briana.

"I'll have to stay with you. No offense, but these old yearbooks have a way of turning up missing."

"I understand," Briana said. "We won't keep you long."

Briana opened the yearbook and started to flip through the pages to the senior class photos. She didn't really expect to find her picture there. Nothing else about her life had proved real. Why should this?

She went through the *A*s quickly. And then started on the *B*s. Bailey. Baker. Barrett. Beatty.

And, suddenly, there it was. Berry. Briana Berry. And above the name, a very familiar ugly mug surrounded by lots of mousy hair.

Briana couldn't believe her eyes. Her brain spun. Her legs shook. She sucked in air, but could not seem to fill her lungs.

"Briana?"

It was Michael's voice, coming as if from a great distance. She shoved the yearbook in front of him, her index finger stiffly pointing.

"Me" was the only word that squeaked through her throat.

Michael looked at the image of the high school student in the yearbook that Briana was pointing to. His eyes dropped to the name beneath it. Then rose again to the picture.

The hair color was not hers, but then, hair color could always be changed. It was the features that were all wrong. This high school girl had a long jaw, a big nose and no cheekbones to speak of. She was nothing like the beautiful woman standing beside him.

And then Michael saw the eyes. And the smile. In them was the intelligence, the strength, the warmth, the wit, the humor, that had already been forged behind that homely young face.

He turned away from the yearbook picture, to the woman who had posed for it those many years before.

"She's you," he said, still feeling the shock of it. "You're her. You're beneath that homely face. And this beautiful one."

She beamed at him—with gratitude, appreciation, and more. A lot more. So much more that he felt his heart come to a halt.

Then her expression changed abruptly. "Michael, I have to go to the Evergreen Nursing Home. I have to find Hazel!"

They yelled their thanks to Mrs. Mifflin as they ran out of the office and down the hallway to the front doors of the high school. Less than a minute later, they were in the rental car and on their way.

Michael could have reminded Briana that they both had already called the Evergreen Nursing Home and been told that no Hazel Doud was in residence. But he didn't.

Ever since he looked at that portrait of Markam and Natalie Newcastle, Michael had suspected that something strange was going on. And now that he had seen Briana Berry's high school picture, he was certain of it.

Briana directed him through the white, wintry streets with unerring ease to the doors of the Evergreen Nursing Home. They hurried up its path and then inside.

The reception area was quiet and deserted looking, its only adornment a green fake Christmas tree with multicolored lights. Michael thought that without the holiday decoration, it would be a dreary, drab place.

"I'm looking for a resident," Briana said to a young man slumped over a copy of *Sports Illustrated,* the heels of his boots propped on the edge of the desk. He wore his dull brown hair in a greasy-looking ponytail that was as lifeless as the expression in his eyes.

"What's the name?" he asked, with all the perkiness of the gray desk and walls surrounding him.

"Her name is Hazel Doud," Briana said.

The receptionist typed the name slowly into his computer, letter by letter, using only one hand. "Nope. She's not here." He slumped back in his chair and redirected his attention to his magazine.

"I'm Briana Berry, her granddaughter. I brought her here in 1990. Please, would you look again?"

An irritated frown puckered his young brow.

"I have looked. If she were here, it would say so on the computer."

Michael stepped forward and flashed his medical identification. He made a statement, not a request. "Check your computer to see if Hazel Doud has ever been a resident."

The receptionist straightened immediately upon seeing Michael's credentials. "Yes, Doctor. Of course, Doctor."

He set the magazine aside and keyed in the request, with two hands this time. He read the response off the screen. "Hazel Doud was a resident here from October of 1990 to December of 1994."

"Where is she now?" Briana asked.

"Six feet under," he announced, with all the warmth of a rock. "She died of a heart attack December twenty-fourth, 1994."

Briana stepped back, an anguished, muffled cry escaping from her throat.

Michael felt an instant tightening in his chest. He moved to Briana's side and circled his arm through hers.

"I'd like a complete copy of Hazel Doud's file," Michael said to the receptionist with a clipped, emphatic command.

The receptionist looked from Michael to Briana and nodded solemnly, finally seeming to tumble to the fact that he had just told someone that her loved one had died. He executed the commands, and the file began to print out.

"Where did they take her?" Briana asked. Michael didn't

miss the catch in her voice. He could guess how difficult it was for her to project a calm front and hold the sorrow inside.

The receptionist consulted his screen. "Lewis Funeral Home."

He handed Michael the printout on Hazel. Michael led Briana out of the nursing home and back toward the car.

With all she had faced, he had never once seen her cry. Until now. A steady stream of crystal tears slipped down her cheeks.

Michael stopped next to the car and wrapped his arms around Briana, bringing her to him, holding her tightly, unable to bear being on the sidelines of her sadness a second longer.

He knew he should not be doing this. But the desire to comfort her was too strong to deny.

She dropped her forehead on his chest with a soft sob. She felt suddenly, inexplicably fragile nestled within his arms. *Fragile* was not an adjective he'd ever thought he'd use with her. Holding this strong woman during her moment of sorrow roused something deep and needy within his soul.

"Hazel would be so ashamed of me," she said into his shirt. "She taught me to laugh, not cry."

"I think she'd forgive you this once," Michael's voice said unsteadily against the fragrance of Briana's snow-sprinkled hair.

He felt her chest expand against his, and then the deepness of her exhalation. She drew back, reached into her pocket, pulled out a tissue, dabbed at her eyes.

"I'm sorry to have fallen apart that way, Michael."

He smiled. "A few tears is hardly falling apart, Briana. Besides, I'm convinced *you* could face the end of the world without falling apart."

Her sigh ended in a smile. "Could we go to the funeral home now? I have to see to the arrangements."

Michael blinked in confusion at Briana's words. "What arrangements?" he asked.

"The funeral arrangements."

"Briana, didn't you hear what the receptionist said? Hazel died December 24, 1994."

"Yes, I heard. It happened Christmas Eve. The first Christmas Eve I wasn't with her! I keep praying that wasn't the reason. The funeral home has probably been trying to reach me."

Michael grasped Briana's shoulders, stared into her face, as the glimmer of an incredible suspicion began to take hold in his brain.

"Christmas Eve, *1994*, Briana. Hazel died three years ago."

"Three years ago?" she repeated, looking at Michael as though he were fading in front of her. "What...?"

"Briana, it's 1997."

Michael watched his words hit her. Hard.

"You're not joking, are you?"

Her question was one of hope—as though he might still take it back, tell her it wasn't so.

"No, Briana. I'm not joking."

The chuckle she managed this time was barely a breath. "Well, looks like I was wrong again, Michael. I'm not missing three weeks out of my life. I'm missing three years!"

BRIANA STOOD ALONE in front of the gravestone as she read its simple inscription:

Hazel Doud
Born December 12, 1912
Died December 24, 1994

What the stone didn't say was that Hazel Doud had been a sweet soul, filled with the strength of gentleness and love. That she had made the world a much more beautiful place simply by being in it.

The snowflakes fell on the frozen ground like a soft benediction, covering the spot where Hazel had been laid to rest. From within their silence and across the years, Hazel's happy voice came to whisper in Briana's ears:

Remember, no tears, my dear! Laugh often. And love a lot.

"I'll remember, Hazel," Briana whispered back, wiping away the moisture from her eyes. "I'll always remember."

And then Briana turned toward the offices of the Lewis Funeral Home, where Michael was waiting with a kind funeral director by the name of Paul, who had given up his Sunday afternoon to help them sort through a three-year-old mystery.

Michael had the door open by the time Briana reached it. When she stepped inside out of the snow, he helped her off with her coat and scarf.

He had understood her need to say goodbye to Hazel alone. And she understood the lingering touch of his hands on her shoulders as the gesture of comfort it was intended to be.

Paul was just returning from a back room. He motioned Briana and Michael to the chairs in front of his desk as he sat behind it.

"I got out the file, as you requested, Dr. Sands," he said. "There were no services for Mrs. Doud. We could find no surviving family."

"What about her granddaughter, Briana Berry?" Michael asked. "The nursing home should have provided you with her name and address."

Paul consulted the thin file on his desk.

"Granddaughter? Oh, yes. Here it is. Briana Berry. She predeceased Hazel Doud by three weeks."

"Excuse me," Briana said leaning forward. "Did you just say that Briana Berry died three weeks before her grandmother?"

"Yes," Paul said. "December third. Some kind of accident in Las Vegas. She was cremated at a funeral home there, to save the expense of transport. Do you want the address of the funeral home that handled it?"

"Yes, by all means," Briana said, leaning back in her chair as the earth tilted all around her once again. "It's not every day that I can get a chance to talk to the people who cremated me."

Chapter Eleven

Getting a flight out of SEATAC back into Las Vegas during the busy holiday season proved the most difficult part of Michael and Briana's traveling arrangements. They took a plane to Salt Lake City, where they changed planes for San Diego, where they in turn picked up a connecting flight headed for Vegas.

After a night of catnaps interspersed with plane changes, they arrived midmorning, worn and weary. The first thing Michael did when he got off the plane was to find a phone and call Nate.

"Well, you were right, Michael," Nate said. "There was a convention for architectural designers at the Mirage three years ago, on the weekend of December third. The hotel shows that Briana Berry checked in, paid in advance by credit card and was just charged for the one night."

"Anything unusual happen at the convention?" Michael asked.

"It went off without a hitch. I called the professional organization for architects. They said Briana Berry was a member until her death three years ago. And that Lee Willix still is. His firm, Willix and Associates, is in Portland, Oregon."

"So now we know why we couldn't find him in Washington."

"There's more. Laura called her editor friend at the newspaper and asked her to look through their archives to see if she could find anything newsworthy that happened at the Mirage around that time. She scored. It seems a dress shop lost its ceiling, severely injuring a couple of customers. They were taken to the hospital.''

Michael's pulse started to race. ''Who were the customers?''

''Newspaper article didn't list their names.''

''What happened to them?''

''Well, that's the strange part. Laura's friend said there was no follow-up story. Seems somebody at the paper dropped the ball.''

''Or the ball got intercepted,'' Michael said, as new suspicions began to rise in his thoughts. ''Nate, where were the injured people taken?''

''Emergency room at Sunrise Hospital.''

''Thanks. And thank Laura for me, too.''

''Michael, hold on a minute. Do you know that Sheldon Ayton has been looking for you two everywhere? He even came by here to ask Laura and me about you this morning.''

''Looks like I was successful in giving his detectives the slip in Louisiana. So what did you tell him?''

''I told him to get lost. And Laura slammed the door in his face for good measure. But I know Ayton has a process server waiting for you and Briana at the institute. And once Briana is served, the court order gives her just twenty-four hours to turn herself in for a psychiatric examination.''

''Thanks for letting me know. I'll be sure to avoid answering any knocks on the door there.''

''Playing cat and mouse with a man like Sheldon Ayton could be a pretty dangerous game.''

''Only if you're the mouse, Nate,'' Michael said before hanging up.

THE EMERGENCY ROOM at Sunrise Hospital was busy. It took a few minutes for them to catch the attention of someone who could direct them to the medical files room.

Once there, the clerk shook her head in response to Michael's request.

"I'm sorry, Dr. Sands. But since you are neither on staff nor have privileges at this hospital, it would be inappropriate of me to give you the names of any of our patients—even past ones—or let you see any of our records without an appropriate court order."

"I understand," Michael said, sending her a deliberate smile as he leaned across her desk. He lowered his voice to a confidential pitch. "But surely it wouldn't hurt to give me the name of the emergency room physician who treated the accident victims?"

The smile was working. The clerk hesitated only a moment before consulting her computer. She looked around before she whispered, "William Cupper."

"Where might I find Dr. Cupper?" Michael whispered back.

"He's on break. I saw him head for the doctors' lounge."

Michael thanked the clerk and led Briana there.

Cupper was easy to spot, since he was the only one in the small room. He was chronologically young, not quite thirty, but already looking emotionally worn and weary. Michael figured it was the emergency room work that was taking its toll.

Michael introduced himself and Briana. Dr. Cupper gestured toward the empty chairs in front of him.

"So what can I help you with, Dr. Sands?"

"I'm interested in some accident victims you treated three years ago—December third, 1994, to be precise. They had been injured in the collapse of a ceiling in a clothing boutique at the Mirage."

Dr. Cupper shook his head. "I get so many emergencies in here. I'm sorry, I don't remember."

"Could you take a moment to check the medical files?" Michael asked.

Dr. Cupper was clearly tired and not eager to rise to the occasion, much less out of his chair. However, Michael was counting on the bond of professional courtesy between doctors winning out. It did. Cupper nodded and headed for the medical records office. When he returned, he had the file in his hands. He plopped back into his chair and scanned the sheets.

"Yes, I remember this now. Two women. Massive head and facial trauma. One D.O.A. One in critical condition. The *lucky* one stayed in a coma for nearly a week. Her face was so bloody and badly mangled, we could barely find the openings for her nose and mouth to put the tubes through. It was a miracle she pulled through."

"What were the names of the two women?" Michael asked.

"Briana Berry and Natalie Newcastle. Berry was the D.O.A. Newcastle was the one who made it."

Michael had been expecting this. He could tell from the look on Briana's face that she had, as well. After what they had learned, this was the only explanation that made any sense.

Dr. Cupper's rounded shoulders suddenly straightened. His eyes went to Briana. "Wait a minute. Didn't Dr. Sands introduce you a moment ago as Briana Berry?"

"Yes, Dr. Cupper," Briana said. "There seems to have been a mix-up. I'm the one you saved in that accident, not Natalie Newcastle."

"A mix-up? No. That's not possible."

"And yet here I am," Briana said with a smile, "in living color, Cinemascope, and 3-D, too."

Dr. Cupper stared at Briana, his look saying that he was still far from convinced.

"You did indicate that both women had serious facial injuries," Michael said. "Couldn't that have contributed to their identities being confused?"

Cupper immediately shook his head at Michael's suggestion. "No, both Ms. Newcastle's mother and brother were at her side. How could they not know?"

"That's a very good question," Michael said. "What notes do you have on the patient through her recovery?"

Cupper took a moment to scan the medical file. "She regained consciousness on the eighth day. Her vital signs were good. But she displayed total amnesia for both the accident and her identity."

"I didn't know who I was?"

"It's not unusual after such a severe head trauma. Full memory is often never restored."

"Where did your patient go from here?" Michael asked.

"As soon as her condition was stabilized sufficiently for her to leave the hospital, her mother and brother had her flown to a specialist in France to begin the restorative plastic surgery. Our chief of surgery recommended the man Chennault—as the absolute best. He can work miracles with a laser."

Michael thanked Dr. Cupper, and he and Briana left the doctor's lounge. They walked down the hall in the general direction of the parking lot where he'd left his car.

"I've been living the life of Natalie Newcastle for the last three years," Briana said as soon as they were alone. "That's why I had that dream of her wedding. I was there, her. At least I thought I was. It's incredible!"

"And there still are a lot of unanswered questions."

"Well, at least I know now I'm not a multiple personality."

"Yes," Michael said. "The suggestion that you were a multiple personality was certainly a clever ploy on the part of Carlie to lead us down that wrong path. It almost worked, too."

"You're right. She had to have known I wasn't her daughter. Why did she pretend I was?"

"She must have had a pretty compelling reason. She got rid of all of Markam's servants, who would have immediately detected the personality differences between you and Natalie. She even had Natalie's portrait with her father thrown out, so that no one would notice the difference in your eye color."

"And she's still trying to maintain the fiction, despite the fact that she knows I've remembered my life as Briana Berry."

"Yes, she must—"

Michael aborted his sentence and grabbed Briana the second he saw the man who had turned into the corridor up ahead. He pulled Briana with him into an empty patient room.

"Michael, what—?"

"Wait!" he cautioned as he eased the door partially closed. Less than five seconds later, Sheldon Ayton walked by.

"Sheldon's mother must be here," Briana whispered, her voice throaty and her breath feathering Michael's chin. He looked down into her crystal eyes and breathed in her lovely scent filling the small space between them.

"Michael, are you all right?" Briana asked.

No, he wasn't. His heart had begun to pound. He could actually feel the blood draining to his feet. He quickly stepped back and made a dive for his disappearing thoughts.

"I'm fine," he lied. "I was just thinking, if Ayton's come to visit his mother for a while, that gives us our opportunity to have a private conversation with Carlie. Come on, Briana. Your surrogate mother has some explaining to do."

BRIANA RECOGNIZED KUEN from the Pettits' video when the manservant answered the door at the Ayton estate. Kuen formally welcomed her home and told her that she would find her "mother" in her suite. Briana ascended the red-carpeted stairs with Michael. The rococo furnishings and family portraits were an exact duplicate of those from her dream.

As soon as Briana entered Carlie's suite, she recognized it as the place of her dream argument. Carlie looked up from some paperwork, her face registering surprise, then pleasure.

"Natalie, honey! You've come home!" She rose and circled Briana in a hug.

"Please, Carlie," Briana said, drawing back out of the embrace. "Don't make this any more difficult than it is."

Carlie looked up at Briana with dismay. "You still don't know who you are?"

"Oh, I know. I'm Briana Berry, an architect from Washington State. Three years ago I came to Las Vegas for a convention at the Mirage. The ceiling of a clothing boutique caved in on me and Natalie Newcastle. We were both badly injured. An ambulance took us to the hospital. I survived. Natalie didn't."

Carlie blinked at her. "Didn't survive? Where are you talking about—"

"I know you switched my identity with Natalie at the hospital."

"Switched what?" Carlie gasped, her hand flying to her heart. It was such a theatrical gesture. And yet the anguish on her face looked so real that it made Briana sick to her stomach.

"Why did you do it, Carlie?" Briana asked. "Please tell me."

"She can't tell you," a voice said suddenly from the door.

Briana and Michael both whirled around to see Rory standing there.

Rory closed the door behind him and came to stand at his mother's side. He wrapped his arm around her waist and turned to face Briana.

"You see, Mama didn't do it. I did."

Carlie gasped again as she looked up into the face of her son. "No, Rory, you can't be saying this is true!"

Rory sighed as he looked into his mother's anguished face. He withdrew his arm from her waist and clasped her hands within his.

"Mama, I'm sorry. I would have done anything to spare you this, believe me. Natalie—the real Natalie—is dead. She died that night three years ago."

Tears fell from Carlie's eyes as she crumpled against Rory in a sob. He pulled her back to her chair and sat her on it, his hands remaining on her shoulders.

"You have some explaining to do, Mr. Taureau," Michael's voice said, and there was a flat command in it that Briana had never heard before.

Rory must have heard it, as well. His chin jerked up. His dark eyes went to Michael's face.

"I had to do it," Rory said, his square jaw jutting out.

"Tell me why," Michael said.

"Mama went to Natalie after Markam died. She just wanted her daughter back, to explain why she had been forced to give her up. Natalie threw her out."

Briana watched Carlie's face. Her wince at Rory's words, and the pain in her eyes, told Briana they were true.

"Six months later," Rory continued, "I found out my knee ligaments had deteriorated. I needed an operation. I had no medical insurance. Mama sold off her house, everything she had. It wasn't enough. We were destitute. Mama crawled back to Natalie, begging for a room in the servants' quarters."

Rory paused to snort in disgust. "She gave us one—the smallest one at the estate—and it came with a hefty price. She made Mama her private secretary, on call twenty-four hours a day, seven days a week, for the next five years. All at no pay. Just room and board."

"That's slavery," Briana said.

"Yes, it was. Only Mama never told me the conditions Natalie had extracted from her. I thought my sister was employing Mama to make it easier for Mama to accept her financial help without feeling dependent. I thought she had softened. I thought she now understood that Mama hadn't willingly abandoned her when she was a child."

"When did you find out the truth?" Michael asked.

"Just before the accident at the Mirage. Natalie had dragged Mama along. I was getting around pretty well by then. I had convinced Natalie to include me on her gambling trips so I could share the burden of her incessant demands on my mama. Natalie was happy to. And why not? It meant she had two slaves to attend to her, instead of one."

Rory paused to exhale heavily.

"Natalie was losing at the tables, in a foul mood. I made

the mistake of telling her it might be a good time to quit before she lost too much. She got angry and told me that she'd have a lot more money if *my* mama hadn't been forging Natalie's signature on checks."

"Was this accusation true?" Briana asked Carlie.

Carlie took a deep breath and nodded as she exhaled.

"The checks were made out to the doctors and hospital, to cover my continuing medical treatments," Rory said immediately, in his mother's defense. "I thought the money was coming from Mama's salary as Natalie's private secretary. I didn't know about her slave contract."

"Until that night," Briana guessed.

"Yes. I begged Natalie not to let her own mama be prosecuted. I promised her that I was nearly well, and I'd be getting a job and paying back all the money Mama took from her. With interest."

"What did Natalie say to your offer?" Michael asked.

"She told me it was too late. She had already advised her accountant of the check forgery. She had him doing a signature verification on all checks issued over the previous six months."

Rory released his hold on Carlie's shoulders. "As soon as we returned to Louisiana, Natalie was going to collect the evidence from him and call the police. I was racking my brain, trying to think of some way to talk her out of it, when the ceiling of the boutique fell in on you both."

Rory stopped to stare at Briana. "I rode in the ambulance. You were both battered and bloodied beyond recognition. I knew it was Natalie who died. When the ambulance attendants turned all their attention to keeping you alive, I got an idea. I switched your purses, put her rings on your fingers, and told the emergency room staff you were my sister."

"What were you hoping to accomplish?" Michael asked.

Rory looked at his mother and shrugged.

"Just to hold back the truth for a while. All I could think of was those forged checks in the hands of that accountant.

With Natalie dead, I feared he would take them right to the police."

Rory directed his next statement to Briana. "You were in a coma, not expected to live. I went to Mama to explain about what I had done."

Rory shook his head, a look of wonder coming over his face. "I found her holding your hand, trying to talk you back to life. After all the humiliation Natalie had put her through, she still loved her. I couldn't tell Mama that Natalie had found out about the checks and what she had planned to do. I just couldn't tell Mama how rotten she was."

"So you let her believe I was Natalie," Briana said.

Rory nodded. "I hired a detective agency to find out about Briana Berry. I learned the only family she—you—had was a grandmother with Alzheimer's in a nursing home. I knew no one would be claiming your body or looking for recompense. Forgive me, but I was glad."

"Why?" Briana asked.

"Because I could contact the insurance company representing the boutique and make them a deal they couldn't refuse."

"Which was?" Michael asked.

"That they pick up all Natalie Newcastle's medical bills, throw in a hundred thousand for pain and suffering, and kill any follow-up news stories that named the victims. I told them I'd have Briana Berry cremated and notify the nursing home of her death. And that would be the end of the matter. They jumped at the deal. Like I knew they would. I let them off dirt cheap."

"Why?"

"Because I needed money quick. And who could it hurt? Natalie was dead. The doctors had no hope for you."

"Why did you make that stipulation about the news stories?"

"I didn't want it to be known that Natalie was in an accident. If her accountant heard, the next part of the plan wouldn't work."

"What was the next part of the plan?" Briana asked.

"To cover the checks my mama forged, of course."

"And how did you do that?"

"I cashed the check I got from the insurance company and sent a typed note from Natalie to the accountant, along with enough money to cover Mama's forged checks, plus ten percent. In the typed note I told the accountant that Natalie had found the forger, gotten reimbursement, along with an apology, and was now satisfied to let the matter drop."

"What did the accountant do?"

"He sent back the checks he had verified as forged, along with a note saying he was glad the matter could be settled out of court. And that was that. He never mentioned it again."

"But your whole plan was based on my subsequent death."

"Yes. When the doctor called Mama and me in the middle of the night to tell us you were not only recovering but had regained consciousness, I thought I'd have to admit everything and go to jail. I was prepared to say I forged the checks. When we arrived at the hospital to find you had amnesia, I sighed with relief. Mama promised you she'd help you rebuild your life as Natalie. For all our sakes, I hoped she would."

"Still, you had to be worried that I might remember who I really was. That's why you told Carlie a story about Natalie thinking she was the orphan, Briana Berry, being raised by her Grandmother Hazel Doud."

"Yes. I made up that story and told it to Mama in those first anxious days when I didn't know whether you would regain your memory. Only I told Mama that it was something I had learned when Natalie was ten and I went to her birthday party."

"So you did see Natalie then?"

"Mama had to stay in the gardener's truck, for fear of being recognized by the servants. She could only catch a glimpse of Natalie. I just joined the other kids. I was so excited to meet my beautiful older sister. Mama had talked so lovingly of her. What a joke. When I said hello to Natalie, she threw cake in my face and called me a dirty name. I walked away from her that day, never having told her I was her brother. When I met her again, seventeen years later, she hadn't changed."

Rory stopped and looked directly at Briana. "We took you to the best plastic surgeon in the world, and he reconstructed your face into Natalie's flawless features. But when you smiled out of that face, you made it lovely to look at for the first time."

Rory's eyes broke away from Briana's face to stare down at his hands, hanging loose by his sides.

"You were so damned nice. Mama wanted to believe it was the near-death experience that changed Natalie into the warm, loving, funny, generous daughter she had always wanted. You can't blame her for fooling herself into believing what she wanted to."

"But you knew the servants would figure out Briana wasn't the real Natalie," Michael said.

Rory nodded at him. "The housekeeper had been around nasty Natalie since her birth. She certainly would have had trouble accepting such a complete personality metamorphosis. That's why I came home from Europe a few days earlier than Mama and got rid of the old servants and any pictures of the old Natalie."

"Because the real Natalie Newcastle's eyes didn't change color like mine?" Briana asked.

"Yes," Rory said. "Mama wanted you to be Natalie so bad, she convinced herself that Natalie had been dyeing her hair all along and that her eyes had always changed color. But I knew others would be more logical and skeptical."

He stopped, took a deep breath. "I know what I did wasn't legal. But I didn't do it for myself. I did it for my mama. And it all worked out for the best, don't you see?"

"Worked out for the best?" Briana said. "Rory, you denied me my identity. My life."

"What life? You were a plain, poverty-stricken struggling architect. Your only family was a grandmother who was so mentally gone she didn't even recognize you anymore. I gave you Natalie Newcastle's beauty and wealth! And a mama who loved you like her own. And a brother who— You were happy with us as Natalie. I swear you were.''

"And would I have been happy as Sheldon Ayton's wife?"

"Mama didn't know who he was when she pushed you into marrying him. When I returned from seeing you in Louisiana, I told her about his detectives, his spying. She understands now.''

Rory stepped toward Briana, extending his hand, a hopeful shine in his dark eyes.

"You don't have to stop being Natalie," he said. "You can divorce Ayton. Come home with Mama and me. The money is all yours. You can have any kind of life you wish. Don't you see? No one need ever know the truth.''

"I'd know the truth, Rory," she said.

Briana signaled to Michael and turned to go.

Carlie's voice rose anxiously behind her. "Don't go! Please!''

Briana stopped, half turned. "Carlie, you can't possibly be willing to go along with this charade now that you know I'm not your daughter?''

Tears trickled down the older woman's cheeks. "I lost my daughter when she was just a babe. You gave her back to me. The love I have felt for you—the love you have shown to me and Rory—was no charade.''

Briana walked over to Carlie and put her arms around her.

"You're right. I don't remember our time together, Carlie, but my heart sure seems to. Thank you for taking care of me, and for caring for me.''

Then Briana quickly released Carlie and walked out the open door, before she could be tempted to stay.

BRIANA HUNG UP THE PHONE at the institute an hour later and turned to Michael.

"According to Natalie's lawyer, she never made out a will.''

"Which means her estate would have automatically gone to her mother. As it will now."

Briana nodded. "I'm going to tell the authorities that this was all just a case of mistaken identity, that no one knew I wasn't Natalie until I suddenly remembered my life as Briana Berry on Christmas Eve."

"You want to keep quiet about the fact that Carlie forged the checks and Rory switched your identity with his dead sister?"

"I don't want to hurt them, Michael."

His eyes were steady on hers when he smiled. Then she watched him purposely turn away.

"I've put in an official request for a copy of your old driver's license record," he said.

Briana leaned her leg against the edge of his desk and watched him not watching her.

"I've also sent a formal request to Dr. Chennault in Paris for your records while you were under his care," Michael said. "Keith is going to get a court order for the accident victim's records from Sunrise Hospital. Once we have everything in hand, we can go to the police and present them with the evidence of who you really are."

Briana's attention wasn't on his words—it was on him. The sun streamed through the windows to halo his head. It turned his tanned skin white-hot, the prominent muscles on his exposed forearms into mounds of gold dust.

His deep blue eyes rose to hers. "Briana?"

She scrambled for a response. "So you're saying I'll soon be back to being me."

"You always were you," Michael said. "Your personality didn't change during the time you believed yourself to be Natalie. Everything we've heard from everyone proves that. You never acted like the mean, vindictive person she was. You remained yourself, warm, sweet, loving—"

Michael caught himself, just not quite in time. He cursed silently as he feigned a cough to give himself some cover. It was so unlike him to make such a mindless mistake. He blamed the far too many sleepless nights fighting his dreams. Of her. He was a man who needed his dreams.

He was a man who needed the woman looking up at him now with eyes that he'd recognize anywhere—on any face.

Of all the women in the world, he had fallen for precisely the one he must not.

He couldn't believe it could happen this way—without conscious thought or intent or action, without a lick of control. A week ago, he would have bet anything that it was impossible.

He would have lost that bet.

Something had happened to him that night Briana Berry awakened in his arms.

He didn't even know precisely what it was. He only knew that when her beautiful, crystalline eyes opened, whatever poured out of them had poured right into his soul.

Briana's heart was thudding hard. He had called her warm, sweet, loving. And from the sound in his voice, the warmth of his rich blue eyes, she knew he had meant it.

And it had been so marvelously unprofessional.

She could not believe how incredibly giddy and weak she felt hugging that knowledge to her. Michael had seen her face, her real face, and he had seen *her* in it.

He had seen who she was inside. And he was attracted to who *she* was.

But he hadn't wanted her to know. That was obvious. As was the reason. He had no intention of doing anything about it. The small slip of the tongue was all that superb control of his would allow.

He was still on the other side of that line he had drawn between them. He still had no intention of crossing it.

"There are your missing memories of the last three years to reclaim, of course," Michael said, looking away from her as he made a heroic effort to keep an even tone. He suddenly realized his hands were shaking, and shoved them into his pockets.

"With the holidays coming to a close, you'll soon be able

to take your pick of a number of very good psychiatrists who can help you to—''

Briana moved to him, standing at the edge of his breath, before she gave any thought to what she was doing. ''Michael, I don't want anyone but you.''

His balsam scent was rich and drugging. His heart was racing right next to hers. Her breasts were nudging his chest, her arms circling his neck, her lips seeking the smooth, firm contours of his, before a second of sanity could intrude to stop her.

It was a hungry kiss, wild, slightly off center, filled with a dizzying need that she barely understood and could not control.

She felt his instant shock, the stiff amazement that hardened his chest and shoulders into a solid brick wall. She tasted panic, and the delectable smoky heat of desire, on his lips before he tore his mouth from hers.

''Briana, please, listen—''

He was pleading for mercy, and she knew it. She did not feel merciful. She felt achy and wanting and way past the point of turning back.

His voice rose in a desperate attempt to sound formal and firm. ''Briana, the affection you're feeling for me is called transference. It isn't real. It won't last. It happens quite frequently when a doctor and patient work closely together—''

''Michael, we've just proved I'm perfectly sane, so I never really needed a doctor. You've refused to take a dime from me, so that means I've never officially been your patient.''

She could feel the tension in his straining muscles, hear the unevenness of his voice. ''Briana, whether you needed a doctor or not does not mitigate the fact that I have been performing as one with you. And as your doctor, I must not—''

''Michael, I didn't fall in love with the doctor in you. I've fallen in love with the man. And just for the record, I've been wanting to make love to you since the moment I first awoke to your kiss, before I even knew who you were or what you did for a living.''

She leaned forward to nip his earlobe lightly with her teeth, and felt the erratic hammering of his heart against her own.

"So if you don't want me, Michael, you're just going to have to come up with a better argument—and fast."

Michael knew he was fighting a battle he couldn't win— nor did he want to. He let out a sound that might have been a sigh of defeat or triumph, or simply a laugh. And then he closed his arms around her and crushed her to him, abruptly and forcefully taking the initiative from her.

Briana's lips parted, exultation driving through her at the fierce demand of his kiss. His mouth was hot and hard and heaven, and his arms were like branding irons around her. He picked her up as though she weighed nothing and set her on his desk. She wrapped her legs wide around his muscled thighs, her breath already ragged, she was so ravenous for him. She prayed he would understand that she had no time to waste on buttons and zippers and soft words.

The blood sung through her veins as his mouth and hands claimed her. She vibrated in harmony with his every caress, totally tuned in to the greedy pleasure of his possession. His tongue licked a trail of molten lava down to her neck as his eager hands pulled open her blouse to expose her breasts. She arched her back, and his thumbs flicked her nipples into pebble points.

When his mouth replaced his thumb, a whimper broke through her lips as a spear of sharp desire pierced her womb.

His hand traveled down the length of her body to the hem of her skirt and then dipped underneath to trail up the inside of her thighs, leaving a path of fire in its wake. When he reached the satin of her panties, he slipped inside.

His intimate touch was firm and focused.

She pulsed in a rich, trembling pleasure beneath the perfect rhythm of his long, hard fingers. His mouth continued to lave her breasts, teasing her nipples as his fingers teased the core of her desire.

She was so wet, so ready. Surely, if Michael didn't take her now, she would go insane. With need.

Please.

She hadn't said it aloud, and yet somehow he seemed to have heard. He plunged inside her, deep and hard, a happy tortured sound tearing through his throat.

She cried out as she came, so full, so fast, it lifted her into an incredible intensity of feeling that seared through her mind in black fire and a cascade of icy white stars.

And he was right there with her.

It seemed a long while later before her thoughts began to return. And then they were mere feathers falling back to earth.

She became aware that her head lay on his shoulder. That she was totally wrapped in his arms as he was in hers. That the wisps of clothing that remained between them were soaked. That the desk was slightly hard beneath her bare derriere. She didn't care.

"Briana," he said, and his voice held a tone of wonder. "Do you know what torture it's been for me not being able to touch you?"

She sighed in pure pleasure at his words. For she had no doubt now that all along he had wanted this—that he had wanted her. And every cell in her body was pulsating with happiness at the thought.

"This can't be comfortable for you," he said solicitously from somewhere behind her ear.

"Are you kidding? I want to be buried this way."

He chuckled as he kissed the top of her head.

"So, Michael, I suppose this transference thing means that I'm going to have to worry about all of your clients falling in love with you?"

He leaned back to look at her, and the warmth of his smile made her heart stumble to a stop.

A twinkle of mischief in the blue of his eyes belied his somber tone. "I think you'll find that most of the men will restrain themselves."

Her chuckle ended in a sigh as his hands moved up her neck and his fingers massaged her nape and scalp. He knew exactly where to touch, and just how much soothing pressure to apply. And all the while his hands worked their magic, he feathered gentle kisses at every pulse point in her neck and throat.

She closed her eyes, sinking farther into the warm, afterglow of his intimate, mind-melting touch.

"I never realized how great it would be to make love with a man who knows so much about anatomy."

"I'm going to burn in psychiatric hell for this," Michael said, but he chuckled against her ear.

"I didn't know psychiatrists have a hell all to themselves. Your touch is absolutely incendiary. When I come visit, I'll bring you some ice water."

His laugh ended with his mouth on hers. It was a tender kiss this time, but it had a growing insistence behind it. And, incredibly, she felt the heat once more gathering inside her, humming through her blood. She was never going to get enough of this. She was never going to get enough of him.

Then the telephone rang, and he grunted an annoyed oath as he drew out of the kiss. "That's my private line. It's only used for emergencies. I can't ignore it, Briana."

She leaned over to nibble at his ear, brushing her breasts strategically against his chest. "Of course you can't."

Michael let out a choked oath, then grabbed for the receiver and barked out an impatient hello.

"It's Nate."

"Nate, this isn't a good time—"

"Michael, Sergeant Vierra is on my other line. She says she's at the institute's door. She's been ringing the intercom for fifteen minutes, and no one's answering."

"For the very good reason that I disconnected the bell chime," Michael said. "I could see Ayton's process server waiting in the parking lot. I have no intention of letting Briana get served before I have all the evidence in hand."

"Sergeant Vierra is not there about the civil matter, Michael."

Michael didn't like the sudden sound in his friend's voice. He steeled himself, knowing bad news was on its way.

"What is it, Nate?"

"Gytha Ayton regained consciousness in the hospital two hours ago. She said she didn't fall down the stairs. She said she was pushed."

"Pushed?" Michael repeated.

"Yes. And she said it was her new daughter-in-law who pushed her. Sergeant Vierra has a warrant for Briana's arrest, Michael. The charge is attempted murder."

Chapter Twelve

"The statement that Gytha Ayton gave the police is pretty damning," Keith said to Michael as they waited for Briana to be processed and released on bail. Michael saw the worried look on the swarthy face of his lawyer friend and knew that he wasn't overstating his concern.

"Let's hear it, Keith," Michael said.

"Mrs. Ayton says that one of her wedding guests, a Carleton Quivert, had been a longtime friend of Markam Newcastle. Quivert also knew Natalie quite well. Yet when Quivert spoke to her at the reception, she didn't recognize him. That puzzled Quivert. The more he watched the way Natalie moved, talked and behaved, the more he became convinced that she wasn't Natalie. He went to Gytha Ayton and told her of his suspicions. Mrs. Ayton went to her new daughter-in-law's room to confront her."

"She accused Briana to her face of not being Natalie?"

"And of tricking Sheldon into marrying her. She said that Briana offered up no denial, no explanation, just stood there staring at her. Gytha stalked out of the room and headed for Sheldon's. She fully intended to tell him that Natalie wasn't Natalie. But she said as she passed by the landing at the top of the stairs, Briana came up behind her and pushed her down."

Michael shook his head. "No way, Keith. I know Briana. Gytha Ayton is lying."

"The police contacted Carleton Quivert," Keith said. "He's given them a statement that corroborates Gytha Ayton's story. He definitely talked to her about his suspicions concerning Briana not being Natalie."

"So Gytha Ayton began to suspect Briana wasn't Natalie. So she confronted her. That doesn't prove Briana pushed her."

"Sergeant Vierra has also found out about the convention three years ago. And the accident at the dress boutique. She's figured out when Briana stopped being Briana and became Natalie Newcastle."

"Great," Michael said. "*Now* she believes her."

"Only she thinks Briana regained her memory a long time ago and decided to remain Natalie in order to continue to have access to the woman's money and the kind of society in which she could meet a rich man like Sheldon Ayton."

"That's nonsense. Vierra must know by now that Briana filed annulment papers from Ayton. If Vierra believes Briana's aim to have been mercenary, how does she explain her actions to get out of the marriage?"

"She thinks Briana panicked and tried to cover her tracks after shoving Gytha Ayton down the stairs."

"Let me get this straight. First, Briana is supposed to have shoved Gytha Ayton down the stairs to keep her from telling Sheldon she wasn't Natalie so she could stay married to the man. Only then Briana immediately runs out and tells everyone she's not Natalie and tries to get her marriage to Ayton annulled?"

"Michael, the police have Briana at the scene with motive, opportunity, and an eyewitness to the crime—the victim herself."

Michael exhaled in exasperation.

"So, legally, what's on our side?" he asked.

Keith rested his hand on Michael's shoulder. "Straight from the hip, Michael. We haven't got a thing. Unless Briana can remember what happened and give us some plausible explanation, it's going to be damn near impossible to win this one in court.''

MICHAEL FLEW BRIANA directly to the institute as soon as she was released on bail. The first thing she did was step into the shower to wash away the smells of the jail—and the feeling of being unclean that came with the kind of accusations that had been made against her.

She didn't believe that she had done what Mrs. Ayton claimed. But if it wasn't true, why would Mrs. Ayton say it was? There had to be some mistake. There just had to be.

Damn it, why couldn't she remember what had happened that night? Why couldn't she remember her time as Natalie?

She found Michael outside, waiting for her in a chaise longue by the pool. He gave her his chair and pulled up another one for himself.

''How do you feel, Briana?''

''About how Alice must have felt when the Queen of Hearts yelled, 'Off with her head.'''

''You still remember nothing of the events of Christmas Eve prior to your awakening at the institute?''

His look, and his voice, were deep, gentle, loving. The psychiatrist shield was gone. She was looking at the man. And he looked wonderful. The worries that had been weighing her down for hours lifted from her shoulders. Somehow, she knew, everything was going to be all right.

''Outside of my dream, all I remember is my time with you.''

Michael's hand rested on hers, strong, warm and reassuring. ''Let's delve into your dream memories, Briana, and get some answers.''

''I don't remember the details of the dream anymore, Michael.''

''With time, dream images always fade. That's why it's so important to record your memories of them right after you awaken from a dream. We have your memories right here.''

Briana noticed then that Michael had brought out the tape machine. He held it in his hand.

"I want you to listen closely and try to recall what you were feeling during the dream images. We're going to begin where we left off."

"At the start of the second dream segment?" Briana asked.

"Yes. Ready?"

She nodded.

Michael leaned over to press the play button.

I was at the top of this awkwardly winding staircase with a deep red carpet, part of a procession, Briana's taped voice said. *On the walls to my left were all these old family portraits.*

Briana listened carefully as her taped voice went on to describe the Ayton estate.

Were you in this procession or watching it, Briana? Michael's taped voice asked.

I seemed to be behind it. Only I turned around and when I turned back, the bridesmaids and ushers were gone.

Were you still at the top of the stairs?

Yes, but the stairs were different, steeper, and it was the older woman who stood with her back to me, the one who had tried to give me the dress that smelled of lavender.

In your earlier dream?

Yes. She was dressed differently, not nearly so fine.

Go on.

The woman was cleaning the stairs with this old canister-style vacuum. The cord was looping around her ankles. She didn't seem to be noticing.

What happened?

I called out to warn her. But she didn't hear me because the vacuum was making so much noise. She tripped on the cord and began tumbling down the stairs.

What did you do?

I watched her fall to the bottom. I wanted to go down to her, but I was afraid. I tried to climb on the banister so that I could slide down. But the banister was too high and I couldn't reach it. I didn't know what to do and I was so scared. I started screaming something.

What, Briana?

I don't know. The dream ended. It made no sense.

Michael turned off the recorder. "Tell me what you think of that dream now, Briana."

"The moment Carlie mentioned Mrs. Ayton's fall, I thought of this part of my dream. I believed that I might have seen it happen. And yet now that I've listened to the tape and my memories are refreshed, I don't think I did."

"Why not?"

Briana focused on the dream details in her mind. "Remember when we went over the first dream about my argument with the two women?"

"Yes. Go on."

"Carlie related the parts of that argument just as I dreamed them. When I saw her, I knew she had been one of the women. And when I saw Mrs. Ayton on the Pettits' videotape, I knew she had been the other. Then, when I walked into Carlie's room at the Ayton estate, I recognized the furnishings that had come from the dream and knew the argument had taken place there."

"So you're saying that the events and images from the dream proved accurate."

"Right. But this dream has distorted images that don't fit what I know to have happened."

"Tell me about those distortions, Briana."

"The staircase, for one. At the first part of the dream it has a red carpet and the stairs go through several turns as they descend from the top floor. It is an exact duplicate of the staircase at the Ayton estate."

"And later?" Michael prompted.

"Later, when I turn back toward the staircase to find the bridesmaids and ushers have disappeared, the staircase is now straight, and it doesn't have a red carpet."

"It's a different staircase."

"Yes. And it seems to loom larger and steeper in my mind's eye—more menacing—as though it's oversize."

"Or perhaps you're smaller in relation to it?"

"Smaller? What do you mean?"

"Think about your dream images, Briana. You see the woman falling to the bottom of the stairs. You want to go down to her, but you're afraid of the steep stairs. You try to climb onto the banister, but it's too high. What do these things tell you?"

"Of course! I feel like a child. A child would be afraid to go down a steep flight of stairs. And it's only as a child that I would have been too small to reach the banister."

"You realize this means you were dreaming of something that had happened to you a long time ago?"

"Then why was Mrs. Ayton in the dream?"

"You said the woman you saw fall was the older woman from your earlier dream argument, but not dressed so fine."

"That's right."

"If she had her back to you and was dressed differently, how did you know that she was Mrs. Ayton?"

"Good question. I think it's just one of those dream identifications you make by some vague pattern or sense that connects the dream image to someone you know."

"I need to know why you made this identification, Briana."

"I've told you everything I remember, Michael."

"Then we'll have to try a little daydreaming."

"Daydreaming?" she said. "How will that help?"

"By releasing your conscious from its sentry duty and giving other parts of your mind a chance to come forward. Lie back. Close your eyes. That's right. Let yourself go limp, loose, as you sink into the cushions. They feel so good, so soft, so comfortable."

Briana listened intently to Michael's voice, finding it deep, dreamy, melodic, mesmerizing.

"The winter sun is warm above, Briana. Bring it inside you. Let its soft light start at your toes and work its way up.

That's right. Its warmth soothes your muscles, relaxing them as it gently drifts through your feet, your calves, your knees, your thighs.''

Michael's compelling voice and pleasant images continued, giving Briana the sensation of a warm light flowing inside her, working its way through her body. She could feel her breathing deepen, her muscles unwind, her nerves quiet.

"You are filled with the light now, Briana. You are calm, contented, and so very relaxed. You will stay that way as you listen to the last portion of the tape once again. You will concentrate on the scene with all your senses. You'll see the woman on the stairs, hear the noise of the vacuum, feel the wood of the banister beneath your hand. You will be there.''

The tape began. Beneath Briana's closed eyes, the images of the dream scene slowly played out, but this time everything did seem so much clearer. She was very small in relation to the woman who approached the stairs. Briana could see the scuff on the woman's white tennis shoes. She looked up at her brown hair, wrapped in a turbanlike scarf. And then Briana caught a whiff of something—something at once both familiar and forbidding.

Briana's heart began to pound. She could see the vacuum cord twisting around the woman's ankles. She yelled. But the loud noise of the vacuum was blocking out her warning. The woman tripped.

"She's falling!''

"Who is it, Briana?'' Michael's voice asked.

Briana could hear the little girl's voice screaming the answer in her head, loud enough to reach across thirty years.

Mommy!

Briana opened her eyes and sat up. She was shaking all over. "My God, Michael, she was my mother! I saw my mother fall to her death!''

Michael wrapped his arms around Briana. "You've faced it, Briana. It's over now.''

He held her close until the awful tremors racking her body subsided. Finally, she drew back out of his arms to see his face. His eyes were so very gentle. "Did you know it was my mother's fall I had witnessed?"

"I only knew it had to be something traumatic that happened to you as a child. You buried the memory very deep, because it was so very painful. Now that it's been released, you'll start remembering other things."

"I do. My mother wore a lavender scent, Michael. I smelled it just now when I relived the dreamed memory of her fall. That must be the reason I never liked that smell. That must also be why I confused her in my mind with Mrs. Ayton. The wedding dress that was Mrs. Ayton's had been packed in lavender sachets."

He kissed her forehead. "Perfectly logical connection."

"Why did the childhood memory surface now, Michael?"

"Because you must have seen Mrs. Ayton fall down the staircase and it triggered what you had seen as a child. You responded as a child would, by running and hiding from the truth."

"So that's why I disappeared from the Ayton estate. How did I get to the institute?"

"I don't know. But the shocks of that night had to have been what succeeded in restoring your memories as Briana Berry and caused you to forget your time as Natalie Newcastle."

"Because if I remembered being Natalie, I would remember seeing Mrs. Ayton fall, and, by association, my mother's fall?"

"Yes."

"It's incredible to believe that I forgot these things on purpose. And I didn't even know I was doing it."

"The mind is an amazing thing, Briana. It possesses many levels of awareness and many levels of which we are not aware. A part of your mind has been protecting you from the painful memories of your mother's death for thirty years. When you were in danger of remembering, it tricked you into forgetting all over again."

"But the memories were in my dreams."

"Because your dreams know you're not a three-year-old anymore. They know you can handle the tragic event you couldn't face then. Dreams are wise—often the wisest part of ourselves. We cannot ever really know who we are in the waking world until we understand who we are in the dreaming one."

"'Discover your dreams and discover yourself,'" Briana quoted, remembering the sign on the entrance to Michael's wing at the institute.

"Briana, you need to remember the specifics of Mrs. Ayton's fall. We have to know exactly what happened."

"But I didn't dream about her fall, Michael. My dream was about my mother's."

"But it was triggered by Mrs. Ayton's fall. They're connected, like two sides of the same door in your mind. We've seen one of the sides—your mother's fall. We need to open that door and get a look at the other side. Lie back. Let's see if we can find those memories that are hiding from you."

Briana reclined back in the chaise longue.

"Close your eyes, Briana. Let yourself feel the warmth of the winter sun flowing through your muscles, soothing them, warming them, relaxing them."

Briana didn't know whether it was because she had just done this, but she found it was even easier to see the white light passing through her and relaxing her from head to toe. She began to float, suspended in the magic of Michael's hypnotic voice.

"You are at the Ayton estate, upstairs on the landing," he said. "You can see the red-carpeted stairs that lead below. The pictures of the Ayton ancestors adorn the walls. The top of the banister is heavy and curved."

Briana found it easy to bring the scene into her mind. Now that she'd seen it in both her dream life and her waking one, the elements were quite familiar.

"Mrs. Ayton is with you," Michael's voice said. "See her."

Fuzzy images, mere flashes, flickered into Briana's mind.

Gytha Ayton's face contorted in anger. Her mouth open, yelling. Briana strained to hear, but the words weren't clear. There was another sound overpowering them.

Then Gytha Ayton turned from Briana and began to march away. The other sound was deafening in her ears. Briana looked down to see that a leash was in Mrs. Ayton's hand. And on the other end of that leash was her dachshund Napoleon.

"Her dog is barking," Briana said. "That's why Mrs. Ayton doesn't hear my warning. She's tripping, falling down the stairs."

Briana opened her eyes and sat up. "Michael, no one pushed Mrs. Ayton. It was the dog leash that tripped her. And the little dachshund fell down the stairs with her."

"No wonder your witnessing Mrs. Ayton's accident brought back the accident of your mother. A dachshund has much the same shape as an old-fashioned canister vacuum. The visual elements were remarkably similar."

"But why is Mrs. Ayton saying I pushed her? She must know I didn't."

"The fact that her injuries were serious enough to put her in a coma for several days makes me doubt that she remembers much about how she fell. Obviously, she's accusing you because she wants to try to hurt you or keep you away from her son. She may even want to believe it could be true that you'd push her."

"Now that we know what really happened, how can we prove it?"

Michael extended his hand to Briana and pulled her to her feet. "I have a few ideas. Come on."

"Where are we going?"

"To see a man about a dog."

"THIS IS G. H. FOOTS, Sergeant Vierra," Michael said as he introduced the little, round man, whose bald head bobbed up and down like one of those spring-necked dashboard ornaments.

"G.H. is the dog trainer and handler from the Ayton estate. He has a statement to give you about Mrs. Ayton's prize show dog, Napoleon, and the injuries Napoleon sustained at the Ayton estate on Christmas Eve."

"What does this have to do with the case against Ms. Berry here?" Vierra asked.

"It has everything to do with it," Michael said. "Mrs. Ayton tripped on Napoleon's leash. That's what caused her to fall down the stairs. Napoleon fell with her and was injured."

Sergeant Vierra turned to stare at the dog trainer.

"I didn't realize the little fella was hurt at first," G.H. said, his head bobbing in nervousness. "I thought he was off his feed because he was missing his mistress. But then I noticed him favoring his right front leg, and the abrasions around his neck."

"When did you notice this?"

"Late Christmas Day. He was dragged down those stairs with her, all right. The vet agrees. He took X rays. Poor little fella's got a sprained leg and a couple of broken ribs."

"Even if the dog fell with her, that doesn't prove she was tripped by its leash," Vierra said.

"No?" Michael asked. "Then how do you explain the fact that a servant had to unwrap the leash from around Mrs. Ayton's ankles before he could free the dog?"

"What servant was this?" Vierra asked, clearly startled.

"His name is Kuen. He found Mrs. Ayton at the bottom of the stairs. Sheldon Ayton came running down the stairs mere seconds later. Kuen removed the whimpering dog to the kennels so G.H. could see to his care and Ayton could see to his mother's."

A frown puckered Sergeant Vierra's brow. "If Mrs. Ayton fell because she tripped on her dog's leash, why is she saying Ms. Berry pushed her?"

"That's a damn good question," Michael said. "Now let me ask you one. Has Mrs. Ayton inquired about Napoleon's injuries?"

"No. She made a fuss with the hospital when she told them she intended to have Napoleon stay in her room and they told her that health regulations prevented it. But she's said nothing to indicate she has any suspicions that the dog is injured."

"If Mrs. Ayton really remembers the facts about her fall, don't you think she would have asked about the injuries her prized pet sustained, the dog companion she's so attached to that she even wants him in her hospital room?"

Sergeant Vierra's mouth was turning mutinous. It was clear that she didn't enjoy learning that she'd been lied to.

"I want to talk to that servant, Kuen," she said.

Michael looked at his watch. "He should be here any minute. When I spoke to him on the phone, he said he would drive here directly from the estate."

Vierra turned to G.H. "Come with me and we'll get your statement on the record."

"Ms. Berry and I would like to sit in," Michael said.

Vierra turned to look at him. "No way."

"Or we can all wait until I call Ms. Berry's attorney," Michael said with a smile. It was a bluff. He had already tried to have Keith here, but had found his friend would be in court all day. Still, the sergeant didn't know Keith's schedule.

Vierra shook her head in defeat. "All right. But you sit quiet, both of you. I ask all the questions."

Michael nodded, pleased that he had achieved his goal. He knew it was important to stay with this and keep pushing Sergeant Vierra to get the charges dropped.

"You go ahead, Michael," Briana said. "I want to be in the parking lot when Kuen arrives, so I can bring him directly up."

It sounded like a good idea to Michael. The more carefully they monitored this situation, the better.

"Where should Ms. Berry bring Mr. Kuen, Sergeant?" Michael asked as he turned back to Vierra.

"We'll be in interrogation room two," Vierra said as she led G.H. toward it.

Briana took note of the room. As she turned to leave, she

felt Michael's hand grasp hers and hold it tightly for a moment. "It's almost over."

As Briana descended in the elevator and made her way toward the parking lot, she could still feel the warmth of his hand.

Almost over, he had said. And then what? They hadn't talked of a future. Not that there had been time, with this charge hanging over her head. Or was Michael simply avoiding the subject because he knew they didn't have a future?

He had told her that he loved his work and it consumed him. He had said he was not a man who would marry.

Falling in love with him had been an absolutely insane thing to do! Still, she could have stopped breathing more easily than she could have prevented it.

If he couldn't return her love, it was going to break her heart.

Briana pushed open the doors of the police station and stepped out into the sunshine. She brought her hand up to shade her eyes as she did a cursory check of the parking lot to see whether Kuen had arrived.

The arm came out of nowhere, wrapping itself across her chest—a hard, strong arm. Briana gasped to find herself suddenly and forcibly pulled back against a man's body, her arms rigidly imprisoned by her sides.

"Don't worry. It's just me," a familiar voice whispered against her ear.

Briana actually gave a sigh of relief when she heard it. "Rory! What are you doing here?"

"I've come to get you. I'm not going to let that bitch Gytha Ayton put you behind bars with her lies. We're getting out of here now. I have our tickets for Dublin. We'll be gone before anyone knows it."

"Rory, it's okay. Dr. Sands is upstairs right now with Sergeant Vierra, straightening all this out."

"Straightening all what out?"

"The Aytons' manservant and the dog handler can prove

that it was Napoleon's leash that tripped Mrs. Ayton and caused her to fall down the stairs."

"I see. So it's Dr. Sands to the rescue again, is it?"

Briana couldn't understand the disappointment in Rory's words. She tried to turn to face him, but his arm still held her firmly against him.

"Rory, let me go—"

Briana's sentence was cut off along with her breath as Rory's hold tightened. His considerable strength was not a surprise. His obvious willingness to use it on her was.

"I can't let you go," he whispered in her ear, his voice suddenly deep and deadly soft. "You don't remember my telling you that on Christmas Eve at the bottom of the stairs, do you? My laying my heart at your feet? It had taken a half bottle of bourbon to give me the courage."

He laughed. It was a bitter sound. "Stupid, huh? A gimp with no money, no profession, trying to win the heart of a woman who had just married a man who would be a billionaire."

Briana's stomach began to crowd her lungs in sudden fear. This wasn't the Rory she thought she knew. And yet, there was some dark intensity here, something that she could see now had always been below the surface of his signs of affection.

Rory continued to whisper in her ear like a lover—a lethal lover.

"You didn't understand what I was saying. You still thought I was your brother. And then Sheldon came along and stood between us again. I knew I had to get you alone. I was in the hall when that bitch stomped out to tell Sheldon you were an impostor. I saw the leash wrap around her ankle. You yelled a warning, but the dog was barking at me in the shadows, so she didn't hear."

"Rory, if you were that close, couldn't you have saved her?"

"Why would I have wanted to save that bitch? I had just

had to listen to her call you the foulest names! She deserved to break her neck for saying such things.''

Odd snatches of forgotten memories were flashing in Briana's mind—memories of her time as Natalie. Times when Rory's touch had lingered on her arm, and the uncomfortable sensations she had felt. A kind of relief that she would be marrying and leaving the estate in Louisiana. Briana was beginning to understand that, even as Natalie, she had sensed something wrong about Rory's regard for her.

''When you saw Gytha Ayton falling down those stairs, you went rigid in shock and fainted,'' Rory's whisper continued. ''I carried you back into your bedroom and waited until everyone's attention was on Mrs. Ayton. I tore his rings off your fingers, dropped them on the bed. Then I replaced the veil on your head to keep the hallway light from awakening you and carried you down the back stairs to Mama's car.''

''What were you going to do with me?''

''I just wanted to take you away from that bastard! I wasn't going to hurt you! You don't believe I would hurt you?''

''No, of course not, Rory,'' Briana lied. His viselike grip *was* hurting her.

''I put you in the back seat and covered you with a blanket. But I didn't have the car keys. When I returned with them, the car was gone. It wasn't until later that I realized I was so drunk that I had put you in the wrong black Lexus. Mama's car was on the other side of the house.''

''Rory, how were you planning to explain all this to me when I awoke?''

''I wasn't planning! I was drunk! I just knew I couldn't let him have you, Nat, you never loved that bastard! I know you didn't!''

''You're right, Rory. I never loved Sheldon.'' At least she could say that truthfully. She was beginning to strongly believe that she had allowed herself to be talked into marriage to Sheldon mostly to get away from Rory.

''Of course you didn't. When I heard you had filed papers to annul your marriage to Sheldon, I thought it would just be a matter of time before we'd all be back together again. But no sooner was Sheldon out of the picture than you turned to Sands! Do you know what that did to me? Do you?''

Rory's arm squeezed tighter. Briana concentrated on breathing through her constricted lungs, trying to calm her rising fear. She had to keep her thinking clear and focused. And to keep placating the man who was crushing the breath out of her.

"You're wrong about Dr. Sands," Briana lied. "I'm just his patient."

"No doctor does what Sands has been doing for *just a patient!*"

"I don't know what you mean."

"He took you into his own apartment! You think I don't know that he hasn't let you spend a dime of Natalie's money? That he's footed the bill for everything, even knowing that as Briana Berry you're penniless and he'll never get any of it back? He's used his friends and influence all over this damn town for you!"

"How do you know what he's done, Rory?"

"Because I had the two of you watched. Every minute."

So many things were becoming clear for Briana now.

"Sheldon never had me followed or spied on, did he, Rory? That was you. It's always been you."

"Yes, it's always been me! When I wasn't with you, I had to know what you were doing. And thanks to your generous checks, I could afford the best private investigators. We shared so much, Nat! We were so close! Then, out of the blue, you accepted Ayton! And Mama was so thrilled. And I couldn't tell her the truth. I knew it would break her heart. And then there was the money. I didn't know who the real Natalie had willed it to, you see."

"Rory, you don't have to worry. Carlie is going to get the money."

"I'm not worried. Not anymore. I tried to forget you. For Mama's sake. But when I saw you marry Ayton, I knew I couldn't. I was too drunk to do it right the first time. But ever since Ayton told me you were at the Institute of Dreams, I've had you watched. I knew the right moment would come—the moment when I could get you alone.''

Briana shivered as his hot breath blew on her neck.

''I thought I could convince you to go away with me when I came to your hotel room in Louisiana. I almost did. But Sands interrupted us. He won't be interrupting us now. We're leaving. We're going to be together.''

''Rory, please understand. I don't return your feelings. I can't go with you.''

''You'll go. You're mine. I created you. I'll see you in hell before I'll let Sands or anyone else have you!''

The last segment of Briana's dream images flashed before her eyes. She now knew who the masked man was. He was the other side of Rory Taureau, this side she was seeing now, a side of dark obsession and cruelty.

She shivered in revulsion.

Rory must have felt that shiver. ''You will learn to love me,'' he said, a wild anger filling his whisper as he began to push her toward a black Lexus in the parking lot.

Briana filled her lungs with air to let out a powerful scream, guaranteed to be heard for blocks. But she never got a chance to let it out. Rory's hand clamped hard and tight over her mouth.

She kicked and fought, desperate to break his hold on her. Rory grunted when her shoe connected with his shin, but he was horribly strong and deadly determined. He held on fast as he dragged her to the car.

Briana looked around, certain there had to be someone witnessing her abduction. But, incredibly, in the middle of the day, in the parking lot of a police station, she saw not one single soul.

''I borrowed a few sedatives from Dr. Neilssen's bag when he arrived,'' Rory said. ''We have a long way to go. I'll make you as comfortable as possible.''

Briana pushed through the icy fear seeping into her body, numbing her limbs. They were almost at the car. She reasoned that Rory was going to have to use one of his hands to open the passenger door. She readied herself to scream and fight like hell for her freedom the second he let up on his hold.

But she never got the chance. Rory delivered a sudden, sharp blow to her diaphragm that literally drove the breath from her body and dropped her like a rock. She lay paralyzed on the pavement, trying to suck air into her lungs, horrified to find she was unable to raise a hand or let out a peep.

Rory opened the passenger door. "I'm sorry. Really. But you gave me no choice. I'm not giving you up."

Hope drained out of Briana along with her flagging strength. She blinked as tears of rage filled her eyes. And almost missed the sudden flurry of motion.

One minute Rory was staring down at her. The next he was leaping back and crouching, his hands balled into fists as he assumed a fighter's stance.

And then Briana saw who he was squaring off against.

Michael.

Her heart pounded in her throat as she desperately fought against the weakness that made her so ineffectual, so unable to help. But it was no use. She couldn't move. She couldn't even speak.

She watched Rory's lightning-fast fists shooting out in sharp, vicious jabs. Time and again, Michael leaped back, just missing being struck by those deadly weapons.

Briana's heart was in her throat. She knew Michael was no match for a professional boxer. Michael's hands weren't even balled into fists. They were making sinuous circular motions as he moved in front of Rory, keeping just out of range.

Then Rory leaped forward in a sudden surprise attack, his right fist on a direct path toward Michael's chin. But the blow never connected. In a move so fast that it registered as a mere blur in her eyes, Briana saw Michael's foot deliver a sharp kick to Rory's middle. The foul oath spewing out of Rory's mouth ended in a choke as Michael's right hand followed up with a chopping blow to his throat.

Rory fell forward, hitting the pavement with a thick,

crunching sound. He lay still, unmoving. Michael stood over Rory's body like a wonderfully fierce avenging angel, the sun a white fire through his hair, the anger a blue devil in his eyes.

And then he was down on his knees beside Briana, cradling her to him, rocking her gently, whispering things she could not hear over the pounding of both their hearts.

MICHAEL FOUND BRIANA standing beside the institute's pool late the next afternoon when he returned from town. She was looking out at the Virgin Mountains and the valley below. He had seen her packed bags in the hallway.

And they had sent a jolt through him.

He had known from the first that he had to let her go, of course. He couldn't try to keep her here. It wouldn't be right. It wouldn't be fair.

His life was the institute. His passion was dreams. He still had so much to learn about them, from them.

He couldn't ask her to live his dream, give up on her own. Everyone had to find their own dreams and be true to them. Without that, life just wasn't worth living.

The sunlight caught the thick waves of her red hair, setting them on fire. She turned when he approached. The color of her eyes had changed to the balmy island blue of her blouse, her cheeks to a white desert sand. The silk of her pineapple slacks made a swishing sound as a smile that said aloha spread her lips.

"Michael."

He'd never known how good a smile could feel, or how wonderful his name could sound. Saying good-bye to her was going to be the hardest thing he ever had to do.

"How did it go with Sergeant Vierra?" she asked.

"Rory Taureau is being charged with attempted kidnapping and assault with a lethal weapon—his fists. Vierra plans on putting him away for quite a while. Soon as he's out of the hospital, that is."

"I'm sorry for Carlie," Briana said. "She called here a

while ago to apologize for Rory. Begged my forgiveness, as though she were responsible. It must be pretty tough being a parent sometimes.''

"I would imagine all the time.''

"How did you beat Rory, Michael? He was a professional boxer, yet he never touched you and you knocked him out.''

"A couple of years ago, while I was teaching a contender for a karate championship to improve his focus and skill through lucid dreaming, I was teaching myself.''

"Your karate client won his championship, didn't he?''

"Rather easily. He'd been winning it for weeks in his lucid dreams. They are a great place for perfecting a skill.'' *But useless when it came to trying to forget you,* Michael thought. "So how did your meeting go with Sheldon this morning?'' he asked aloud.

"Let's just say I won't be exchanging Christmas cards with the Aytons next year. However, Sheldon's agreed not to fight the annulment. And I've agreed to forget the fact that his mother tried to make me into a felon.''

Michael kept his voice even, formal. "I understand Lee Willix has asked you to join him in his Oregon architectural firm. Are you going to accept?''

She turned back to the view, a small frown on her forehead. "I told him I'd think about it. He wants me to come see him and his wife and their three-year-old daughter.''

So that was where she was going. To Oregon. Damn.

"Maybe, before I go, you could teach me to lucid-dream?''

She was giving him an opening. He knew it. He also knew he couldn't take it. He couldn't ask her to share a life that was less than it should be. He couldn't take advantage of her feelings for him.

The cell phone in Michael's pocket peeled away. He snapped it open—irritated, angry, unhappy.

Briana listened to the affirmative and negative grunts that comprised his side of the conversation. And all the while, her heart was sinking because she knew he wasn't going to ask her to stay.

She had been very foolish to think he might, of course. She

was going to walk away from this beautiful desert with one hell of a broken heart.

Michael finally flipped the phone closed. "That was Nate. We've unraveled the mystery of how you got from the Ayton estate to under my tree. Rory placed you in the Lexus of Laura's uncle, Everett Thaw, by mistake."

"That short, pudgy man you pointed out on the Pettits' tape?"

"Yes. Everett had driven halfway home before he heard you make some sound from the back seat and finally realized that he had a sleeping stowaway. He panicked."

"I don't understand. Why would he panic?"

"Everett is not exactly what you'd call a clear thinker. He reads intrigue and Machiavellian motives into everything. He didn't know what you were doing asleep in the back seat of his car. But whatever the reason, he knew he didn't want to be involved. So he decided to drop you off at the institute and pretend ignorance."

"How did he get in?"

"He says the guard left the door to the rotunda unlocked. It's possible. Anyway, Everett carried you inside, laid you under the Christmas tree, and then drove away as fast as his Lexus would go."

"He sounds like a charming man," Briana said with a small chuckle. And then, because that message out of that silly fortune cookie kept repeating in her mind—*Dreams can come true*—she turned to face Michael for one last try.

"Still, however unintended, Everett Thaw did me a very big favor that night. He brought me to you."

Michael couldn't resist her smile, or the love pouring out of her eyes.

He reached for Briana, pulled her into his arms, said the precise words he had sworn he never would. "Please don't go. Stay here. Marry me."

Briana's heart stumbled unsteadily as she grasped his shoulders, leaned back to see his face, her words no more than a breath. "Michael, what are you saying?"

"There are plenty of architectural firms in southern Nevada. We're experiencing an incredible building boom. You can associate with a firm here, or start your own. My parents left me a million when they died. I've added several more to it. It's all yours. Marry me, Briana."

Briana's heart had begun to race with happiness. But it just about stopped with his next words.

"Darling, I promise I'll do my best to be the right kind of husband and father. And if it means giving up the institute and getting a regular job to be there for you and the kids, so be it. I can't let you go, Briana. I need you more than anything."

"But you don't want to be a father."

"I want to be your husband. I understand how important children are to a woman. I won't shortchange your needs."

She looked into the deep, sincere blue of his eyes and knew he meant it, too. He was ready to sacrifice even his dreams for her. Tears came into her eyes as her heart filled with so much love that she found it hard to speak.

"Michael, do you remember when I told you that my two brothers died young, before I was even born?"

"Yes. And the tragedy was too hard for your father to face. I would face that if I had to, Briana. I would face anything for you. I swear."

Yes, with all her heart she believed he would. And with all her heart, she knew she would never ask it of him.

"Michael, the reason my brothers died so young was because they were born with an inherited blood disorder. Their immune systems were unable to resist infection. Their short lives were pure hell. Male children in my family are the ones who become ill. Females are carriers. *I'm* a carrier, Michael. I've known it since I was twenty. I won't bring a child into a world of agony. I never planned to have children."

Michael stared into her lovely crystalline eyes, stunned by her words.

"But I will tell you this, Michael. If I wanted children, I would never marry you—no matter how much giving you up would break my heart. Because I could never let you give up the institute or your work in dreams. It's what makes you who you are. It's what makes you the man I love."

All along Michael had firmly believed that he was falling for the one woman he must not. Now he knew he had fallen for the one woman made for him.

What astounded him most was that his dreams had known it from the first. It was ironic. He, who had preached for others to listen to their dreams, had failed to listen to his own. Until now. He gathered her close—very, very close.

"Briana, I love you. With everything I am, I love you."

She sighed, at the incredible joy of his words, the feel of his arms.

"Yes, but will you still love me when my mousy brown roots start to show?"

She felt his chest quiver against hers as his amused puffs of air darted past her ears.

"Darling, you can go to a plastic surgeon and get your old features back, for all I care. All I ask is that you don't go so far that I have to start calling you Brian."

Briana chuckled delightedly. And then his mouth covered hers, molding it to his own.

Her lips parted willingly beneath the strong demand of his. The heat of his hands, the hardness of his body, his bold possession, all washed through her mind, telling her what her heart had known from the first time she found herself in Michael Sands's arms, being awakened by his kiss.

That dreams did in fact come true.

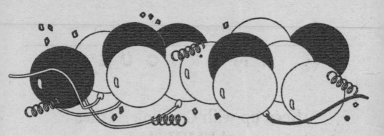

Ring in the New Year with

New Year's Resolution:
FAMILY

**This heartwarming collection of three
contemporary stories rings in the
New Year with babies, families and
the best of holiday romance.**

Add a dash of romance to your holiday celebrations
with this exciting new collection, featuring bestselling
authors **Barbara Bretton, Anne McAllister** and
Leandra Logan.

Available in December,
wherever Harlequin books are sold.

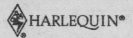

HARLEQUIN WOMEN KNOW ROMANCE WHEN THEY SEE IT.

And they'll see it on **ROMANCE CLASSICS**, the new 24-hour TV channel devoted to romantic movies and original programs like the special Romantically Speaking—Harlequin™ Goes Prime Time.

Romantically Speaking—Harlequin™ Goes Prime Time introduces you to many of your favorite romance authors in a program developed exclusively for Harlequin® readers.

Watch for **Romantically Speaking—Harlequin™ Goes Prime Time** beginning in the summer of 1997.

If you're not receiving ROMANCE CLASSICS, call your local cable operator or satellite provider and ask for it today!

Escape to the network of your dreams.

See Ingrid Bergman and Gregory Peck in *Spellbound* on Romance Classics.

DEBBIE MACOMBER

invites you to the

HEART OF TEXAS

Join Debbie Macomber as she brings you the lives
and loves of the folks in the ranching community
of Promise, Texas.

If you loved Midnight Sons—don't miss
Heart of Texas! A brand-new six-book series
from Debbie Macomber.

Available in February 1998
at your favorite retail store.

Heart of Texas by Debbie Macomber

Lonesome Cowboy	February '98
Texas Two-Step	March '98
Caroline's Child	April '98
Dr. Texas	May '98
Nell's Cowboy	June '98
Lone Star Baby	July '98

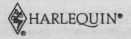

HARLEQUIN®

HPHRT1